"I'm so glad you c

"I am, too."

Did Maggie have any id.........y she was? Her hazel eyes looked tired but happy. Maggie Young was a beautiful woman, and he didn't have to be in love to appreciate that.

"Well, I just wanted to say thank you again. For everything."

"You are welcome. Good night, Maggie." Clayton waited until she shut the door and then prepared for bed. He heard her moving about her room for a moment or two and then the house was silent. His brain went into overdrive in the quiet.

What had he been thinking? Marriage? Responsibility of the ranch? Firing the foreman and taking over his job, along with his own responsibilities as a Pony Express manager? He'd been sent here to do the job of Pony Express manager.

He'd not shirk his duties as a Pony Express employee, he'd not allow harm to come to his new family and, most important, Clayton Young would not fall in love with his pretty new bride.

Distance. That was what he needed to keep between them. If he didn't get close to Maggie, his heart wouldn't betray him.

Rhonda Gibson lives in New Mexico with her husband, James. She has two children and three beautiful grandchildren. Reading is something she has enjoyed her whole life, and writing stemmed from that love. When she isn't writing or reading, she enjoys gardening, beading and playing with her dog, Sheba. You can visit her at rhondagibson.net. Rhonda hopes her writing will entertain, encourage and bring others closer to God.

Books by Rhonda Gibson

Love Inspired Historical

Saddles and Spurs

Pony Express Courtship
Pony Express Hero
Pony Express Christmas Bride
Pony Express Mail-Order Bride
Pony Express Special Delivery

The Marshal's Promise
Groom by Arrangement
Taming the Texas Rancher
His Chosen Bride
A Pony Express Christmas
The Texan's Twin Blessings
A Convenient Christmas Bride

Visit the Author Profile page at Harlequin.com.

RHONDA GIBSON

*Pony
Express
Special
Delivery*

HARLEQUIN® LOVE INSPIRED® HISTORICAL

Recycling programs for this product may not exist in your area.

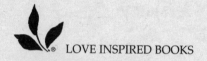

LOVE INSPIRED BOOKS

ISBN-13: 978-0-373-42539-6

Pony Express Special Delivery

www.Harlequin.com

Printed in U.S.A.

This is the Lord's doing; it is marvelous in our eyes.
—*Psalms* 118:23

To my readers: Thank you so much for reading my books. You are forever in my heart.

To James Gibson, my real-life hero.
I will love you, always.

Thank You, Lord, I give You ALL the glory for each and every book.

Chapter One

Wyoming
Winter 1861

Clayton Young's horse, Bones, slowly picked his way down the dirt road that led to the Fillmore Ranch. The leather of the saddle on the horse's back squeaked and shifted as the horse stumbled a bit. Clayton patted the horse's neck. "Good job, Bones. Hang in there. We're almost to the barn, ole boy, and then we'll see what can be found to eat in our new home." Clayton straightened up and drew in a deep breath.

This was the third and final day of his journey. The Fillmore Ranch offered much in the way of comfort, or so he'd been told. Right before he quit, the previous relay station manager, Bill Evers, had said the ranch had been his easiest assignment with the Pony Express.

Clayton sighed. This assignment was his last job with the Pony Express. The telegraph lines and offices were swiftly taking over the Express's routes. Why send your mail by pony when it could go by train in a day's time or wire in mere minutes? People were whispering that the Pony Express was in financial distress and would soon be extinct once telegraph lines were completed from the East Coast to the West. Because of all the talk, Bill had found another job and quit the Pony Express. He had a small family and couldn't afford to be out of work even a day.

Unlike his friend Bill, Clayton didn't have a family to support so he figured he'd stick with the Pony Express to the end. Then he'd pursue his dream of becoming a doctor. He'd saved almost every dime of the money he'd earned working for the Pony Express, and that would hold him over for a while after this job ended.

Bones began traveling up the hill. Clayton leaned forward in the saddle. Like this road, it seemed that shortly after Christmas his life had become an uphill climb. His fiancée, Eunice, had broken off their engagement and quickly married the banker's son, and then he'd learned that the Pony Express could shut down at any moment. Mixed emotions warred for his attention. On one hand, he'd miss the stability the Pony Express had brought to his income and his life. On the other hand, he'd be free to pursue doctoring, something he'd dreamed of doing for as long as he could remember.

He topped the hill and saw the ranch house below. The sun was lowering in the west, casting rust-colored rays over the barn, yard and two-story house. It was a nice place with a couple of large trees in the front and what looked like fruit trees off to the side.

Pleasure and a tiny spiral of hope teased his mind. This was his chance to start over. With blessings from the Lord and hard work, he just might see his dream of becoming a doctor come to fruition.

Movement below drew his attention. A little girl ran from the house to the barn. Clayton figured that was five-year-old Dinah. Bill had said the little girl was the sister to Jack Fillmore's young wife. Jack had died three months earlier and left a widow behind.

He gently touched his knees to Bones's ribs. The horse took his time easing down the hill. All the while, Clayton watched the child. She exited the barn pulling a mustang pony behind her. What was a five-year-old girl doing messing with a horse? His gaze swept the rest of the yard and surrounding area. Where were the ranch hands? Where was Jack's widow?

His gut clenched, a sure sign that all was not well at the ranch. "Let's go, ole boy."

Bones heard the words *let's go* and tore down the hill like the ranch was on fire. Being a Pony Express horse, Bones had been trained by Clayton that when his rider said "let's go," he was to move fast. Clayton would have grinned, if he weren't concerned about the child below.

He knew the exact moment the little girl spotted him. She stopped in her tracks, wrapped the horse's reins around the wagon and ran at top speed toward the house. She had barely made it onto the front porch when Bones skidded to a stop below her.

Clayton saw her hand tremble as she reached for the doorknob. He knew a scared little filly when he saw one, and his instincts kicked in just as they did when he sensed Indians and bandits on the Pony Express trail. What he needed to do now was keep calm and find out what the trouble was.

He spoke in a soft, even voice. "You must be Dinah."

The little girl nodded.

"I'm Clayton Young and I was sent to manage the Pony Express station. Is Mrs. Maggie Fillmore here? Bill told me she would show me the ropes."

The little girl turned loose of the door and rushed toward him. "My sissy just had…um, the baby's having trouble breathing." She paused in uncertainty.

Big tears welled up in her eyes and ran down her chubby cheeks, and a tiny dimple peeked through strands of hair that had fallen from her braids. "He's not crying or nothing. Sissy says we have to get to town where the doctor lives." She twisted her small hands in her dress in agitation. "I have to hitch the horse to the buggy so we can get Sissy and the babe to Doc Anderson."

Bill hadn't mentioned that Mrs. Fillmore was with child. Clayton forced himself to remain calm, knowing that the babe might already be dead. "Tell you what. Why don't you take me to the baby and let me see if I can help?" He saw the indecision on her face and slid off his horse. "I've doctored my brothers for years. Please, let me help your sister." Clayton wrapped his horse's reins around the porch post.

Dinah nodded and held the door open. When she started up the stairs, Clayton could no longer remain calm, and he slipped past her two steps at a time. If the baby had turned blue, he might already be too late.

Clayton followed the sound of weeping and entered a room of pure chaos. Linen was strewn over the floor. A pan of water sat on the floor beside the bed, and sitting on the side of the bed wearing a dressing gown was a larger version of Dinah. She held the still baby in her hands. Her mournful weeping filled the room.

The setting sun shone through the window behind her, creating a halo of sorts, and golden ringlets tumbled across her shoulders, reaching almost to her waist. When she looked up at him, pure unadulterated grief twisted her features, and without a word she held the baby out to him, silently begging for his help.

Clayton gently lifted the baby to his chest. A white line circled his tiny mouth, and his lips held a tinge of blue. Clayton laid the baby on the bed and with his little finger pulled down on the lower lip.

Carefully, using the edge of the sheet, he cleared the child's air passages. The baby kicked and then gagged. Clayton turned him over and lightly swatted his bare bottom. The baby emitted a weak cry, followed by high-pitched, angry wails. Clayton turned him back over and placed the boy, full of life, in his mother's arms.

Clayton released the pent-up air in his lungs. He knew a moment of intense satisfaction and peace. A frail smile touched the woman's lips as she examined her newborn son. She yawned and her eyelids drifted down. Clayton gently lifted her and the baby, and he eased them back onto the bed. She may have been too weak to stand, but he noticed the grip on her baby had not lessened one bit. Clayton pulled the covers over them both and started to straighten up the room.

As he turned with the pan of water, he noticed the little girl standing in the doorway, silent sobs shaking her body. He set the pan on the dresser and picked Dinah up.

In the corner of the room sat a rocker. He dropped

into it, holding her. Clayton rocked, occasionally rubbing her hair as he'd seen his adoptive mother, Rebecca, do with his sister many times.

His gaze moved to the woman on the bed. She'd fallen into an exhausted sleep with the baby cradled against her. He felt Dinah relax in his arms. Her eyelids drooped and finally her breathing relaxed into that of gentle slumber.

Clayton laid his head against the back of the rocker and propped his feet on the footboard of the bed. The chair tilted to a perfect sleeping position. The room now lay in shadows as the sun completed its final descent. Clayton felt exhaustion pull at him but remembered that he couldn't sleep. The horses were still outside and needed tending.

He lowered his boots, stood up slowly and carried Dinah to the bed. Clayton laid her on the opposite side of Maggie Fillmore. Maggie's blond hair rested against her cheek, and she had dark circles beneath her eyes. How long had she labored alone?

Protective vibes for the sleeping trio filled him as questions plagued his mind. Where were the men who should have been close to the ranch house? Why hadn't the widow had another woman with her during her birthing time? Would he be able to protect his heart from this precious family?

Maggie awoke with a start. The smell of bacon wafted up the stairs. No, not up the stairs. There was no way the odor could travel that far. She turned her head and saw a plate of eggs, bacon and toast resting on the table.

She sensed Dinah stirring at her back. "Sissy?"

"I'm here." Maggie reached behind her and touched the little girl, all the while focusing on the baby who slept so contentedly next to her. Several times during the night, she'd drawn him close to nurse.

"Where is Mr. Young?" Dinah sat up and leaned over Maggie's shoulder. "Did he fix us breakfast?"

Maggie heard Dinah's stomach growl. Poor little mite hadn't had anything to eat since noon the day before. Maggie's pains had been so great during labor that she hadn't been able to make it back down the stairs. "I'm not sure who fixed this." Maggie handed her a strip of the crispy bacon.

"Hold up, half-pint."

In the doorway stood the man who'd saved the baby's life the night before. Maggie pushed herself up, bracing her back on the headboard and holding on to the baby. Her body ached in places she never knew could hurt.

He came into the room carrying two more plates of food. He held the smaller plate out as if offering it to Dinah. "I brought you your own breakfast."

Dinah returned the strip of bacon to Maggie's plate and scooted from the bed. She hurried around the end to take her plate. "Thank you."

He brushed his hand across the top of her blond head. "My pleasure." His blue gaze swung toward Maggie. "I hope you don't mind that I made myself at home in your kitchen."

She watched as he walked to the rocker at the foot of the bed. He pulled two forks from his back pocket, handed one to Dinah and then eased into the rocker. Dinah followed and sat at his feet.

Maggie frowned. Dinah wasn't the type to take to

a stranger as she was doing with this man. Was she infatuated with him because he'd saved the baby's life and fixed them breakfast?

He said a quick prayer over the food and then looked up at her. His piercing blue eyes met hers. He waved his fork in the direction of the food. "You should probably eat it while it's hot."

She pulled the plate and fork to her. "Um, who are you?" Maggie set the plate on the edge of the bed. The fact that he'd prayed over the food surprised her. She'd not been much for going into town for church, and Jack had never shown an interest either. Had God really answered her prayers last night and sent a godly man to save her baby's life?

"Oh, I'm sorry. Name's Clayton Young. I'm the new Pony Express station manager. I suppose I should have introduced myself last night, but I forgot with the urgency of the situation and all." He shoveled egg into his mouth.

Maggie didn't know what to say to that, so instead replied, "Thank you for saving the baby."

Clayton grinned. "Thank God, ma'am. He's the one who saved the boy. I was just the instrument He used." He winked at Dinah. "Isn't that right, half-pint?"

Dinah smiled around a mouthful of eggs and nodded happily.

Maggie studied the pair. It was as if they shared a secret. She sampled the bacon. It was good. Mr. Young seemed to be able to fry meat as well as save babies.

"Have you come up with a name for the little tyke?" Clayton Young asked.

Her gaze moved to the infant. He needed a name, but Maggie didn't know what to call him. She'd been struggling with that for a couple of months now. Jack might have liked the boy named after him, but Maggie didn't want to call him Jack Jr. She'd thought about the men in her life. Her father's name was Paul, but he wasn't anything like the apostle. That name would only conjure up bitter memories of the man who'd run off with another woman and left her mother heart-broken. She'd not known her grandfathers so had no names to choose from there.

Clayton cleared his throat. "Well, I'm sure there is no rush."

Maggie looked up at him. The only man who'd ever done anything for her was a total stranger, and he sat across the room from her. "Maybe I'll name him Clayton, after you."

Clayton shook his head. "That's not a good idea."

"Why not?" Dinah asked.

He set his now-empty plate on the floor. "Well, every time his mother would call, 'Clayton!' I'd come a-runnin'. When boys are little their mamas have to call their names a lot."

"Oh." Dinah looked to Maggie. "I like the name James."

Maggie looked down on her newborn's sweet face. His lips were puckered in sleep. "What do you think of the name James, baby?" His eyes opened and he yawned.

Dinah clapped her hands. "He likes it."

Maggie snuggled the baby's face and felt his small lips move across her skin. He smelled sweet and warm. She looked up with a grin that quickly faded. Mr. Young looked as if he'd swallowed a bug. "What's the matter, Mr. Young? Do you not like the name James?" She didn't know why it mattered to her if he liked the name or not, but it did.

"I like it just fine."

Dinah reached over and took his hand in hers. "Then why do you have that frowny face?" she asked.

He grinned. "I'm sorry. I didn't mean to have a frowny face. It's just that my full name is Clayton James Young."

Maggie didn't know what to think when the baby kicked his legs and made what to every new mother sounds like a happy noise. "If you don't want me to name him…"

"No, it seems the little man likes his new name. If you want to call him James, that's all right with me." He stood and collected his and Dinah's plates. "Now, if you ladies will excuse me, I have a kitchen to clean up and a stew to get on the stove. Then I'm going into town to get the doctor so he can look over baby James." He nodded once and then left the room.

Maggie heard his boots clomp down the stairs. She looked to Dinah, who stood by the door watching him leave. "Dinah, come here for a moment."

Dinah hurried to her bedside. "Do you want me to help you get dressed, Maggie?"

Maggie shook her head. The baby began to fuss for breakfast. She swung her legs to the edge of the bed and then stood slowly. "No, I'm curious. You seem to like Mr. Young."

Dinah nodded. "He's a nice man."

She eased into the rocker. "What makes you say

that?" Maggie moved the now-howling baby to a more comfortable position. He immediately stopped crying with the warmth of breakfast filling his small tummy.

"He saved baby James and rocked me to sleep last night."

Maggie's head came up as concern filled her heart. Men weren't to be trusted, so why had he taken it upon himself to comfort Dinah? "He did?"

"Uh-huh. I was scared and Mr. Young picked me up and rocked me while I cried. I went to sleep and he put me in bed with you." Dinah smiled. "He told me everything was going to be all right. And it is." Dinah jumped on the bed. Her smile filled the room.

Maggie rocked the baby. Not only had he saved James, but he'd also soothed Dinah's fears. He'd made them all breakfast and was already planning a trip to town to bring back the doctor. What kind of man was Clayton James Young? Unfamiliar words whispered through her heart: *the kind who took care of the people around him.*

She didn't need that kind of man in her life. He'd turn out just like all the others who had let her down. Maggie refused to be hurt again, so she hardened her heart against Clayton Young.

Maggie cuddled the baby close. Her job was to make sure that she could hold on to baby James's ranch. Gus Fillmore, her late husband's cousin, had insisted on becoming the ranch manager and she'd let him because he'd promised to keep her up-to-date on the running of the ranch. Maggie's new fear was that he'd soon begin to demand ownership. She couldn't allow that. With Jack's dying breath, he'd asked her to make sure baby James would inherit the ranch, and she'd promised to do just that. It was a promise she intended to keep.

Chapter Two

Clayton made his way out to the barn. There were no riders scheduled for arrival so he felt all right about going to town to get the doctor. But he didn't feel comfortable leaving Maggie, Dinah and the baby alone. His gaze moved about the front yard once more. Still no ranch hands. Where was everyone?

He'd been so tired the night before that all he'd managed to do was put the horses away and return to the house. He'd checked on Maggie and the children then returned downstairs, where he'd fallen asleep on the settee. Clayton hadn't seen anyone other than Maggie and the children since his arrival.

The trip to town could wait a few more minutes. He entered the barn and saw that the horses had already been fed and watered. In a matter of minutes, Clayton saddled his horse and headed out to find the ranch hands.

It didn't take long to spot two men working on the south fence. They were both bent over when he rode up. "Morning." Clayton stopped Bones and leaned on his saddle horn.

"Morning. You must be the new Pony Express manager."

The taller man took his hat off and wiped the sweat from his brow.

"That I am. I'm looking for the foreman."

"I'm Gus Fillmore." The shorter of the two men stood up. He shaded his eyes as he looked up at Clayton. "What can I do for you, Mr. Young?"

"To start with, you can call me Clayton." Clayton extended his hand.

Gus took it and squeezed hard, then released Clayton's hand. "We're kind of busy here, Clayton." He indicated the fence behind him.

Clayton nodded. "I can see that." He paused until he had the man's full attention then asked, "Did you know that Mrs. Fillmore had the baby last night?"

"Nope." Gus motioned for the other cowboy to get back to working on the fence. "Maggie's family ways are no concern of mine."

"That so?" Clayton watched as the two men returned to their work. How could Gus not think that his boss having a baby didn't concern him? And since they had the same last name, Clayton knew they were kin by marriage, so why didn't Jack's relative care about his wife?

"Yep. This ranch is my only concern." He grunted as he lifted a log into place.

Clayton shifted in the saddle. "What if she'd had complications?"

Gus turned to eye him. "You a doctor or something?"

"Not today. But I am concerned that no one was around when Maggie was having her baby."

Gus snorted rudely. "Look, Young. My job is to run the ranch, yours is to run the Pony Express, and Maggie is none of our concern."

"I see. So, if she had died in childbirth?"

Gus shrugged and then spit. "Then we would have buried her and continued on with the running of this ranch." He locked eyes with Clayton. "Now, if you will excuse me, I have a job to do."

Clayton nodded. He turned the horse back toward the ranch house. Gus Fillmore had made it clear he didn't care what happened to Maggie but that he did care about what happened to the ranch. If Maggie had died giving birth to baby James, would Gus have claimed the ranch as his? Clayton was pretty sure the callous, uncaring man would have done just that.

Clayton thought about the situation at the ranch. His concerns for Maggie and the children's welfare grew. He couldn't help but wonder if Gus had deliberately made sure no one would be around when Maggie went into labor. Had the man been hoping she'd die giving birth?

Maggie moved slowly about the kitchen. Coming down the stairs had taken much longer than ever before. She'd not expected to be quite this sore after having the baby.

"You all right?" Dinah asked. Worry etched her little face.

Maggie smiled at her little sister. "I'm fine. I just had a baby and I'm still a little sore."

"Oh." Dinah climbed up on one of the chairs at the table. "Are you sure you can make bread?"

Maggie nodded. "It's bread-baking day. I can do

it." She wrapped James tightly in a blanket and laid him in an oval washtub on the table in front of Dinah. "Keep an eye on the baby. If he wakes up tell me, all right?"

Dinah stood up on the seat. "I'll watch him real good, Sissy."

Her smile widened at the seriousness in Dinah's voice. "I know you will, sweetie. Thank you." She walked to the cabinet and pulled out a tin of beans. "Here, Dinah, why don't you make sets of five beans? Be sure and pull out all the rocks and dirt clods."

"All right, Sissy. I like playing with the beans." Dinah took them and began sorting them. It seemed she'd decided to separate them by color and size today.

Maggie grinned, happy that Dinah was unaware she was learning how to count and doing a simple chore at the same time. Grabbing a tin scoop, she heaped flour along with two generous pinches of salt into a large creamware bowl. Maggie then pressed her fingers into the mound of flour mixture and dug out a hole. After brushing her hands on her apron, she reached into the pie safe and pinched off a corner of yeast, crumbling the moist leaven into the center of the flour. With the milk properly scalded, she added a spoonful of bacon grease, stirring until the ingredients melted together.

While the mixture cooled, she wiped down the counter with a damp rag, set a bowl in front of Dinah to put her sorted beans into and then returned to her baking. She gently tapped the side of the pan to ensure a lukewarm temperature, then poured the thickened milk into the well of flour. Waiting for the yeast to dissolve, she gradually added a generous handful of sugar.

Weariness eased into her sore muscles as she worked. She forced her thoughts away from her discomfort and focused her attention on the liquid mixture foaming merrily in the center of the flour. Satisfied she'd waited long enough for the yeast to develop, Maggie folded in the dry ingredients.

Bread-baking day was her favorite day of the week. She loved the silky texture of the flour, the way the dough gradually came together beneath the heels of her hands to form a smooth, flexible ball. The way the yeast smelled reminded her of days spent in the kitchen with her mother before their world fell apart, happy and comforting. She put the dough into pans and then slid the two loaves into the oven.

"Baby James is awake, Sissy." Dinah rubbed the baby's head.

"Thank you, Dinah." Maggie lowered herself into the chair beside her sister and picked the baby up out of the washtub. The growing fatigue of the simple action of making bread pulled her to slump in the chair. She pressed the baby to her chest. He snuggled into her neck, bringing a sweet feeling of deep love for the infant.

"Is he hungry again?" Dinah asked. She studied the small rows of beans in front of her.

Maggie checked the baby's diaper. He was still dry. She cuddled him close and leaned her head back as he nursed. Her eyes felt heavy, so she closed them. She'd just rest them a little while the bread baked.

"Sissy?"

Maggie jerked awake. How long had she been

sleeping? The baby rested in her arms. "I'm sorry, Dinah. I fell asleep." The smell of baking bread filled the small kitchen.

"I think the bread is finished." Dinah stood in front of the stove holding a dish towel.

She tucked the blanket around the baby once more and placed him in the washtub. Her back ached as she stood. "You're right. It is ready to come out." Maggie pulled the bread from the oven and sighed. "Dinah, I think I'll take the baby and go lie down."

"You want me to do the dishes?" Dinah asked.

"No, sweetie. Why don't you come upstairs with me? You can play with your doll and blocks while I take a nap." She tugged on the girl's ponytail. "Then we'll get up and put those beans on to boil."

Dinah put the beans into the bowl Maggie had supplied earlier. She yawned. "Maggie, how come baby James sleeps so much?"

"He's new to the world. He's going to be doing a lot of growing, so he needs to sleep. You used to sleep a lot, too."

Carrying the baby, Maggie made her way back up the stairs, each step painful and slow. Dinah tagged along behind her. "You remember when I was a baby?"

"It was only five short years ago," Maggie reminded her. She continued placing one foot in front of the other until she finally reached the top of the stairs.

The front door opened below them. Maggie turned to see who had entered her house. Gus stepped inside. She frowned. When had Gus become so bold as to enter without knocking?

"Aw, Maggie. It's good to see you are up. I take it

the baby is in good health?" Gus walked across the room and stopped at the foot of the stairs.

Maggie tightened her hold on the baby. "Yes. What did you come to the house for, Gus?"

He laughed. "Always getting straight to the point, huh, Maggie?"

She didn't answer him. Maggie waited for him to continue. From experience, she knew he'd continue whether she answered or not.

"Now that the baby is here, you have even less time to invest in the ranch. Sell it to me, Maggie. I'll give you a good price and you and the kids will be able to live a life of comfort for years to come." He advanced farther up the stairs.

Dinah hid behind Maggie's skirt.

Maggie understood the little girl's fear. Most often Gus's eyes blazed his anger at whatever situation they were confronted with, but today, cunning and desire to own the Fillmore Ranch shone clear as day. She shook her head. "Thank you, Gus. I'm sure that your offer would be generous, but I promised to keep the land for baby James. I can't sell it."

His jaw clenched. "Jack is dead. He'll never know if you kept your word or not." He leaned a hip on the stair railing.

"You're right. He is dead. But I am not. I made a promise to him and I will not break it. This ranch belongs to Jack's son and I won't sell it, not to you, not to anyone." As confident as her words sounded, inwardly Maggie trembled.

Gus's face turned bright red. His jaw clenched and unclenched several times. He stood taller and fisted his hands at his sides. His eyes blazed with anger and loathing.

Maggie tightened her hand on the railing. "Please let yourself out, Gus."

He jerked around and headed to the door.

Just as his fingers touched the bar to open it again, Maggie said, "Oh, Gus. I'd like to see the ranch ledger. Please have one of the men bring it to the house this evening."

He jerked the door open and slammed it shut behind him.

Baby James awoke with a start. His small face puckered as if he'd bitten into a persimmon. Then he opened those same lips and wailed out his displeasure at being awaken so rudely.

Maggie wanted to join the baby in his tears but knew she had to stay strong for Dinah's sake. She patted the baby's back and made shushing noises.

"Come along, Dinah." Maggie led the way to her bedroom. Once inside, she closed the door and locked it. Her hand trembled as she changed the baby's diaper.

"Maggie, why does Uncle Gus want the ranch so bad?" Dinah had scrambled up on the bed with her rag doll.

"All men want to own land, Dinah. Gus thinks this ranch should rightfully belong to him since it was his cousin's." Maggie shuddered to think how far Gus might be willing to push to get the Fillmore land.

Dinah picked up her doll and hugged it close. "But you aren't going to give it to him, are you?"

Maggie wrapped the baby up tightly. She lay down

on the bed and then cuddled James close again. "No, this land belongs to James."

"I'm glad." Dinah yawned. "I don't much like Mr. Gus." Her eyes drifted closed.

Maggie wished she could fall asleep as quickly as Dinah and the baby. Her mind was having no part of rest at the moment. She knew Gus Fillmore wasn't going to give up on owning the ranch. Today he had showed just how badly he wanted it, and the depth of that desire scared Maggie.

How far would Gus go to get his cousin's ranch? And how was she going to stop him from taking it? Her thoughts went to Clayton Young and the doctor. Did she dare close her eyes and rest until they arrived?

In town, Clayton spotted the doctor's shingle hanging on the doorpost of a small house. He dismounted. After tying the horse's reins to the hitching post, he entered the front door. A bell over the entryway clanked his arrival. Clayton's gaze moved about the waiting room that appeared to be empty.

A side door opened and the doctor motioned for Clayton to follow him into the examination room. He was a tall man with thinning hair and sharp gray eyes. "Is this an emergency?" he asked.

Clayton shook his head. His gaze moved over the country doctor. The dark-haired man was older than Clayton had expected, with grass-green eyes. He wore a white coat over his regular clothes, and a stethoscope hung around his neck.

"Then you won't mind if I wash up, will you?" He turned and moved to the washbasin beside the examination table.

"No, sir."

Clayton felt as if he were right where he belonged. His gaze traveled over the examination table. A cabinet sat to the right where he assumed the doctor kept medication and medical instruments. A desk and chair stood on the other side of the room.

Clayton's gaze moved to a bookshelf that rested beside the desk. Its shelves were packed with volumes of books and loose papers. He imagined the books were filled with all kinds of cures and advice to help the sick.

"Have you had any doctor training?" The elderly man finished washing his hands then moved to the desk.

Clayton turned his attention back to the doctor. "No, sir. But I've read a couple of medical books and was the family doctor." He grinned as memories of his brothers' cuts and bruises came to mind. When you grew up with six adopted brothers, you tended to stay busy with bandaging and sewing up gashes.

Thankfully, nothing serious had come up. Clayton's grin slid from his face. If it had, he wouldn't have known what to do. Josephine, his brother Thomas's wife, had known more about healing than he had when one of the other Pony Express riders had arrived with a gunshot wound. The event had forced Clayton to realize that he needed more schoolin' if he intended to be a doctor.

"I thought as much, the way you are eyeballing those books."

Was he so transparent that the doctor had read his desire to become a doctor just by watching his expression when he'd looked at the books?

He held out his hand. "I'm Charles Anderson and the only doctor for miles around."

Clayton took his hand and shook it. Doc Anderson's handshake wasn't as forceful as Gus Fillmore's, but then again, the doctor didn't have anything to prove. "Clayton Young."

"Ah, the new Pony Express manager out at the Fillmore place. Bill mentioned a new man would be arriving soon."

"Yes, sir." Clayton released the other man's hand.

"So, if you don't mind my asking, what were you doing reading medical books and behaving as the family doctor?" He tucked his hands in his front pockets.

Clayton studied his face. "Our farm is about fifteen miles from town. If someone got hurt or sick, I took care of them."

"And the books?"

Clayton pushed away from the window. "I've wanted to be a doctor since forever. Ma bought me a few books. Typically animal care books, but most of the practices are the same." Clayton still remembered the first time his adoptive mother, Rebecca Armstrong, had given him a book. He'd thought her the most wonderful person alive. Still did, if truth be told.

The doctor surprised him with a burst of laughter. "Well, that's the first time I've heard that, but all considering, you might not be too off with your thinking." He rubbed his chin. "So, what brings you to my office?"

"Mrs. Fillmore had her baby last night."

The doctor stood taller. "Did the delivery go well? How's the baby?" He began grabbing items and thrusting them into a black bag. "Why didn't you speak up sooner?"

Clayton grimaced. "I wasn't there for the delivery. The boy seems to be fine this morning and I got distracted with all your questions."

Doc Anderson slowed down and looked at Clayton. "I'd better go out anyway and check on Maggie and the babe."

Clayton grinned. "My thoughts exactly. That's why I'm here."

The doctor gave him a funny look, then walked over to the bookcase. He chose two books and dropped them into his big black bag. "My buggy is sitting beside the house. It's already rigged up. I was about to go to the Harper place, but they can wait until I examine Maggie and the baby."

Clayton followed him through the waiting room and out the front door. He watched the doctor lock the door and drop the key into his front pocket. "I'll wait here."

The doctor nodded and then walked to the side of the house.

A few minutes later, Clayton found himself riding beside the doctor's buggy. He wasn't sure he'd ever want to use a buggy for house calls. It was quicker to just jump on the horse's back and ride.

"I hear the Pony Express may be shutting its doors soon," the doctor said in way of conversation.

"Yes, sir. I've heard that, too."

"Do you have any plans for your future?" He clicked his tongue to get the horse pulling his buggy to go a little faster.

Clayton grinned. "I'm hoping to become a doctor."

"Figured as much." The doctor nodded. "I don't know if you've noticed, but I'm getting up there in years." He kept his gaze on the horse's back.

Clayton answered, "No, I didn't notice."

The good doctor laughed. "Well, be that as it may, I've been thinking about retiring in a few years. Think you might be interested in becoming my assistant, if the Pony Express doesn't pan out?"

Was this God's way of blessing his plans of becoming a doctor? Clayton swallowed. This was just the opportunity he'd prayed about. "I would be honored, but I can't leave the Pony Express right now."

"No, I don't reckon you can. But, if you are serious about becoming a doctor, I'll be happy to loan you a couple of books. Maybe you can study those and then we can talk more about your future." He dug in his bag and pulled out one of the books.

Clayton rode the horse close to the buggy and leaned down to take the book Doc Anderson held up to him. Then he straightened and examined the soft calfskin cover. It was light brown with the words "*The History and Treatment of the Diseases of the Teeth, the Gums, and the Alveolar Processes*, by Joseph Fox" on both the front of the book and the spine.

"In my line of work, I'm often called to pull teeth or doctor a tooth that has infection in it. That's probably one of the best books you can find right now, so don't lose it."

Clayton flipped it open and was happy to see that there were numerous illustrations of teeth and different forms of decay. "I'll take good care of it." He slipped it into his saddlebag.

"See that you do. Here's the second book I want

you to study." He held up a smaller book for Clayton to take.

Clayton took the book and silently read the cover. *The Family Doctor: A Counsellor in Sickness, Pain and Distress, for Childhood, Manhood and Old Age. Containing in Plain Language, Free from Medical Terms, the Causes, Symptoms, and Cure of Disease in Every Form...with Engravings of Medicinal Plants and Herbs* by Henry S. Taylor. It never failed to amaze him that books came with such long titles. This one would be interesting to read. He just prayed that with his Pony Express duties he'd have time. "Thank you, sir. How long can I keep them?" He ran his finger over the raised lettering of the title.

"As long as you need. That one is fairly new. Came out last year, but I have an older one that says pretty much the same thing. Just remember to take good care of it. Books aren't cheap, you know."

Clayton nodded. He added the book to his saddlebag. His thoughts went to Maggie and the kids. "Doc? How well do you know Maggie Fillmore?"

"Well enough, I reckon. Why do you ask?" His gray eyes searched Clayton's face.

"I met Gus Fillmore and he seems to not like the widow. Is there anything I should know about her?" That wasn't exactly what he wanted to ask but felt it was a good starting place.

"Gus Fillmore is Jack's cousin. He'd hoped to inherit the ranch and when he didn't, he offered to buy it from Maggie. She refused. I'm sure Gus is still a little sore about all that and is holding a grudge."

Just as he suspected. Clayton nodded. "I think you're right." He focused on the road home and even tapped Bones's side with the heel of his boot to get the horse to go a little faster.

The doctor urged his horse to do the same.

Clayton didn't like the idea of Gus Fillmore having ill feelings toward Maggie. He didn't know her very well, but what he did know, he liked. She'd braved having a child on her own, then had the sense to tell her younger sister to get help, and when he'd arrived, she'd trusted him to make the baby breathe. Maggie seemed like a strong woman, but would she be strong enough to keep Gus Fillmore from taking over the ranch?

Chapter Three

It seemed as if Clayton had been in town far longer than he needed to be, if he were concerned about baby James. Maggie's eyes were drifting closed when she heard the men arrive in the front yard. She pushed herself up into a sitting position.

The baby stirred in her arms and Dinah awoke with wide eyes. The little girl had slept for over an hour.

Maggie reached over and brushed the blonde hair from her eyes. "Sweetie, I think Clayton and the doctor have arrived. Would you go look out the window and make sure it's them for me?"

Dinah came awake instantly. She scrambled off the bed and ran to the window. Her little hands tugged at the drapes.

Maggie grinned as the girl disappeared behind them.

"It is Clayton and the doctor." Dinah came out. "Want me to go open the door for them?" She ran to the bedroom door and waited for an answer.

"Yes, please."

Maggie listened as Dinah ran down the stairs. A

few moments later she heard the doctor's voice and sighed. Now she could relax. Clayton was back, and the doctor would make sure the baby was healthy.

Over the last couple of months, the older gentleman had fussed and insisted she come see him on the first Monday of every month. Yesterday, this time, she would have loved to have had him close but instead had faced having baby James alone.

A soft knock sounded on the door. She called, "Come in."

Doc Anderson entered first. "Well, hello, Maggie. I wasn't expecting you to have that little bundle for another week." His gray eyes searched Maggie's.

Maggie smiled at him. "I know. Baby James came a little earlier than we expected. Not only was he early, but his coming into the world wasn't as easygoing as we'd hoped."

The doctor glanced with concern from Maggie to Clayton. "What happened?" He walked across the room and took the baby from her arms.

Hadn't Clayton told the doctor how he'd saved the baby's life? She watched as Dinah slipped into the room and took Clayton's hand in hers. Her little sister pressed against his leg. Obviously, Gus's visit had scared her more than Maggie had realized. Or was the little girl simply happy to see the man responsible for James's well-being?

Maggie pulled her gaze from the pair and explained the difficult delivery in a low tone, wishing Dinah were in the other room. Her voice cracked as she told him how the baby wouldn't breathe for her.

She looked to Clayton and said, "Thankfully, Mr. Young arrived and saved him."

The doctor turned to look at Clayton. "Is that right?" It wasn't really a question as much as an expression of admiration.

"It wasn't really me, sir. God used me to help the child." Clayton's neck and cheeks turned red under the doctor's interested gaze.

"Well, then I'm glad the good Lord sent you when you were needed the most."

Maggie searched Clayton's face. So, he believed in giving God credit for what he'd done. It gave her comfort to think that Clayton might be a God-fearing man.

Doctor Anderson turned to face them once more. "Clayton, why don't you take Miss Dinah downstairs for a little while?" He didn't give Clayton time to answer before he spoke to her. "Maggie, I'm going to examine you both and make sure that you're healthy enough to get back to a regular routine."

Worried blue eyes met hers. Maggie said, "Dinah, you can stay if you want to."

"No, I want to go with Clayton." She clung tighter to his hand. "He'll keep me safe."

Maggie moved her eyes to search his. Had he heard the fear in Dinah's voice? What would he think if he knew just how badly her cousin-in-law wanted the ranch?

Clayton nodded. "I can use her company in the horse barn, if that's all right with you."

Maggie knew he'd take care of Dinah and for a brief moment allowed herself to dream that he really could keep them all safe. "Thank you."

Half an hour later, the doctor and Maggie walked out onto the front porch. "Now, don't forget, Maggie, this first week rest downstairs until bedtime at night. Stairs will delay your healing. And no lifting anything heavier than the baby. If there are any indications of sickness in either of you, call on me right away. Otherwise, I'll expect you to come into town in about six weeks so that I can check on the babe."

"I will. I'm glad we are both doing well. Thank you, Doctor, for coming out."

Clayton felt Dinah's small hand slip into his once more. They walked across the yard to the house.

"Is baby James all right?" Dinah asked.

Clayton laid a hand on her shoulder. His gaze moved from the doctor's to Maggie's.

"He is a happy, healthy baby," Maggie answered. Her smile seemed to brighten the already sunny afternoon.

The doctor cleared his throat to get Clayton's attention, then said, "Mr. Young, I'd like a few minutes of your time." He motioned for Clayton to come closer to the porch.

Clayton felt his face burst into flames as he realized the doctor had caught him staring at Maggie. He had no business staring at a new mother, even if she was the prettiest woman he'd ever met. Where were his manners? He walked up onto the bottom porch step.

"You did a fine job with the baby."

Clayton rested an arm on the porch railing. "Thank you. But like I said, it was God's doing, not mine."

The doctor nodded. "Yep, that's how I feel every time a life is spared." His gaze moved off into the distance for a moment. "I'm glad you were here for these two. Read and study those books I gave you. I've a feeling you are going to be a great doctor." Doctor Anderson stepped around Clayton and into the yard where Dinah still stood.

"Thank you, sir. I will."

The doctor knelt in front of Dinah. "Thank you for helping Clayton out in the barn while you waited for us. Here's a bit of candy for all your troubles." He handed Dinah a small peppermint stick and grinned at her before standing again.

Dinah looked to Maggie, who nodded her permission for the child to keep the candy. Clayton tried to hide his grin as the child immediately stuck the treat in her mouth.

"What do you say?" Maggie asked.

She pulled the candy out with a frown, then said, "Thank you, Doctor Anderson." Dinah turned her attention back to the candy.

"Did you know that peppermint is good for an ailing stomach?"

Clayton watched as Maggie opened her mouth to answer but then realized that the doctor was talking to him and not her. He answered, "Yes, sir. It's also good for colds. Ma always kept a little peppermint around for hot tea when any of us came down sick."

The doctor slapped him on the back. "She sounds like a wise woman. When you get done with the books, come on back to town for more."

He turned to Maggie. "Remember what I said, get

some rest over the next few days and ease into your regular routine."

"I will, Doctor. Thank you." Maggie motioned for Dinah to come to her. Dinah looked up at Clayton one more time and then walked slowly to her side.

Clayton frowned. Dinah had told him that Gus had come by the house earlier in the day and that he was a mean man. He planned on talking to Maggie. Dinah seemed really scared of the other man. He waved goodbye to the doctor.

"Clayton, would you like to come in for dinner? I baked bread to go along with your soup." Maggie rocked the baby in her arms.

"Sissy makes the best bread. She's teaching me, but mine isn't as good as hers," Dinah said around a mouthful of peppermint.

He grinned down at the sticky-faced girl. "I'm sure your bread is pretty tasty, too." Then Clayton looked back to Maggie. "I would love to eat with you lovely ladies." He stepped back and opened the door for her to pass.

Dinah followed close behind her sister. "No, I put too much salt in last time."

"Well, you are learning. My first pot of soup wasn't too good either." Clayton smiled at Maggie. "Why don't you sit down and Dinah and I will set the table."

She looked tired. "Thank you." Maggie moved to one of the hardwood chairs and eased into it.

It didn't take long to set the pot of soup on the table and slice up the now-cooled bread. "My ma makes this soup all the time. It's one of my favorites. I hope you like it." Clayton set a bowl in front of Maggie.

She yawned. "I'm sure it will taste wonderful."

"Didn't you get any rest while I was gone?" Clayton asked, handing Dinah a spoon. "Careful, half-pint, it's hot."

"I rested but didn't sleep."

He eased into his chair. "Dinah mentioned that Gus stopped by today."

She nodded. "He did."

"Can I say the prayers?" Dinah asked.

Maggie smiled tiredly at her. "Yes, dear."

Dinah prayed over the food and thanked the Lord that her Sissy and baby James were going to be all right. She ended with, "and please don't let mean Gus have baby James's ranch. Amen."

Shock filled Maggie's face. "Dinah, you don't need to worry about Gus. He isn't going to get James's ranch."

The little girl frowned and dipped her spoon into the soup. "I don't know. He was mad when he left." Her hand shook as she raised the spoon to her mouth.

"Is Gus the reason you weren't able to sleep this afternoon?" Clayton handed Dinah a thick slice of bread.

Maggie inclined her head toward Dinah as if to say now was not the time to discuss this. "No, I just had a lot on my mind."

"I went to sleep, Clayton. I had a dream that I got to ride a horse with you," Dinah said, taking a big bite out of her bread.

Clayton smiled. "That sounds like a nice dream."

Dinah went back to eating and chattering about her dreams.

Maggie ate silently. Her eyes drooped as if exhaustion drifted over her like a soft morning fog.

When Dinah finished eating, she asked, "Sissy, can I go play with my dolly now?"

"Yes, I'll be up in a little while to read a story and get ready for bed." Maggie pushed her bowl back. She reached over and picked up baby James.

"I'll take care of the dishes tonight. You rest up for that climb back up the stairs." Clayton began cleaning the table. He placed the bowls and cups in the washtub. The sound of Dinah going up the stairs filled his ears. As soon as she was up, he said, "I talked to Gus this morning and asked why there were no men stationed at the house yesterday."

"What did he say?"

He heard the weariness in her voice. "That he needed all the men to repair the fences."

"Did you tell him I'd had the baby?"

Clayton nodded as he filled the pan with hot water. He saw a bar of soap and shaved a few slivers into the water. "I did."

She exhaled. "Well, that explains his visit today."

"What did he want?" Clayton turned and faced her. He leaned against the sideboard and waited for her answer.

Maggie laughed bitterly. "He wants the ranch."

Clayton turned back around. He'd known Maggie only two days and already he cared about her and the children. Not in a romantic way but in the way a friend would care for another friend. He made quick work of the dirty dishes and put the last one in the drainer to dry.

When he turned again, Maggie and the baby were

asleep. Her face had softened in sleep, and she looked very young. Clayton felt a surge of protection for her and the child. He hated that Gus was using his status as a relative of her husband's to bully the young widow. If all Dinah had told him was true, there was no doubt in his mind that that was exactly what the other man was doing. Still, it was none of his business. His job was to keep the Pony Express moving, and he intended to do just that.

As if she sensed his gaze upon her, Maggie stirred. Her hazel-green eyes opened slowly. She looked up at him. "I'm sorry, I dozed off."

Clayton was thankful that she felt comfortable enough with him to fall asleep in his presence. "Nonsense. You have nothing to be sorry about."

She groaned as she balanced the baby and stood. "I guess I should get my family to bed. Tomorrow will come soon enough."

He nodded. "I agree." Clayton laid the dish towel to the side and took the dirty water to the back door where he tossed it into the yard.

"Thank you for—" she looked about the kitchen, then focused on his face once more "—everything."

"It was my pleasure." Clayton returned the dishpan to its place and then asked, "Do you need help getting up the stairs?"

She shook her head. "No, you've done plenty. I'll just bolt the door after you."

Clayton nodded. He stopped by the door to slip into his coat. "If you need anything, call out or send Dinah and I'll come runnin'."

Maggie followed him slowly. "I will."

He opened the door and grinned at her. "See that you do."

At her nod, Clayton turned and walked off the porch. He stopped just off it and listened until he heard the wooden beam fall across the door.

The full moon lit the yard, making it easier for him to find his way to the barn. He pulled the big door open and entered. The smells of hay and horseflesh filled his nostrils.

He walked to the back room that was to be his new home.

It was small with a cot and table. The cot had a homespun quilt on the top and a pillow of sorts. The table was low to the ground and had a small mirror over the top. A washbasin rested in the middle of it, and he noted several nails filled the back wall.

His bundle of clothes rested on the cot where he'd thrown them the night before. Clayton saw the pot-bellied stove and a small rack of wood beside it. He made his way to the stove and began making a fire. The coldness in the air hinted that winter wasn't finished with the ranch just yet.

After starting the fire, he opened the bundle of clothes and hung up his pants and shirts. One nail was bigger than the others, so he took off his coat and hung it on that nail. His extra pair of long johns, he folded and placed on the far end of the table. He set his razor and comb beside the washbasin. Lastly, he pulled out the small Bible that Seth, his adoptive father, had given him and laid it on the bed.

Clayton sat down on the edge of the bed. In the last forty-eight hours, he'd delivered a baby, comforted a

little girl, and became friends with the local doctor
and the young widow woman.

He'd decided he disliked Gus Fillmore almost the
moment he'd met him. Gus had seemed arrogant and
uncaring. By confronting Maggie when she was weak
from having the baby, Gus had shown his greed for
the ranch.

Clayton decided he'd protect Maggie and her small
family from Gus and his greed. How was he going to
do it, though? He had no proof that Gus meant Maggie any harm, but something in his gut said that Gus
would be more than happy to get rid of the widow and
her son as well as sweet Dinah.

The next morning, Clayton felt as if he'd ridden
the Pony Express trail hard. He'd tossed and turned
throughout the night as his thoughts turned into night-
mares of Gus Fillmore kicking Maggie and the children off the ranch. He went through the morning
chores and then met his first Pony Express rider.

He was a young man with a wild head of curly red
hair. From the ledger Bill had left behind, Clayton
had learned the boy's name was Sam and that he was
skilled at avoiding the Indians. That was good information for a Pony Express station manager to know.

"Did you have any trouble?" Clayton asked as they
exchanged horses.

Sam bounded into the saddle. "Nope. Any news
from the other direction?"

"Nope. Safe journeys." Clayton slapped the horse
on the rump and Sam was well on his way to the
next station.

He turned back to the barn with the spent horse.
Standing in the doorway was a man who looked to

be in his early twenties. Muscles filled his shirt and chest.

"Mr. Young, would you like for me to take care of the horse for you?"

Clayton continued to walk the horse toward the man. "You seem to have me at a disadvantage. Seems you know me but I have no idea who you are." He continued into the barn. It was nice of the stranger to offer to take care of the Pony Express horse, but until he knew whom he was talking to, Clayton wasn't about to turn over Pony Express property to the man.

The man followed him into the barn. "I'm sorry. Name's Hal. I work for Mrs. Fillmore. I usually take care of the horses." He held out a big beefy hand.

Clayton took his hand and shook it. "From what I've seen you do a good job, Hal."

"Much appreciative." Hal picked up a pitchfork and began tossing fresh hay into the horse's pen next to the one Clayton and the spent pony stood in.

Clayton filled a feed sack with oats and hung it over the horse's stall door. Then he proceeded to brush the animal down as it ate. "Where have you disappeared to the last couple of days?" he asked.

Hal stopped shoveling and leaned on the fork. "Boss had us fixing fences."

"They're all fixed now?" Clayton continued brushing as if the question he'd asked was of no importance at all. He hoped Hal would talk freely about the running of the ranch. For Maggie's sake, Clayton prayed all was going well.

He shrugged. "I reckon. Boss says we are to go back to our regular chores."

"I thought you said you worked for Maggie. Who

are you calling 'boss'?" Clayton ran his hands down each of the mustang's legs.

He listened as Hal answered. "Oh, I do work for Maggie. At least, she's the one who pays me. But the real boss is Mr. Fillmore. He gives the orders and does the hiring and firing."

"Gus Fillmore?"

"Yes, sir."

Clayton continued examining the mustang for any sign of stress on its legs and body. As if talking to himself, he said, "I wonder why everyone can go back to work as usual today."

"Probably because the boss had to run into town today. Figured we knew our jobs well enough to get back to them."

Clayton stood and brushed the mustang's back. "How many men work for Mrs. Fillmore?"

"Just five. Me, Bud, ole George, Abraham and the boss." He grinned across at Clayton. "Ole George is our cook. He'll have breakfast ready here in about ten minutes."

Clayton hadn't given much thought to whom he'd eat with. He'd just assumed he'd cook his own meals, but now that he thought about it, there really wasn't a kitchen in his room, or even a makeshift kitchen.

"Did Bill eat with you boys or fend for himself?"

Hal put the fork back against the wall. "Bill didn't like the boss too much, so Ole George would have me bring him a plate."

Clayton nodded. "I see." He knew that the Pony Express supplied him with food, but he hadn't received a shipment yet.

"Would you like to meet the other men or should

I bring you a plate later?" Hal asked as he walked toward the exit.

Clayton put his brush away and followed him. "I'd like to meet everyone." If he was going to protect Maggie from Gus, Clayton planned on finding out just how loyal Gus's men were to him.

Chapter Four

A week later, Maggie's mind was on the ranch. Things had fallen into a routine she could handle as she recuperated from childbirth. Clayton had checked on her and the children every day. He took his meals with the men but seemed ever watchful of the house. Whether his scrutiny was intentional or not, it afforded Maggie with a peace of mind she hadn't felt in a long time.

She was having a hard time keeping Dinah out of the barn. Her little sister seemed to adore Clayton. It was all Maggie could do to keep the little girl out of his and the Pony Express riders' hair. But if she scolded Dinah, Clayton rushed to her defense and assured Maggie that Dinah was no trouble and was not in the way; that he liked having her underfoot.

Her thoughts returned to the running of the ranch. Gus had been right when he'd said since she had two children to take care of she wouldn't have time for overseeing the ranch. How was she going to make sure Gus was doing a good job? She wanted to go out and ride the fence lines, but with an infant, that wasn't going to happen. And her body would never handle riding a horse; at least not the way she felt now. Was this normal? Perhaps she'd ask one of the ladies in town when next she went for supplies. It would be so nice to have another woman's opinion on the changes that had taken place in her body. She sure couldn't ask any of the men.

Maggie felt her frustration grow. Everyday chores were difficult with two children underfoot. Each night she fell into bed exhausted. The doctor had said she should be able to do routine work within a week. He'd also advised her to let Clayton help as much as he wanted.

Could she do that? Maggie stroked the baby's tiny hand. She fretted that she didn't really know Clayton Young. Other than the fact that he'd saved the baby, gone to town to retrieve the doctor and that Dinah liked him, Maggie knew nothing else about the Pony Express man.

Well, that wasn't entirely true. Before he'd left, Bill Evers, the previous Pony Express manager, had come up to the house and asked if he could visit with Maggie for a few moments. She'd agreed and offered him coffee and cookies. While the man had eaten almost a full plate of gingersnaps, he'd told her that his replacement was a nice young man who would be a great help around the place.

Her gaze moved to the window at the front of the house that looked out toward the barn and bunkhouse. So far, Bill had been right. She'd seen Clayton repair a corner of the barn roof, build a small fence around the chicken coop, as well as gather eggs during the last week.

Maggie frowned. On the other hand, Gus Fillmore neglected most of the chores. He had tried to stake his claim to the ranch the day of Jack's funeral, but when he'd discovered that Jack had a will and had left the ranch to his unborn child, Gus had stormed off so angry he could spit, but later returned and offered to stay on and help.

She would have loved to have sent Gus packing as soon as her husband had been buried, but since most of the men had quit and she'd been so sick with her pregnancy, Maggie had allowed her late husband's cousin to stay on. Now with hindsight she wished she hadn't.

Bill, the former Pony Express manager, had warned her to keep a close eye on Gus and the ranch books. Maggie had intended to ask Gus about the ranch ledger, but he'd found reasons to be gone before dawn and back long after she and Dinah had gone to bed. After a while, Maggie had given up on him bringing the ledger to her and planned on going in search of it after the baby was born.

The day she'd gone into labor, Maggie had been surprised to discover not one of the hired men anywhere near the house when she needed someone to go get the doctor.

Tears pricked the backs of her eyes at how close she'd come to losing her son. She kissed his soft downy hair, which looked as if it were going to be honey colored, much like her own. The light wisps tickled her lips.

Maggie hugged him closer. Her love for James far surpassed the realization that if the baby had died, she and Dinah would have possibly been forced by Gus to give up the ranch, as well.

She watched from the window as a Pony Express rider came thundering into the yard. Clayton met him with a fresh horse and a smile. They exchanged a few quick words, and within moments the rider's horse raced back onto the trail. Clayton glanced toward the house and then began to return to the barn.

Impulsively, Maggie hurried to the front door and called out to Clayton. When he looked in her direction, she yelled, "When you are done with the horse, would you come to the house? Please."

He nodded, then continued to the barn. In the kitchen, Maggie filled a plate with sugar cookies. She made sure the coffee in the pot was still hot.

She gazed down into James's sleeping face. His small features looked more like hers than her late husband's. Even though they were closed, Maggie knew his eyes were the only thing that resembled his father. They were dark blue, unlike her hazel eyes that often held more green than any other color. She hurried up the stairs and laid him in his dresser drawer. Dinah lay on the bed fast asleep. Maggie usually enjoyed a nap with the children but knew she needed to get out of the habit of sleeping the afternoon away.

Making sure both children were covered, she walked back down the stairs. She hadn't spoken more than ten words with Clayton in the last five days but knew that now was the time. After a week of living and eating with the ranchers, he should know how the ranch was being run and could tell her if all was well. At least she hoped he was as observant as his predecessor had been.

Half an hour later, Clayton knocked on the front door. Maggie hurried to let him in. "Thank you for coming to the house." She led the way to the kitchen.

"What can I do for you?" he asked, eyeing the plate of cookies and the two cups that rested on the table.

She smiled as she picked up the coffeepot. All men were the same when it came to cookies and coffee. "Well, for starters you can have a seat and help me eat these cookies." She poured hot coffee into the two cups.

Clayton's rich laughter washed over her like warm water on a cold day. She felt goose bumps swell on her arms.

"I'll be happy to put away a few of those cookies for you." He moved to the table and waited for her to indicate which chair to take. She waved him to the one on the end, and then Maggie joined him.

When he was seated, Maggie said, "Help yourself." She pushed the plate closer to him.

Clayton picked up a golden-colored cookie and bit into it. He grinned. "These are very good."

"Thank you. They are my grandmother's recipe." She took a sip of the warm coffee.

His eyes narrowed. "Why are you trying to sweeten me up?"

She laughed. "Am I that transparent?"

Clayton chewed, then swallowed. "Let's just say I know a bribe when I taste one. Ma used to ply us boys with cookies when she wanted information."

Maggie nodded. "I think I would like your ma."

"I'm sure you would. Everybody loves Ma." He washed the first cookie down with a big gulp of the coffee. "So, what do you want to know?" His blue gaze met hers.

She sighed and put down her cup. "As you know, I can't very well get out with the children to check and see for myself what Gus is doing to James's ranch. Bill used to come and give me updates on how things were going so I was hoping you would do the same." Maggie waited to see if things were as bad as she felt in her heart that they were. She hadn't seen the books in over three months. She prayed the ranch finances were in order.

Clayton set his cup down and reached for another cookie. "Well, according to Hal, Gus isn't around much so hasn't given any orders other than for the men to do what they normally do. I've noticed that the calves haven't been rounded up or branded and there are a lot of repairs on the place that are being neglected."

Maggie leaned forward in her chair. "How many calves do you think we have this year?"

It seemed to Maggie that Clayton was doing a mental head count. "I've seen about three hundred, more or less."

"That sounds about right. Gus said we lost over half the herd this winter and that's about half of the calves Jack said we'd have this year."

Clayton's eyes narrowed. "How did you lose half the herd?"

"Gus said that last big snow we had trapped some of them in the gully and they froze to death. He and the men couldn't get to them because of the weather." She sighed. "We took a big loss on them."

"If you don't mind my asking, how is the ranch

making money?" Clayton pushed the plate away as if he'd lost his appetite.

"Jack always took the cattle to market in the late spring, but with us losing half the herd, I'm not sure what Gus has planned." She hated admitting that she didn't know what would happen next.

Clayton's frown deepened. "Maggie, there aren't enough cattle on this ranch for a cattle drive to anyplace."

She shook her head. "We are a small ranch. Every spring Jack teamed up with our neighbor, Mr. Morris, and they'd take our cattle and his to market."

"Doesn't it seem odd to you that half the herd froze to death in the gully? Isn't the gully supposed to help protect them? And where were the men when the cattle were freezing?"

Clayton's blue eyes had hardened to deep sapphires.

Maggie realized just how little she knew about her own ranch. She sighed. "I don't know."

"I'm not trying to be rude, Maggie, but why haven't you asked Gus these questions?"

She swallowed. "I didn't know what to ask at the time, and lately, he isn't talking to me."

Clayton nodded. "Yeah, I noticed he hasn't been to the house. I just assumed that you two meet once a month instead of weekly."

Maggie shook her head. "No, he's still sore because I won't sell the ranch to him."

They sat in silence for several minutes. Then Clayton said, "You could fire him. Since the Pony Express riders come through about every two or three days, I would be happy to help you with the running of the ranch. At least until you can find someone who would do an honest job for you."

Maggie hated to admit it, but Clayton really was a good man. Not a man whom she'd ever fall in love with or want to marry. Jack had been a good man but he hadn't loved her. Her marriage to him had been out of his desire for an heir and her need to put a roof over Dinah's head. Then just as she'd started to fall in love with her husband, he'd up and died. Maggie didn't want to feel the disappointment of lost love again. But he seemed to really want to help her. "Thank you, but I don't feel like I can do that at this time. Gus wouldn't leave quietly, and since he's Jack's relative he might go as far as to try to take the ranch away from me legally. To be honest, I'm not sure if I have a legal right to the land."

"Did Jack have a will or a piece of paper saying the ranch belonged to the child?" Clayton reached for another cookie.

Maggie nodded. "Yes. Right after the funeral Jack's lawyer called both Gus and me to his office. He had Jack's will. Jack had left the ranch to our unborn child and given Gus a hundred dollars. Of course, Gus wanted it all, but the lawyer said that as long as the baby lives, he legally owns the land." She watched as he finished the cookie.

"Well, doesn't that answer your question? Sounds like you do have a legal right."

She shook her head. "No, James has the legal right. Not me."

Clayton drank the rest of his coffee and stood up. "You know, maybe we should make a trip to town and check with Jack's lawyer. I think that as long as you are James's mother, you have as much right to this land as he does."

She stood also. "I guess it wouldn't hurt to ask." Maggie followed him to the door.

Just before leaving, Clayton turned to face her. "Maggie, I'll do what I can to help you with Gus." His blue eyes softened into clear blue pools.

Maggie's heart skipped a beat. Her palms grew moist. She wiped them on her apron. Confusion clouded her mind. What was it about Clayton Young that had her brain turning to mush?

Clayton walked to the barn. He didn't understand why he cared so much about this family. But the thought of Gus Fillmore taking advantage of Maggie and the children infuriated him.

Over the last week, he'd tried to keep to the barn and do the job of Pony Express manager but had found himself watching the house and wondering what Maggie and Dinah were doing.

He missed his family and decided maybe that was why he felt protective of Maggie and the kids. Clayton went to his room and picked up one of the medical books Doc Anderson had given him. Flipping through the pages, he couldn't focus on the book. His mind continued to drift to Gus, Maggie and the turmoil with the ranch.

He tossed the book onto the cot and pulled his coat and hat back on. Not expecting another rider for a couple of days, Clayton decided he needed to get some fresh air.

Bones snorted his greeting.

Clayton chuckled and said, "You miss our rides,

too, don't you, ole boy?" He saddled the horse and led him outside.

Within a few minutes, Clayton was riding the fences of the ranch. He wasn't sure what he was looking for but felt the need to have a good look around.

The ranch was flat in most places, and after riding about a mile he circled around and came upon the river. It gurgled along, and new green grass and shrubs lined its banks. He continued and was pleasantly surprised to come upon a wooded cove with the river running past and a pool of clear water that had washed out a peaceful inlet.

Clayton dismounted and allowed Bones to drink his fill while he looked about. He inhaled the fresh air and closed his eyes to enjoy the sweet sound of running water behind him. His shoulders relaxed and his thoughts moved to visions of having a picnic with Maggie and the kids in this spot.

His eyes snapped open. What was he thinking? This wasn't his family. He had no business thinking about family picnics. Still, he liked Maggie and the kids. What would it hurt to have a picnic with them? Who said a man and a woman couldn't share a meal together and enjoy this wonderful fresh air? As friends, of course. Just friends.

Bones snorted a warning. Clayton turned and saw Gus riding in his direction. Clayton remounted Bones and waited for the ranch foreman to arrive.

"I see you've found my favorite spot on the ranch," Gus said as a greeting. "What are you doing so far away from the barn?"

Clayton leaned on the saddle horn. "Getting fresh

air." He looked about at the new leaves and grass. "This is a nice spot."

Gus stared at him. He tilted his hat back. "Don't you have the Pony Express to take care of?"

What was Gus getting at? Clayton tightened his grip on Bones's reins and answered. "Obviously, you don't know how the Pony Express works." He looked about to let the thinly veiled insult sink in.

The other man shifted in the saddle. "Just like you don't understand the workings of a ranch."

"It's interesting that you should say that. I've been around a ranch or two, Gus, and I know enough to know that you are short on the amount of cattle that should be roaming these pastures and that your excuse to Mrs. Fillmore is weak." He sat up straighter in the saddle. "I also know it's branding season and you haven't started." Clayton had the satisfaction of seeing the shock on Gus's face turn to anger. "Is there a reason you don't want me out here riding the range?"

Gus shifted in the saddle again and ignored the question. "You are free to roam around as much as you like, Young. Just don't get in the way of my men and our jobs. As you have kindly pointed out, we have work to do." He turned his horse to leave and then turned to look over his shoulder. "I suggest you focus on your job and let us do the same." He spurred his horse and left at a gallop.

Clayton had hit a nerve with the foreman. Gus hadn't answered his question and had clenched his jaw. His shoulders had squared and he'd tightened his grip on the horse's reins as if it took all that he had not to ball up his fists and swing a punch. Clayton's ride had been relaxing until he'd met up with Gus.

Man and horse picked up where they'd left off and continued their exploration of the ranch. The Fillmore Ranch was a decent-size spread, but Clayton hated that the oversize pastures were sparse in cattle. Baby James's inheritance was being underused, meaning less money would be coming into the family.

When Clayton arrived back at the ranch house, he noticed a horse tied to the hitching rail in front of the porch. Dinah played on the porch with a rag doll and some blocks. She looked up and saw him and came running.

"Hi, Clayton!"

He slid off Bones's back. "Hello, half-pint. I see you have a visitor."

Dinah looked over her shoulder at the house. "Yep, a man from the bank."

"I see." Clayton led Bones into the barn.

Dinah followed, swinging her rag doll by its arm. "Sissy asked me to go outside to play while she talked to him."

Clayton took off the horse's saddle. "Well, I'm glad she did. Now you can tell me your doll's name."

"Oh, this is Charlotte. Sissy was going to name baby James Charlotte, if he was a girl." She hugged the doll close.

"That's a pretty name." He rubbed Bones's black-and-white coat. Clayton wondered why Maggie hadn't had a boy's name picked out for the baby since she'd already had a girl's name chosen.

Dinah nodded. "Yeah, it's Mama's name."

He looked at the little girl over Bones's back. Sadness filled her pixie-like face. Poor little mite.

"Dinah! Clayton!" Maggie called from the house.

"Sissy is calling us," Dinah said.

They left the barn together. Clayton watched as a well-dressed man rode away toward town. Maggie stood on the porch holding the baby.

Dinah ran ahead. "I was in the barn with Clayton."

"I saw that." Maggie rocked the baby. When Clayton got close enough, she asked, "Can you hitch a horse up to the wagon for me? I need to go into town."

The tremble in her voice tore at him. "Sure. Would you like for me to go with you?"

"Can I go?" Dinah asked.

"Of course you are going, Dinah." Maggie frowned at the little girl. She then turned her attention to Clayton. Uncertainty filtered through her voice. "I don't want to take you from your work."

"No more riders coming in today," he said. "I wouldn't mind going, and I can take Doc Anderson back one of his books."

"Thank you. We'll be ready in just a few minutes." Maggie turned to go back inside. "Come along, Dinah. We'll change our dresses and fix your hair up pretty."

Clayton grinned as he went back to the barn. If he'd learned anything about Dinah, it was that she liked her hair fixed and her dresses kept clean. He chose a brown mare to pull the wagon. She was an older horse with white socks. He'd worked with her a few times in the corral, and she'd been very obedient. Clayton hitched the horse to the wagon and then pulled it up to the front of the house.

As he waited for them to come out, Clayton wondered why someone from the bank had come to see Maggie. Why did she need to run off to town as soon as the banker had left? Did the trip have anything to do with the ranch or Gus? Whatever the reason, Maggie was shaken up by it. He had so many questions that only Maggie could answer.

Chapter Five

Maggie gently pushed the last comb into Dinah's hair. The long strands hung about Dinah's shoulders in soft waves. Then Maggie looked at herself in the mirror. She wore a soft cream-colored dress. It was probably the best she had short of the wedding dress that hung in her closet. Pulling her hair up and back, Maggie pinned it into place. She allowed strands to fall about her face. If she couldn't talk Mr. Jones at the bank into extending her loan, she might just lose the ranch.

Tears stung the backs of her eyes. According to Lucas Dillon, the man Mr. Jones had sent out, Gus hadn't paid the bank loan in three months. Mr. Dillon had said that if she didn't get to the bank and make a payment today, Mr. Jones would have no choice but to foreclose on the ranch. The thought sped her up. It was already early afternoon. They had to hurry to town before the bank closed.

She bundled James up in a blue blanket and hurried Dinah out the front door. Clayton sat on the wagon, waiting. His horse, Bones, was tied to the back of the wagon. Maggie couldn't help but notice that he was dressed in black pants and a white shirt and he'd traded out his brown work boots for shiny black ones.

"You ladies look very nice," he complimented, jumping from the wagon. He scooped Dinah up and set her in the bed of the wagon. Clayton handed Dinah her rag doll. "You left Charlotte in the barn."

"Thank you." Dinah hugged the toy close to her chest.

Then Clayton turned and held out his arms to take James.

Maggie handed the baby over and allowed him to cradle James in one arm while assisting her with the other. Once she was seated, Clayton returned the baby to her and then climbed back onto the wagon.

He grinned over at her. "If I didn't know better, I'd think we were headed to Sunday services, but since it's not Sunday, I'm curious why you lovely ladies are dressed up." Clayton clicked his tongue, and the mare started toward town. Bones followed.

"I need to go to the bank." Maggie's voice cracked. "It seems my foreman hasn't been making the bank payments." She looked down at the baby. Thankfully James had managed to sleep during the climb into the wagon.

Clayton's jaw worked. "You left the bank business to Gus Fillmore?" he asked.

She nodded. "I was sick and the doctor told me to stay home. No trips to town. I trusted Gus to take the payments into town." Maggie glanced over her shoulder and was pleased to see that Dinah was playing with her doll and didn't seem to be paying attention to the adult conversation.

He blew air out. "And he didn't do it?"

She turned back to face forward. "Mr. Jones sent one of the bank tellers to tell me. I don't know what I'm going to do if he doesn't give me more time to pay the bank the payments that are past due." Maggie hated this. She didn't want to tell Clayton all her problems but needed to talk to someone before facing Mr. Jones.

"How are you going to make those back payments?" he asked.

Maggie sighed. "I could sell a few head of cattle and maybe some of our horses."

"And what about Gus? And the missing money?" His jaw worked, and Clayton's blue eyes had turned to blue ice.

She sighed again. "I've been thinking about Gus."

"And?"

"It's my word against his. I have no proof that I trusted him with the money. I doubt I'll ever see that money again." Tears pricked her eyes, and she ducked her head. Gus had stolen her money, and she knew that he'd swoop in and take the ranch, as well.

Clayton nodded. When they arrived in town, he pulled up to the bank. "Would you like me to come in with you?"

Maggie felt like she should say no but heard herself answer, "That would be nice. Thank you."

After setting the brake, Clayton jumped from the wagon. He helped Dinah down, then reached for James once more. Maggie swallowed hard as she took his hand. Warmth filled her hand and arm. The bank loomed above her, and she wanted to turn around and go home. Women shouldn't have to face bankers who wanted to foreclose on their children's inheritance.

Dinah took her hand and Clayton placed his hand at the small of her back. His strength seemed to come through his touch, and she walked into the bank with her head held high.

Mr. Jones was a tall man with wide shoulders, narrow hips and silver in his black hair. He strolled toward her the moment she walked through the door. "Good afternoon, Mrs. Fillmore. I'm glad to see you were able to make it to the bank on such short notice." He held out his hand for her to shake.

Maggie waited for him to release her hand and lead them into his office before she spoke. As soon as the door was closed behind Clayton, who still held James, Maggie said, "Mr. Jones, I'm sorry that the payments weren't made on the ranch. My foreman assured me that he'd taken care of them."

Mr. Jones walked behind a large mahogany desk and sat down. "I trust you brought the payments with you." He motioned for her to sit down in one of the two chairs in front of him.

Aware that he didn't care why the payments hadn't been made, Maggie sank into the soft leather. "No, sir. I didn't."

Mr. Jones folded his hands over the papers on his desk. "I trust you have the money."

Maggie shook her head. "No, sir. I do not."

"Then how did you plan on making the payments?" He looked from her to Clayton.

Clayton had moved into the room but hadn't come any farther than the closed door. He held the baby in the crook of one arm and Dinah's small hand in his other hand. His blue eyes were as hard as ice. Thankfully, Dinah hadn't sensed his anger.

She cleared her throat to get the banker's attention focused on her once more. When he looked to her, Maggie said, "Mr. Jones, I need time. Time to collect the money."

He shook his head. "I'm sorry, Mrs. Fillmore, but I can't give you more time. You have ignored my messages in the past and refused to come into town to straighten out the matter. I've left word with Gus and told him we needed you to come in. After three payments have been missed, we can no longer carry the ranch. You know that."

Maggie felt her heart sink. She'd do anything not to break her promise to her late husband, even beg the banker to give her an extension. "Please, Mr. Jones. I need more time. Gus never told me of your requests. This is the first I've heard that the payments hadn't been made, and I haven't had time to get the delinquent funds gathered."

He stood. "I'm sorry, Mrs. Fillmore, but if I don't have the money by closing, we'll have to foreclose. Maybe you could ask your late husband's cousin for the money. Gus has shown great interest in the ranch. He's a good man. I'm sure he'll be willing to loan you the money."

Maggie stood. There was no doubt in her mind that Gus could come up with the money. He probably still had it and was waiting until the bank took the deed from her and then he'd pay whatever it took to get the ranch back. Sadly, it was her money that he'd use, but no one would be the wiser. She sighed.

"Thank you for your time, Mr. Jones." Maggie walked toward the door.

The air in the office was stifling. She felt weak in the knees.

"Mrs. Fillmore, I hope you can find a means to pay the loan before the bank closes today."

Maggie's stomach turned. She hadn't needed Mr. Jones's reminder that she had to make the payment before closing time. Maggie knew she had no means to pay the money back. Where would she go now? What was she going to do? She had two children to take care of and, thanks to Gus Fillmore, no home for either of them.

Red-hot anger boiled in Clayton's veins. As soon as they were back outside, he growled, "If I wasn't a Christian, I'd beat the money out of Gus Fillmore. He has it coming."

Maggie reached to take baby James from his arm. "I know how you feel, but what's done is done."

She sounded beaten. Tears ran silently and swiftly down her cheeks. Dinah watched her sister and soon she too was silently crying.

Clayton hated to see a woman cry. He pulled Maggie to him and let her tears flow into his shirt. Dinah leaned against his leg and also wept. He wasn't sure if the little girl understood what was going on or if she simply had a tender heart and couldn't stand to see her big sister so broken.

After a few minutes, Maggie sniffled and looked up at him. Clayton led Maggie to the bench in front of the bank. Maggie sat down with a heavy sigh. Dinah continued to hang on to his thigh. He bent down and picked her up. "Maggie. I'll loan you the money to make the payments." He swallowed hard. He'd been saving his money since day one of working with the Pony Express and knew he'd have enough to cover whatever her payments were.

Dinah laid her head on his shoulder and stuck her thumb in her mouth. In the last couple of weeks, he'd never seen her suck her thumb. He hugged her against him, hoping to offer the little girl comfort.

"I can't let you do that." She wiped her face with the corner of James's blanket and then looked up at him.

He knelt in front of her. Dinah continued to cling to him. Clayton lowered his voice so that passersby wouldn't overhear him. "Why not?"

Her hazel-green eyes stared deeply into his. "For several reasons. One, it wouldn't look right for a stranger in town to pay my debts. Two, I'd still have Gus Fillmore to deal with, and three, I'm not sure I could ever pay you back."

"One, no one has to know it was me who gave you the money. Two, you can always fire Gus, and three, I'm in no hurry to get the money back." He searched her pretty face.

She shook her head. "I'll know." Tears filled the depths of her eyes once more. "I promised Jack I'd protect James's inheritance, and now I've let them both down."

Clayton wanted to protect her and the kids. He didn't want to fall in love with her and he really didn't want to do anything foolish, but at the same time Clayton knew he'd never let Gus have James Fillmore's ranch. His fiancée had taught him that women were fickle and money would set them to running into another man's arms. Nope, he wasn't about to fall in love with Maggie, or any other woman for that matter. "No, you haven't. I've got an idea, but you'll have to agree to it."

He looked to Dinah, who shivered against him. Clayton tried to shield her small body from the cold wind. He softened his voice and offered the little girl what he hoped was a warm smile. "Dinah, dry your eyes and let's go to the restaurant and get a big slice of peach pie."

She rubbed her face on the sleeve of her pretty coat. "All right, Clayton. I like peach pie."

He turned back to Maggie. "We've got a couple of hours yet. We'll go have dessert and coffee and figure something out." Clayton expected her to protest but instead she stood up, wrapped James tighter in his blanket and nodded.

Maggie started walking down the boardwalk. "The closest restaurant is at the hotel. I've been there a couple of times and they make a pretty good peach pie."

"Yours is best," Dinah said. She looked up at Clayton with big hazel eyes.

"Sissy makes the bestest pie crust."

"I'm sure she does." He watched the gentle sway of Maggie's dress. Was it crazy to go to the extremes he was about to, just to help her keep her word to her late husband? Or had God intended this all along?

Maggie pushed through the door of the Grand Hotel where warm air enveloped them. Clayton and Dinah followed. He was curious as to why the hotel was called Grand. It wasn't all that big and he'd seen fancier ones.

She turned to the right and walked into the small restaurant. Once they were all seated, she said, "I can't even begin to think of a solution, Clayton."

The waitress took their orders of coffee, milk and pie. As soon as she left their table, he leaned toward Maggie. "What if I told you I know how to take care of the back payments, get rid of Gus and make sure that James keeps his inheritance?"

Her eyes turned a deep shade of green. "I'd say that would be wonderful." Maggie tucked James closer to her. She smiled down into the baby's open eyes.

"You might not like my plan."

She smiled across at him. A heartwarming smile that made him think his plan might just work. "Well, I won't know until I hear it."

The waitress brought their drinks and pie on a large tray. She set Dinah's milk in front of her before serving the adults their coffee.

Dinah picked up her milk and took a big drink. She smiled with a milk mustache. "It's cold."

"And the pie is warm." The waitress winked at Dinah. She set a dessert plate in front of each of them and then left once more.

Clayton took a deep breath and then said, "We could get married."

Maggie dropped the pie-laden fork she'd just raised to her lips. "Excuse me?"

He rushed the words past his lips before he lost his courage. "It wouldn't be a real marriage. I'm not looking for love and I'm not even sure if marriage is fair to you, but it will take care of your current problems."

Dinah looked from one adult to the other. "You going to marry Clayton?" she asked. Her innocent question reminded them that the little girl was old enough to understand their conversation.

"I don't know, Dinah. We're just talking. Go ahead and eat your pie." Maggie smiled at the little girl.

Clayton tried to read Maggie's face. What must she be thinking? Was she going to hold out for true love and lose the ranch? Unable to decipher her expression, he took a bite of the dessert. Its sweetness coated his tongue and caused his stomach to churn. Or was it the present topic that had his belly in knots?

Dinah looked to Clayton. Seeing him chewing, she nodded and went back to eating.

He felt Maggie's gaze upon his face. She asked, "How is it not fair to us? You are the one who would be giving up your freedom. I can't ask you to do that, Clayton."

"I believe I was the one who brought up..." He paused, then whispered, "Marriage."

She frowned. "Yes, but..."

Clayton stopped her. "Look, I'm not giving up anything. My fiancée left me for the banker's son. Which is fine because I want to be a doctor, and as a doctor, I wouldn't really have time for a real family anyway. I'm not interested in falling in love, so it isn't hurting me at all. But you have to realize that love is off the table, and as a doctor, I will be away from you and the kids a lot of the time."

She swallowed hard, then admitted, "I'm not interested in love either. The only reason I married James's father was to put a roof over our heads. Don't get me wrong. Jack was a good man and never mistreated us, but it wasn't a love match. I answered his mail-order bride ad and shortly afterward came to the ranch.

We were married six months and then he died." She paused. "You should probably know, I really don't trust men not to leave when the going gets tough, and I have no intention of falling in love either. Not now, not ever."

Clayton's impulse was to tell her that as long as she wanted him to be around he'd not leave her. But the hurt in her eyes spoke volumes, and he knew she'd never hear him over the echoes of the disappointments in her past. "So, are you saying a marriage of convenience would work for you?"

"How will it help my situation?"

So, she wasn't ready to commit to his suggestion just yet. "Well, I could catch the bank up with your payments, and if I'm your husband there wouldn't be any gossip. You can fire Gus and explain that your new husband is taking over running the ranch until James is old enough to take the reins. And then, we'd make sure that the ranch grows and will be something James will be happy to inherit." He returned to eating his pie. Maybe if he let her have a few minutes to think about it, Maggie would see that this was her only solution.

Dinah gulped her milk. "Sissy, can I have some more pie?"

Maggie pushed her untouched dessert toward her sister. "You can have mine. I'm not hungry."

"Thanks." Dinah pulled the plate to her and began eating once more.

"What about your dream to be a doctor?" Her soft question took him by surprise.

Clayton's head came up and his gaze met hers across the table. "I'll still study while working for the Pony

Express and the ranch. When the Pony Express stops, I'll continue helping you with the ranch while studying to be a doctor. I'm not giving up on that dream."

She took a sip of her coffee. After several long moments, she asked, "Are you sure you want to do this?"

He didn't know what more he could do besides propose to her. Clayton pushed his chair back and walked around the table. He knelt on one knee and asked, "Maggie Fillmore, will you marry me?"

Chapter Six

Maggie felt as if every eye in the restaurant was watching them. She answered, "Yes."

The room exploded in clapping hands. People nodded their congratulations to them. Clayton stood and grinned down at her. She had to admit, as far as future husbands were concerned, she'd found a handsome one.

She almost groaned when the traveling preacher stood up and walked to their table. "Well, Maggie Fillmore. Congratulations. I've been praying the right man would come along and marry you."

She looked up at Clayton, who grinned as if he was the happiest man in the room. "Thank you, Reverend White."

"How soon did you two plan on being wed?"

Maggie swallowed.

Clayton answered, "I'll marry her today, if she'll have me."

The minister turned to look at her. She knew that the sooner she married Clayton, the better. Maggie nodded. "I would like that."

"Well, then, let's walk over to the church." He turned to leave. Lifting his voice, he announced, "Maggie Fillmore is getting married today. Let as many people know who you think would like to attend. We'll be performing the service in about thirty minutes." He continued out the door as if his inviting the whole town to her wedding was an everyday event.

Clayton laughed. "Well, he doesn't waste any time, does he?"

Maggie shook her head no. She looked to Dinah, who hadn't spoken during most of their conversation. "What do you think, sis? Is it all right with you if I marry Clayton?"

Happiness lit up her sister's small face that looked so much like their mother's. Maggie wished her ma were there. For the hundredth time, she silently asked the Lord why her mother had died. Why she'd been left to raise Dinah on her own and why her father hadn't loved her enough to stay with the family. Dinah had suffered much loss in her young life. Maggie hoped that their new life with Clayton would bring some stability to the little girl's world.

Dinah nodded. She scooted down from her chair and came to stand beside Maggie. "Will we have to move out of our nice house?"

Clayton knelt in front of Dinah. "No, you can stay in the ranch house. If it's all right with Maggie, I'll move in with you two."

"Of course it's all right with me." Maggie pushed her chair back, along with the sorrow of losing her mother and father. She stood. "I suppose we'd best hurry or the preacher's going to think we've changed our minds."

An hour later, Maggie stood on the church steps with her new husband. Clayton had said his vows with his shoulders pulled back and his gaze locked on her face. He now held baby James and was looking down on the child with warmth in his pretty blue eyes. Dinah stood beside her also looking up at Clayton. It was obvious that Dinah adored her new brother-in-law.

Clayton turned his gaze upon her and smiled. "Are you ready to go to the bank, Mrs. Young?"

The warmth in his eyes for James seemed to include her. But Maggie knew he'd never love her. He'd said as much. She nodded. "But first we have to get through our well-wishers." Maggie looked out at the people who stood in front of the church. It seemed as if the whole town had come to witness her wedding.

Clayton tightened his grip on James, took her hand in his and proceeded to walk down the stairs of the church. He stopped at the bottom and smiled at the crowd. "Thank you all for attending our wedding. We will see you all Sunday at worship services. If you will excuse us, I need to get my new family back to the wagon and home where we will start our lives together."

Maggie clung to Clayton's hand as he led her and the children through the center of the cheering crowd. The thought that Clayton would probably make a good politician brought a smile to her lips. She felt people reach out and pat her shoulder or touch her hair as she passed.

For the first time since Jack's death, Maggie felt as if this was her hometown. She saw the ladies from her quilting bee and stopped long enough to receive their hugs and promised to be at the next meeting.

When they got back to their wagon in front of the bank, Clayton stopped. "Shall we go in and show Mr. Jones our paper from the preacher? Then I'll have him transfer the payments for the ranch from my account to James's."

She smiled up at him. "Mr. Jones never did like the fact that I was a woman with a bank account and loan at his bank. He'll be much happier now dealing with you."

He nodded. His blue eyes hardened, but he grinned at her just the same. "Well, it will always be yours and James's ranch. The ranch stays in your names, but I'll be happy to represent you both from now on."

She felt at a loss for words. Any other man would have demanded she put the bank note in his name, giving him ownership. Maggie swallowed around the lump in her throat. "Thank you."

Clayton put his arm around her shoulders and gave her a gentle squeeze. "My pleasure." Then he led them into the bank.

Mr. Jones looked surprised to see them back in his bank. "Can I help you, Mrs. Fillmore?"

Clayton stepped between them. "It's Mrs. Young now, and we are here to pay the mortgage on the ranch."

Disbelief filled the other man's face, but he led them to his office. This time Clayton stepped over the threshold first while his new family followed. Mr. Jones shut the door behind Maggie and Dinah. "So, I assume we will be transferring the deed to the ranch to you, Mr. Young?" He pulled papers from the side drawer of the desk.

"You assumed wrong, Mr. Jones. The ranch belongs to James Fillmore. The papers need to read that Maggie Young is James's guardian and will be controlling all transactions regarding the ranch." Clayton handed James to his mother. "As his mother, that is the way the papers should read."

Maggie saw the challenge in Clayton's eyes. Mr. Jones saw it, too, and nodded. "I see. How do you intend to catch the loan up?" He glanced at the wall clock as if to remind them that their time was running out.

"I will be pulling the funds from my account, which was transferred here two weeks ago, to pay for the past three months and the balance of the ranch, as well." Clayton leaned his hip against the large desk.

Maggie and Mr. Jones both gasped.

Mr. Jones wrote on a scrap of paper and then held it up for Clayton to see. "Are you sure you have the funds to cover such a large expense?"

"You are welcome to look at my account, Mr. Jones. I'm sure you will see that there are sufficient funds to cover the payments and the remainder of the mortgage."

"Very well. Please, have a seat and I'll be back in a few minutes." He hurried out of the room.

Maggie walked across the wood floor. She felt like a woman who'd just been given her freedom. "Clayton, are you sure about this? That's a lot of money."

He reached out and took her free hand. Clayton gently pulled her to him. "Maggie, I never want you to worry about money or losing the ranch again."

"But I don't know when I'll be able to pay you back."

Clayton leaned his forehead against hers. "Maggie, I don't want to be paid back. I want you and James to make the ranch so successful that Mr. Jones will wish he'd married you."

She gasped and pulled back. Did Clayton mean he wished he'd not married her? Maggie saw the teasing, happy glint in his eyes.

"Honey, it did my heart good just now to see that man's face when I told him I was paying off the ranch, and when you make it successful, Mr. Jones will think twice before harassing you again." He chuckled.

Maggie couldn't contain her joy at knowing the ranch would be paid off and her son's future secured. She giggled just as Mr. Jones returned.

He looked from her to Clayton and lifted his chin. "We're closing now, so the paperwork will have to wait until tomorrow to be completed."

Clayton stood to his full height. "No, that doesn't work for us. You see, payment was demanded by the end of the day. If Maggie hadn't returned, you would have taken possession of the ranch and sold it to Gus Fillmore for the amount of past-due payments. So, we will finish our business today, Mr. Jones." His blue eyes no longer held warmth but cold, hard determination.

The banker backed out the door once more. "I'll see if that's possible."

Dinah joined Maggie. She tucked one hand into Maggie's and the thumb of her other hand into her mouth, a sure indicator that she felt unsure of the circumstances taking place. Her hazel eyes searched Clayton's hard face.

Maggie gave Dinah's hand a gentle squeeze. She sat down in the closest chair and pulled the little girl to her side. "Clayton is buying the ranch for James. That's good, isn't it?"

Dinah nodded but didn't remove her thumb.

Mr. Jones arrived back in the room. His face was flustered, but he held a stack of papers in his hands. "Mr. and Mrs. Young, I'll need you to sign these papers and then we'll all be free to go home."

Home. Maggie couldn't wait to get back to the ranch. Back to her cozy house where life would return to normal. She stood to sign the papers. As she wrote her new name, Margaret Elizabeth Young, across several pages, she wondered if life would ever be normal again. For the second time in her life she was married to a stranger.

Clayton carried his meager belongings into the ranch house. His room was next door to Maggie's. A door connected the two rooms. She'd explained that before Jack had died, he'd had the door put in so that they would have their new baby close when he was born.

He heard Maggie talking to Dinah in the little girl's bedroom across the hall, so he continued through Maggie's room and into his own. On the ride back to the ranch, they'd agreed to keep the fact that theirs was a marriage of convenience a secret from the children and the ranch hands. He opened the adjoining door and stepped into the room.

It was small with a small bed and dresser. He laid

his belongings on the bed and looked about. Better than the barn, he reminded himself as he walked over and looked out the window. He could see the well and large tree and realized his room was right over the kitchen. Soft footsteps sounded behind him.

"If the room is too small, we can switch." Maggie stood in the doorway.

Clayton shook his head. "No, this is fine. It's much nicer than the barn, and I'm sure it will be warmer also."

Maggie nodded. "I'll show you something." She walked into the room. "I think you'll like this during the winter months." When she came to the back wall, she stopped and knelt.

For the first time, he noticed a handle beside the wall. Intrigued, Clayton stepped closer so he could get a better view.

She looked up and smiled. Then Maggie pulled on the handle, and a square opened up in the floor.

Clayton looked down into the kitchen. His gaze questioned hers.

Maggie sat back on her heels. "In the winter, you can open this and the heat from the stove will rise and warm the room. Isn't that clever?"

"Very." He examined the door in the floor.

"Jack was a kind man. He wanted to make sure that the baby didn't get too cold up here. So he cut a hole in the floor and then made the door to cover it so that it's hidden, unless you know where to look." She smiled up at him.

She was beautiful. Her hair still hung about her shoulders and she'd yet to change into her normal housedress. Green eyes sparkled with joy. Was the joy from sharing the door with him? Or was she reliving happy thoughts about her late husband?

Clayton lowered the door back into place. "Maggie, would you mind telling me more about your relationship with Jack?" He held his hand out to her.

Maggie took his hand and allowed him to help her up. She dusted off her skirt and then answered. "What would you like to know?"

Clayton sighed. "Never mind, it's not important." He couldn't understand why he'd asked about her late husband. What had he hoped to learn?

"I don't mind telling you, Clayton. I'm just not sure where to start." She sat down on the edge of his bed.

He leaned against the wall and crossed his arms. Clayton wished he'd never asked. When he was around Maggie he felt as if he did and said the stupidest things.

Maggie smiled at him. "I believe I told you I arrived here as a mail-order bride. Jack wanted an heir to leave this ranch to, and I needed a roof over Dinah's head. Jack was a good man. He treated me right, doted on Dinah, and then when he found out about the baby...well, he became even kinder. He added the door and then opened the floor to let in heat for the child." She looked to her folded hands.

Clayton said, "He sounds like a wonderful man."

"He was." She looked up. "Jack wanted the best for baby James. He cared about family."

Clayton saw the troubled look cross her face. "Is that why Gus was working on the ranch?"

Maggie nodded. "Gus showed up one night and told Jack he needed a loan. Jack would give the shirt off his back to anyone he thought needed help, so you can imagine my surprise when he refused to give Gus money but told him he'd hire him on as a ranch hand." She walked over to the window and looked down at the ground. "Gus was madder than an old bull. He yelled so loud that Dinah and I could hear him all the way up here. Said he was kin and that as kin Jack owed him."

Clayton picked up his Bible and put it on top of the dresser. "What did Jack say to that?"

He opened his saddlebags and pulled out his clothes.

"Said he didn't owe Gus anything. Asked if he wanted the job or not."

He nodded. "And Gus took the job."

"Yes, but he immediately began bossing the other men around and even tried to tell Jack how to raise cattle. But Jack was patient with him." She turned from the window. "Then when Jack died, Gus told me that the ranch was rightfully his. I refused to argue with him. Jack had told me he'd been to town and had drawn up papers with the lawyer there. After the funeral, Gus and I went to the lawyer's office and listened to the reading of the will."

Clayton placed his saddlebags in the bottom drawer of the dresser. "That's when Gus discovered the ranch belonged to baby James."

"That was a little over three months ago. I got sick and Doc Anderson said I wasn't to think or do anything more than take care of Dinah and myself until the baby was born." She laid her hand on her now-flat waistline.

"I take it that's when Gus decided to become your foreman?"

Maggie nodded. "I don't think Jack would have let him stay here, if he'd known that Gus would try to take the ranch."

"And that's why we need to pay him his wages and send him packin'." Just thinking of the man irritated Clayton. How could Gus sleep at night, knowing his actions would have left Maggie and the children homeless? Didn't the man have a conscience, or any sense of right and wrong? The more Clayton thought about it, the madder he became.

Once more, Maggie nodded. "How soon do you think it will be before he finds out we're married?"

Clayton had been thinking a lot about Gus. The ranch foreman left every day. He'd learned from the other men that Gus usually rode into town. With the money from the bank payments, Clayton figured Gus was going to the saloon and either drinking or gambling the money away. Since none of the men complained he was drunk when he came back in the evenings, Clayton was pretty sure that Gus was gambling. The saloon was the meeting place for both drunks and businessmen. By now the banker or someone who worked at the bank had undoubtedly already spread the news. "He probably already knows."

"Do you really think so?" She wrung her hands in front of her. Worry creased her brow.

Clayton crossed the room and pulled her into a hug. "Don't fret, we'll do this together."

"Sissy, baby James is crying." Dinah walked into the room.

Maggie pushed against Clayton's chest. She stepped back and smiled at the little girl. "Thank you, Dinah." Then she hurried from the room.

Dinah followed. "You're welcome. I think he's hungry. I'm hungry, too." Her voice drifted farther away. "Now that Clayton lives here, too, will you be sleeping in your bedroom again? With baby James?"

Maggie's voice was muffled. Clayton walked to the doorway and tried to hear her answer. But her soft voice was too muted to hear her reply. Why had she moved into Dinah's bedroom with her? Had she been worried she would go into labor in the middle of the night and need the little girl to run to the bunkhouse and let Gus know? That made sense, but she'd had the baby over a week ago. Why hadn't she moved back into her bedroom earlier?

Chapter Seven

Maggie relaxed in her favorite rocker in the sitting room. She listened as Clayton read the story of Jonah and the whale to Dinah. Clayton read with such enthusiasm and animation that Dinah was mesmerized. Maggie hoped he knew Dinah would be requesting he read more stories.

The two were so cute sitting on the settee with the Bible in their laps. Maggie picked up her knitting needles and the stocking hat she was making for James. She loved the pale blue. The color would bring out the blue in the baby's eyes even more.

As she added stitches, Maggie marveled at the changes in her life during the last year. Her first husband had died, her son had been born and today she'd remarried. A year ago, she'd been happy just knowing that she and Dinah had a roof over their heads. The fire crackled comfortingly, but it couldn't quell the uneasy feeling of knowing that soon Gus Fillmore would have to be confronted and fired as the ranch foreman.

As if her fears were coming to life, the sound of

boots pounded across the front porch. It was late for visitors, and the only person who would come to the house at this time would be Gus. She looked across the room at Clayton, grateful for his presence. Knowing Gus, the situation was bound to escalate.

Clayton closed the Bible and said, "Dinah, why don't you head upstairs? It's getting late."

Someone pounded on the wood, causing Dinah to jump. The little girl's gaze moved to the front door. She looked up at Clayton.

"Go on, I'll take care of our late-night visitor."

Dinah grabbed him and hugged tightly. Then she released Clayton and smiled. "All right." She slid off the settee and looked to Maggie.

Maggie gave what she hoped was a reassuring smile at her little sister. "I'll be up in a few minutes to say good-night prayers. Get ready for bed, and then you can play with your baby doll until I come up."

The knocking on the door began again. Dinah dashed up the stairs.

When she was safely in her room, Clayton pulled the door open.

Gus stood with both hands resting on the door-jambs, one on each side. His head had been hanging down between his outstretched arms. He looked up and frowned.

Maggie stood to the side where she could see everything the two men did and hear every word. Gus glared at Clayton. His sides heaved as if he'd run to the house.

"Gus, is something wrong?" She took a step closer to the door but caught the slight shake of Clayton's head, so she stepped back to the rocker.

Gus dropped his arms to his side. "I've come to talk some sense into you."

Clayton continued to block him from coming inside.

Cold air entered unbidden through the open door. Maggie rubbed her arms. "What do you mean?"

Realizing that Clayton had no intentions of inviting him inside, Gus huffed, "I hear you got married in town today." His tone was accusing.

Clayton finally spoke. "That's right. And, we've been talking and now that I'm Maggie's husband and living here on the ranch, we no longer need a ranch foreman."

Gus's head snapped backward as if he'd been punched. "He's speaking for you now?" he demanded, his gaze locking with hers.

Maggie straightened her shoulders and stood a little taller. "No. I should have fired you months ago. You are a thief, Gus Fillmore, and if Jack were alive—" She let the rest of her words hang in the air.

Clayton's back stiffened and his legs locked into place.

Gus didn't deny that he was a thief. Instead, he balled his fists and took a swing at Clayton's face.

Maggie realized Clayton had anticipated Gus's next move. Her quick-witted new husband ducked and then punched Gus in the stomach. She gasped and then covered her mouth to contain any other noises that might erupt and scare the children upstairs.

The foreman doubled over with a grunt and stumbled back a few steps. Clayton followed him and shut the door behind them.

Maggie rushed to the window and watched as Gus

continued to back off the porch. Clayton kept his fist balled and his gaze locked on the former foreman. "You're fired, Fillmore."

"You can't fire me. I quit."

Clayton stepped to the edge of the porch. "I just did. Don't step foot on James's ranch again."

Gus spun on his heels. "I'll get my things and be out of here."

Maggie could only assume he was headed to the bunkhouse. Clayton said, "Leave now, Gus. I'll send your things to town in a few days."

Gus snarled over his shoulder, "You can't do this, Young."

Clayton crossed his arms over his chest and didn't answer.

Maggie watched from the window as Gus climbed on his horse, which had been tied to the hitching post. Had he come straight from town and not even taken the time to put away his horse? It seemed that way.

Gus snarled, "I'll be at the Grand Hotel. If you don't supply my personal belongings by tomorrow night, expect a visit from the sheriff."

Clayton nodded. "I would love a visit from the sheriff. Why don't you come, too? I'd like for you to explain to him what happened to the last three bank payments Maggie asked you to pay."

Gus kicked his horse in the ribs and shot across the yard. Maggie waited until he was out of sight and then opened the door. She walked out to stand beside Clayton. "He's pretty angry. Do you think he'll be back?"

Warm blue eyes met hers. His voice held an edge that sent a chill down her spine. "If he's smart, he won't."

She rubbed her cold hands together. "I hate to say it, but I don't think we've heard the last of him."

Clayton draped an arm about her shoulders. "Don't worry about him. I'll make sure he never bothers you or the children again."

Maggie wondered how he planned on keeping that pledge. She knew Gus, and he wasn't a man to give up so easily. Clayton's arm felt warm about her shoulders. Maggie nodded. "I'll try not to." Even as she said the words, Maggie knew she could no more keep her pledge than he could.

She worried her bottom lip as they walked back to the front door. Would Clayton be able to keep Gus at bay? His pledge had sounded sincere, but in her experiences, no man had ever stayed long enough in her life to keep his promises. She wasn't about to start hoping Clayton was any different.

Maggie had lost all trust in men and their ability to stick around. Clayton's promises were just as empty as those of all the other men in her life. She glanced up at his profile. What would it be like to trust him? Maggie ducked her head and fought off the intriguing thought. She hardened her heart. It was better to not trust him or any man. The thought saddened her.

"I'm going to walk out to the bunkhouse and update the men on what has happened today. Is there anything you want me to tell them?" Clayton opened the door.

She stopped and turned to face him on the other side of the doorway. "Tell them I hope they will continue to work here at the ranch but if they choose to move on, I'll understand. A couple of them are friends of Gus's." Maggie sighed. "I just hope we can trust them now that he is gone."

"I'll tell them." He tucked a strand of hair behind her ear, then quickly lowered his hand. What was he thinking? They weren't really married, and she couldn't possibly want him to touch her in such a manner. But there was a sadness in her eyes that he couldn't resist.

Was she unhappy that Gus Fillmore was out of her and the kids' lives? He shook the thought off. No, Maggie had expressed her dislike of the man earlier. Clayton found himself wanting to hug her close and chase away all her sadness.

She lowered her head and said, "Thank you," then proceeded into the house and up the stairs to where the children waited.

Clayton closed the door and then hurried across the dark yard. The chill in the night air bit into his skin. He should have grabbed his coat off the nail beside the door. What was it about Maggie that made him feel as if he would protect her with his life? And that made him forget even the simplest of things, such as his coat.

At the pace he was walking it didn't take long for Clayton to get to the bunkhouse. He squared his shoulders and entered without knocking. The men inside looked up at him. There were questions in their eyes but none of them spoke. Not even Hal, who normally talked his arm off.

"Care if I join you?" he asked the room in general.

George, the cook and man who took care of the chickens and pigs, stood. "You're always welcome here. Would you like a cup of coffee?" He limped toward the woodstove where two coffeepots sat.

His steps reminded Clayton that George was the oldest of the group and the man he needed the most. Seeking out counsel from the oldest man in any group was just good practice. At least that's what his stepfather, Seth, had told him a few weeks ago. Seth had never led him astray before. Clayton intended to heed his advice.

Remembering to answer George, Clayton nodded and said, "I'd appreciate one." He walked farther into the room.

The older man nodded and picked up a tin cup. He filled it from the nearest pot and then walked to Clayton. "We missed you at supper." He handed Clayton the cup.

What had caused the man's limp? It hadn't been there at breakfast. "Thank you." Clayton took a sip, then said, "I am guessing you all know that Maggie and I got married today." He waited for each of them to nod. "A few moments ago, I fired Gus Fillmore. He stole from the ranch and, as you all know, he has not been doing his job."

The men looked at each other and nodded.

Hal spoke. "Well, I, for one, am glad to see him go."

Again, the men nodded. Clayton looked each of them in the eye. "Maggie wanted me to tell you that she hopes you will continue to work for the Fillmore Ranch but understands if you want to quit."

"I can't speak for the rest of the men, but I'm not going anywhere," George said. He sat down on his cot with a grunt. "Gus Fillmore wasn't an easy man to work for, and there was no love lost from me at his departing."

"I agree with George. I'm staying," Hal said. "I enjoy working with the horses."

Clayton couldn't help wondering if Hal was afraid he'd change his current duties. He reassured the young man. "You do a good job with them, Hal. I can't imagine replacing you. Glad you're staying on."

Bud and Abraham exchanged looks. Bud was the younger of the two, and his features expressed the indecision he was feeling. These were the two young men whom Gus had used for grunt work. If it was a hard job, Bud and Abraham were the ones who were assigned to do it.

Abraham looked to Clayton and said, "I'll stay. This ranch is my home. I'll do everything in my power to see that it succeeds."

Clayton nodded in his direction and then said to the group as a whole, "I'll expect complete loyalty to the Fillmore Ranch." His gaze moved to Bud, who studied the checkerboard between himself and Abraham.

The young man spoke softly. "Gus is my friend. I don't always agree with his actions, but I can't say that I won't remain his friend."

Clayton walked over and rested his hand on the young man's shoulder. "I'm not asking you to give up your friendship. Your loyalty to Gus speaks volumes. What I'm asking is your word that you will be more loyal to the ranch, work hard, and respect Maggie and the children. I don't think that is too much to ask."

Bud looked up at him. "No, sir, it isn't."

Clayton smiled. "Does that mean you are staying on, too?"

"Yes. I'll not do anything that will mess things up for Mrs. Fillmore, I mean, Mrs. Young or the kids."

Clayton squeezed his shoulder gently. "See that you don't." Then he turned his attention back to the men. "Thank you all for staying. I'm going to be the new foreman but will need all your help. And since I'm asking for more from you, I'm willing to pay you a dollar more a month."

The men's eyes lit up. Their voices chorused together as they all offered thanks in their own way.

When the room had quieted once more, Clayton continued. "I'll be hiring a couple more hands, as well." His gaze met Bud's and Abraham's. "The workload around here will now be distributed evenly."

Abraham nodded his thanks. Bud simply grinned.

Clayton decided to learn more about the men now in his care. Hal, he knew, was a little slow in his thinking but was very good with horses. But he knew nothing else about the man. It would be good to find out where he came from and how he ended up here at the Fillmore Ranch.

Bud and Abraham were young. Did they have families they were supporting? Parents they were sending money to?

And as for George, his story would be interesting. He was a great cook but not a big talker. Clayton finished off his coffee. He returned the cup to the sideboard and then nodded. "I think we are all going to do just fine. I'll be working right along beside you."

They all nodded their approval.

He looked about the room and spotted Gus's bunk. It was a little farther from the other men's and seemed to have more room for his things. Clayton walked over and flipped through a box under the cot. As he suspected, the ranch bookkeeping book was at the bottom.

Aware of the other men watching him, Clayton opened the book to find lines of accounting records. He also saw where each calf had been listed. Gus had gone so far as to draw the calf's facial markings and done the same to the matching cow to indicate which calf belonged with each cow. It was a good practice, one Clayton hoped to continue.

He closed the book and turned back to face the men. "Hal, would you pack up Gus's personal belongings and bring them up to the house in the morning?"

"Be glad to."

"Good." Clayton turned his attention back to the oldest member of the group. "George, do you have a moment to step outside?"

"Yes, sir." George pushed himself up from the cot and limped toward him. He stopped just inside the doorway and began to pull on his warmer clothes.

"Good night, men." Clayton led the way outside. The cold air nipped at his face and hands. He tucked his hands into his pants pockets and turned to face George.

The older man grinned at him. He wore a nice big coat, scarf and a hat. "Next time you come out for a visit, you might consider grabbing your coat," the man teased.

"That's good advice." Clayton walked toward the empty corral. George limped behind him.

"On second thought, let's head up to the house." Clayton bypassed the corral. He slowed his speed and waited for the older man to come along beside him. "What's wrong with your leg?" he asked.

The older man glanced sideways at him. "Yesterday I dropped a knife and cut my leg. It's fine."

Clayton shook his head. "I'll be the judge of that."

George grunted. "So now you're a doctor, too?"

"What? You don't think I wear enough hats already?" Clayton led him around to the side of the house where they entered the kitchen. "Step into my office."

"Funny." George walked into the warm kitchen. "Think I could have a cup of coffee?"

"Sure. While I'm getting it, roll up that pant leg. I want to see that cut." Clayton closed the door and then walked to the stove, where he retrieved the pot and a cup.

George rolled up his pant leg. "It's not pretty," he said, revealing a red, angry-looking cut.

Clayton set the cup on the table and poured coffee into it. "Nope, it isn't. We'll need to clean it up." He returned to the stove, placed a pot on the front burner and then picked up the water bucket. "Be right back. Going for fresh water."

"Take your time. It's nicer in here than out in the bunkhouse with those rowdy boys." He pulled his coat off and took a drink of coffee.

Clayton returned. "We'll heat this up and then clean out that wound."

George nodded. "Mrs.—" he paused "—Young sure makes a good cup of coffee."

Clayton laughed. He wasn't sure if he'd ever get used to Maggie being called Mrs. Young, but he had to admit, George was right about her coffee. "That she does."

After Clayton cleaned up George's wound, the two men sat in silence as they enjoyed the coffee. Clayton's thoughts turned back to George's earlier words about getting away from the other men for a while. He remembered the days of sharing the bunkhouse with his brothers. They were all pretty rowdy, and he could only imagine how much they got on his older brother's nerves.

"I thought you brought me up here to talk," George reminded him.

Clayton set his cup down. "I did." He studied George's face. "How old are you?" he asked.

George chuckled. "Not real sure. I think I'm about seventy. Why do you ask? Planning on firing me because I'm old?"

Clayton chuckled. "Nope. That never crossed my mind. I was thinking about moving you out of that bunkhouse and into the barn. But if you think that might make you look old or give you too much privacy, maybe I should leave you where you are."

"The barn? Why?"

Clayton knew he had to give the man the respect he deserved. "Well, today I may have bit off more than I could chew. I'm now a husband, a ranch foreman and a Pony Express station manager. I'm not sure there is enough of me to go around. I need help."

George chuckled. "Well, at least you have the smarts to know you need help." His faded gray eyes searched Clayton's. "What did you have in mind for me?"

"Would you be willing to move into the room in

the barn? Still be the ranch hands' cook and if I'm not here when the Pony Express riders come, make sure the exchange of horses goes smoothly? I moved out today so it's all yours, if you want it." Clayton looked in the cookie jar and pulled out a fistful of ginger-snaps. Then he walked back to the table.

George took the cookies Clayton offered him. "What other duties would I have?" he asked.

"Only one." Clayton silently thanked the Lord for this thought. "I'll be helping the men, and I need someone to watch out for my new family." He looked toward the sitting room. "I don't trust Gus Fillmore not to cause problems here on the ranch or with Maggie."

"Protect your family?" George stuffed half a cookie in his mouth and waited.

Clayton nodded. "I can't leave them unprotected."

George grinned. "And I'm guessing this is between you and me. The missus isn't to know?"

"I'd prefer she didn't, but if she should ask, we'll be honest and tell her. For now, I don't want her worrying about Gus or anyone else." Clayton savored the sweetness of the gingersnap. Maggie would understand, but he had the feeling she wouldn't appreciate knowing that he'd used one of the men to babysit her and the kids when he was gone.

George extended his hand. "I'd be honored to protect the family in your absence. Mr. Fillmore always treated me well. I'll watch out for his kin in return."

Clayton shook the older man's hand. He hadn't earned George's respect yet and understood the man was telling him so. Instead of commenting on that,

Clayton said, "Thank you. Let me know if that leg gets worse. Especially if you see red streaks running."

Half an hour later, Clayton lowered the beam across the door, locking his new family inside. For the first time in his life, Clayton felt proud. He'd saved the ranch, married a pretty lady, and talked the men into staying and working the property. He'd lightened the workload of an older, respected man and was able to clean up the knife wound. All in all, it had turned out to be a good day.

Maggie had left a lantern lit for him downstairs. Clayton picked it up and made his way up the flight of steps. Since the house was sleeping, he went to his room through the hallway entry and flopped across the bed.

"Clayton?"

He glanced toward the door that adjoined the two rooms. "You can come in, Maggie." Clayton sat back up.

She opened the door and he could see that she'd brought the makeshift crib from Dinah's chest to the bedroom. "I just wanted you to know that I've moved back in here."

Clayton nodded. "Can I ask you a question?"

Maggie smiled. "Of course."

"Why did you move out of your bedroom in the first place?" He pulled off one boot, placed it at the foot of the bed and reached for the other.

"The baby was due and I didn't want to be in here alone when he came. I'd thought about moving Dinah into this room but she wanted to stay in her room, so I started sleeping in there." She grinned. "We were going to take a nap the day he was born, so I lay down with Dinah on her bed and the next thing I knew I was in labor and no one was here to help me but my little sister." She paused and offered him a bigger smile. "I'm so glad you came along when you did."

He took the other boot off. "I am, too."

Did Maggie have any idea how pretty she was? She wore a dressing gown and her hair had been released from the many combs she'd worn earlier in the day. Her hazel eyes looked tired but happy. Maggie Young was a beautiful woman, and you didn't have to be in love to appreciate that.

"Well, I just wanted to let you know we are in here and to say thank you again. For everything."

"You are welcome. Oh, and you'll be happy to know we did not lose a man after firing Gus. Bud is young and still wants to be Gus's friend but has sworn his loyalty to the Fillmore Ranch. I hope you don't mind, but I offered George the room off the side of the barn. He's a little older and could use the quiet space. Plus, he'll be able to help me and Hal with the horses."

"Of course George is welcome to the room." Maggie's smile lit up her eyes. "I'm glad the rest of the men decided to stay, too. I was a little worried. We used to have seven men working for us, but right after Jack died, three of them quit." She yawned. "Well, if you will excuse me, I need to get some sleep."

"Good night, Maggie." Clayton waited until she shut the door and then prepared for bed. He heard her moving about her room for a moment or two, and then the house was silent. His brain went into overdrive in the quiet.

What had he been thinking? Marriage? Responsibility of the ranch? Firing the foreman and taking over his duties, along with his own responsibilities as a Pony Express manager? He'd been sent here to do the job of Pony Express manager. Clayton silently vowed to do the best job as husband, foreman and Pony Express manager that he could. Seth had taught him that family always comes first. His family was new but they were now his responsibility.

He'd not shirk his duties as a Pony Express employee, he'd not allow harm to come to his new family and, most important, Clayton Young would not fall in love with his pretty new bride. Distance. That's what he needed to keep between them. If he didn't get close to Maggie, his heart wouldn't betray him.

Chapter Eight

Two weeks later, Maggie buttoned up Dinah's light-weight coat and smiled. "I'm glad we are going to town today, aren't you?"

Dinah's pigtails swung back and forth. "Uh-huh." She clung to her rag doll. "Do you think Billy Fisher will be at the store today?"

Billy Fisher was a cute little boy with shiny black hair and twin dimples in his cheeks. The same age as Dinah, Billy enjoyed playing with the little girl. He had a two-year-old brother and a ten-year-old sister. Being the middle child seemed to make him appreciative of having Dinah as a friend. He was also the store owner's son. Since Billy and his family lived above the store, there was a good chance Dinah would see her friend.

"Maybe. Why?" Maggie stood and looked at baby James. In the last week, it seemed as if he'd grown several inches. His little body had filled out some, and his cheeks held a rosy color. Deep blue eyes looked up at her.

"I like him. He's fun to play with." Dinah skipped

to the door. "I'm going to go see if Clayton has the wagon up to the house yet." She put her little hands on her hips and shook her pigtails. "And if he don't, I'm gonna help him." Then she turned and sped out the door.

Maggie called after her. "Don't get underfoot, Dinah." She grinned at the change in Dinah since Clayton had come into their lives. The little girl had grown sassier, but Maggie didn't mind. It was so much better than the timid child she'd been.

She scooped James up and grabbed her purse from the bedpost. She loved being with the kids, but a day in town with adults would be a real treat. Clayton had taken to working late, eating, spending a little time with the kids and then retiring to his room. It felt like he was deliberately avoiding her.

Maggie knew they were practically strangers but had hoped to spend more time with him in the evenings, talking about the ranch or just sitting in the same room while he read and she sewed. She realized that she was comparing their pretend marriage with the life she'd spent with Jack. It hadn't been a perfect marriage, but at least they'd talked. Maggie missed that.

She decided not to think on the past but focus on what she intended to buy at the general store. Flour, sugar, coffee, needles, thread and, if possible, a couple of skeins of yarn. At the rate James was growing he'd need new clothes, so maybe she should add a couple of yards of material to the list. She'd had little time to sew during her pregnancy while she'd been so ill. Baby James had few things to wear.

Since the ground was still frozen it was too soon to

think about her summer garden. Instead she decided to focus instead on the house and the kids. Sewing would keep her mind occupied, and the housekeeping, cooking and laundry would keep her hands busy during her times of loneliness.

Maggie walked slowly down the stairs. Her motherly instinct was to be very careful not to trip or drop the baby. She breathed a sigh of relief as her boots touched the sitting room floor. Her gaze moved to the couch. Should she grab one of the blankets off of it for the ride home?

Dinah came running back into the house. "Clayton says he's ready when you are."

"Slow down, Dinah. Ladies do not run in the house." She wrapped the baby's blanket tighter around him. "Grab the brown blanket off the couch, please."

Dinah blushed at the gentle scolding. "All right, Sissy. I'm sorry I runded in the house." She walked across the room and pulled the blanket from the couch. Dinah wadded it up and then returned to Maggie.

Maggie led the way outside. She waited for Dinah to follow and then shut the door.

Clayton met her at the foot of the porch steps. He held his arms out for James. His gaze met hers and he grinned. "Ready?"

She handed the baby over and nodded. "I have several things I want to get at the general store." Maggie turned to take the cover from Dinah. She gave the little girl a hug and thanked her for getting the blanket. "You are such a good girl, I think we'll get you a stick of candy. Any kind you want."

"Thanks, Sissy." Dinah hugged her back and then

pulled away. "Did you hear that, Clayton? Sissy is going to let me have any candy I want."

He smiled. "I did hear that. Your sister is very generous." Clayton followed Dinah to the wagon and stood behind her as she scrambled up.

Maggie joined them. She waited until Dinah was in the bed of the wagon and then began her own ascent. Once seated, she tucked her skirts around her legs. She turned to face Clayton. He handed baby James up to her. "Thank you."

Clayton pulled himself up on the seat beside her and bobbed his head in her direction. "My pleasure." Then he slapped the reins over the horse's back.

"I've asked George to round up the calves while we're gone. Tomorrow I'll ride over to the Morris ranch and see when they will be taking their calves to market," Clayton said. He glanced over at her.

Maggie nodded. "I'm sure he won't mind if we add ours to the trip."

Clayton looked over his shoulder at Dinah. "I've decided that Bud and Abraham can go on the drive with the Morris men, if that's all right with you. I'd like to stick close to the ranch."

He was worried that Gus would return and make trouble for her and the children if he went, too. "That sounds good to me. Jack didn't always go on the drives and both Bud and Abraham have gone in the past."

"Good, then I'll make the arrangements." Clayton turned his attention to driving the wagon.

The remainder of the trip to town went swiftly. Maggie enjoyed the cool breeze in her face. The temperatures were warming up each day. She spotted what looked like new buds on the trees and longed for summer. Maybe she would ask if the general store had gotten any seeds for gardening after all.

Clayton pulled up in front of the store and set the brake. He jumped down and helped Dinah from the wagon. "Stay on the boardwalk."

"All right." She wrapped her arms around her doll and waited.

He turned back to the buggy and took baby James from Maggie. She felt his broad hand on her back as she climbed from the wagon. Once on solid ground again, Maggie turned and took the baby from Clayton.

His eyes met hers as he handed the child over. "I'm going to walk over to Doc Anderson's office. I intended to return his book the last time we were in town, but a few urgent matters occupied my mind that day." He grinned broadly and his dark eyebrows arched mischievously. "Like giving up my freedom to become a married man."

Maggie swatted him with the diaper she held. "Behave yourself, Clayton Young. No one held your hand to the fire."

He let out a long, exaggerated sigh. When she stepped aggressively toward him he held both hands up in surrender. He chuckled and a trace of laughter remained in his voice when next he spoke.

"I'll be back in a bit to get you and the kids. Don't worry about loading the wagon. I'll take care of that when I return." Clayton reached under the seat and pulled out the books he'd borrowed from the doctor.

Maggie asked, "Is there anything I can get for you?"

Clayton stepped up beside her. "Not that I can think of. You and the children take your time. I'll be back in a bit." With long purposeful strides, he walked in the opposite direction of the store.

Maggie watched him go. Why did she want him to talk to her so much? Most of the time, he seemed to be pushing her away, and she understood that to some degree. Yet at others, like just now, Clayton drew her in and made her feel wanted, cherished. The truth was, she was afraid to get too close to him, too. But she also needed adult conversations. Would he understand when she confronted him later? She hoped so, because Maggie refused to sit idly by while he ran the ranch and interacted with men all day but ignored her in the evenings.

Clayton dragged his feet as he walked to the doctor's office. He rubbed the spine of the book in his hand with his thumb. This was one of the hardest decisions he'd ever made, but for the sake of his new family, Clayton would give up doctoring. The Pony Express and the ranch kept him so busy that he had no time to study. The ranch alone was becoming a full-time job. He'd fallen into bed each night without cracking open the medical book.

Doc Anderson came out of the building just as Clayton arrived. "Well, hello, Clayton. Good to see you." His gaze moved to the book. "Have you finished that book already?"

"No. But since Maggie wanted to come to town for supplies today, I decided to go ahead and return the book." He walked toward the doctor with the books extended.

The doctor crossed his arms over his chest. He

looked strange with the big black bag tucked under one arm. "You haven't finished reading it?"

Again, Clayton answered, "No."

"Then why are you bringing it back? Was it too hard for you to read?" He fixed his gaze on Clayton's eyes.

Clayton smiled. "No, I've just decided I don't have time to study doctoring right now." He squirmed under the doctor's steady scrutiny, aware that the doctor had been reading people's expressions for years and even now was trying to decipher what Clayton was thinking. Was his face readable?

Doc Anderson dropped his arms but didn't take the book. "I'm headed over to the sawmill. One of the men out there has a nasty cut. I thought I'd go see how he's doing. Why don't you come along?"

Clayton looked back toward Main Street. "I left the family at the general store."

"Won't take but just a few minutes and it will give us time to talk about this decision of yours." He walked past Clayton.

Raised to obey his elders, Clayton followed. He tucked the book under his arm.

When Clayton came even with him, the doctor said, "You know, son, if you wait until you have time to study, you will never study."

Clayton rubbed his chin. "I believe I've bitten off more than I can chew," he confessed. "The ranch is a lot more work than I expected. Along with my Pony Express job there is no time for studying, and I don't know how to make more time in a day." He paused. "Do you?"

Doc Anderson laughed and then said, "I'm a doctor, not a clockmaker."

Puzzled, Clayton frowned. "Then what is the purpose of me going with you?"

"To help, of course."

Clayton hurried to keep up. "I'm always willing to help."

"Just as I suspected." The doctor led the way to the sawmill, his head held high and the black bag in his hand swinging as he walked.

Clayton shook his head and continued onward to the sawmill. Once there he followed the doctor inside.

They were met by the owner. "Here to see Marshall again today, Doc?"

"Yep. Joshua, is he in the back?"

Joshua nodded to Clayton.

The doctor looked from one man to the other. "You two had a chance to get acquainted yet?"

"Can't say I've had the pleasure," Clayton answered, extending his hand. "I'm Clayton Young."

"Joshua Kimball. Nice to meet you." His handshake was firm yet respectful.

Clayton nodded. "I'm working out at the Fillmore Ranch, so I may be needing a few items come spring."

The doctor snorted. "He's more than the foreman."

"That so?" Joshua narrowed his eyes at Clayton.

"Don't be thinking he lied to you. He's the foreman all right, but he's also the Pony Express station manager and Maggie's new husband." The doctor grinned as if he'd just introduced the town mayor.

A lopsided grin touched Joshua's face. "Good. Maggie needs a good man to help her out around there. Gus Fillmore is about the most worthless piece of human flesh I've ever known."

Inwardly, Clayton sighed. He'd been afraid Joshua was one of Gus's many friends. His shoulders relaxed and he returned the man's smile.

"Well, if you two are just going to stand there grinning like a couple of dandies, I'm thinking it's time we go check on Marshall." He turned and walked through another door at the back of the small building.

Clayton followed. When they stepped out into the yard, he was amazed at the size of the sawmill. There were logs and various boards of all kinds stacked about. Two men worked near the oversize saw and two others stacked boards against the back wall of the building. His gaze moved about the large space. It was bigger than the main barn at the ranch and seemed airier. The smell of fresh sawdust and pine resin made him want to build something. He shook his head. All he needed to add to his schedule was a building project. But, boy, it sure was tempting just because of the smell.

Doc Anderson headed toward the two men who were stacking boards. "Marshall, how's that ankle feeling today?"

The younger of the two looked up. He waved. "Howdy, Doc. It is still sore but I think it's better." He sat down on a pile of boards and began removing his work boot.

Clayton watched as Marshall revealed a jagged cut across his ankle. It was red and swollen. This was better? And just sore?

"What do you think, Clayton?"

He looked up and realized the doctor had been

watching his expression. Clayton knelt in front of the injured man. "I'm Clayton Young. Do you mind if I get a closer look?"

Marshall nodded his consent.

Clayton picked up his foot and felt along the wound. Heat radiated from the cut. He gently pressed and it opened. Clayton looked up at the doctor. "Infection has set in."

Doc Anderson frowned and nodded. "Have you been washing the cut every night like I told you to?" he asked Marshall.

"Naw, washing it isn't going to make it feel any better."

Clayton slowly lowered the man's foot. "The washing isn't to make it feel better. It's to clean the wound so that we won't have to cut your foot off later." He stood.

The man yelped. "Cut my foot off? Doc, who is this lunatic?"

Doc Anderson frowned at the man. "He's studying medicine and is right. I didn't tell you to wash it so that it'd feel better. Warm soapy water cleans up cuts and keeps them from getting worse."

Marshall began putting his boot back on. He frowned up at Clayton. "Ain't nobody gonna cut off my foot."

Clayton chuckled. "I didn't say we were. I said that keeping it clean will prevent it from having to be cut off."

He ignored Clayton. "I ain't never heard of washing a cut so that it will get better."

Doc Anderson nodded. "No, probably not. Most doctors don't have folks keep a wound clean. But I've discovered in my years of doctoring that if the patient follows my orders and washes the wound, it gets better faster." He dropped a firm hand on the young man's shoulder. "Why don't you stop by my office after work? We'll get you cleaned up and prevent Clayton here from chopping off your foot." He laughed, taking the sting out of his words.

"Yes, sir." Marshall pulled his boot back on. He stood.

Clayton saw him wince and frowned. It was obvious Marshal was in pain. He wanted to do something to help him feel better. How had the young man gotten the cut in the first place? And how long ago?

"Well, I suppose we should get you back to town, Clayton." Doc turned to look at Marshall. "And I expect to see you as soon as you get off work. Don't make me come back here tomorrow, or I might just bring my butcher's knife and finish off that foot for you." His voice held a hint of teasing, but his eyes remained steady on the young man.

"I'll be there," Marshall said.

Clayton and the doctor walked back to the doctor's office. The doctor remained silent and seemed to be deep in his own thoughts. Clayton's thoughts went to Marshall and his infected ankle. He wanted to help the young man, and that longing outweighed his desire to ranch. How was he going to give up his dream of becoming a doctor?

Doc Anderson said, "You know, you could always hire a new foreman for the ranch."

He chuckled. "Do you know anyone looking for a ranch job? Because I sure don't." Clayton ran his hand over the book. Why did he feel this desire to read the silly thing from cover to cover? Why had talking to Marshall reminded him that he was put on this earth to help others?

"Not off the top of my head. But I'm sure with a little word of mouth, we could find someone." The doctor stopped in front of his office. "Look, Clayton, I'm not here to tell you how to run your life, but I saw your face today. You were curious and wanted to look at that wound. Then you were a tad angry to learn he hadn't followed doctor's orders, and last, you simply wanted to help him. You still do."

Clayton nodded.

The doctor leaned against the whitewashed fence. "Why do you want to be a doctor?"

The question took Clayton by surprise. "I hate to see others suffer."

"And who did you see suffering?"

Clayton used the tip of his boot to scrape a mud clod off a rock. How did a man tell another man that he'd watched his parents die from a high fever? Clayton had only been eight but had decided then and there that if he could learn how to make people better, he would. "My parents."

The doctor nodded. "For me, it was my sister. She fell in the river and drowned. We pulled her out but she strangled on the water in her lungs. I vowed on the spot that I'd do everything in my power to learn how to keep people from drowning and dying." He grew silent for a few moments. Clayton assumed he was reliving the past. Then the doctor continued. "At the time, I didn't realize what I'd promised, but as I studied I realized that if I could save one person, my sister's death wouldn't be in vain."

Clayton understood the doctor's feelings. Every time God allowed him to help someone else get through a sickness or saw their bodies healed, he felt as if he were honoring his parents. To others that might seem foolish, but it made sense to him.

The doctor cleared his throat. "Son, I'll help you fulfill your promise to them, but neither one of us is getting any younger so we have to do it now." His gaze moved to the book in Clayton's hands.

He nodded. "All right. I'll try."

Doc Anderson slapped him on the back. "That's all anyone can ask of you."

Clayton left the doctor's office feeling good about his decision but also worrying about the ranch. How was Maggie going to feel when he suggested that they hire a foreman to take over the running of the ranch? Would she think he'd lied to her? After all, he'd said he could take care of the ranch, the Pony Express and their family.

Chapter Nine

Maggie jiggled baby James. The little fella had woken up ten minutes earlier and was demanding lunch. She looked about the general store for a quiet corner. Seeing none, she wished Clayton would return. She'd thought he'd be gone only a few minutes, but those minutes had turned into an hour.

Over the baby's meowing cry, Dinah said, "Sissy, I'm ready to go."

She looked down at her little sister. "I know, I'm about ready, too."

Mrs. Fisher looked up from the front counter. "I'm sorry Billy isn't here to play with you today," she said to Dinah. "He and his papa will be back tomorrow."

Dinah looked up at Maggie with big eyes. "Sissy, can we come back tomorrow?"

Even though she hated to disappoint the little girl, Maggie answered honestly. "I'm afraid not, Dinah. We'll be back Sunday for morning services."

"Aw…that's not fair. I want to come back and play," Dinah fussed.

"Don't sass your sister."

James quieted his cries and turned his little head about as if looking for the source of Clayton's voice. Maggie turned around. "When did you come in?"

He grinned. "A few moments ago." Clayton laid his hand on Dinah's shoulder. "Long enough to hear this one sassing you."

Dinah grinned up at him. "I didn't mean to sass." She turned her gaze on Maggie. "I'm sorry, Sissy."

Maggie shook her head. Dinah's sour face changed faster than a kitten could lap up milk. She looked from Dinah to Clayton. She noted that he held two books in his hand. "How was your visit with Doc Anderson?"

Clayton picked up a spice bottle and took a whiff. He curled his nose at the strong smell. "Good. He said to keep studying." He replaced the bottle.

"Can we go now?" Dinah tugged at her hand.

Maggie nodded. She was ready and so was James. He'd begun fussing once more.

"Mr. Young, I have your supplies all boxed up." Mrs. Fisher indicated two large boxes and a smaller one that sat beside the counter.

He grinned. "Thank you, Mrs. Fisher." Clayton set his two books on top of the larger boxes. "Dinah, would you mind carrying the smaller box?" he asked.

The little girl skipped toward him. She tucked her doll under one arm and then took the box from him. "Look, Sissy, I'm helping."

Her pleased face melted Maggie's heart. Since Clayton had arrived, Dinah had become a happy little girl again. Maggie wished her sister could have known their father better. He'd been a kind man with a big heart. But then, he'd left them. Mother always said that she hadn't been surprised. The woman he'd left with had a sad story and knew how to manipulate her father to get him to do anything, including leaving his family. Ma had insisted it didn't mean that Papa hadn't loved his girls, just that he'd felt sorry for the other woman and her children.

Maggie didn't care what his reasons were. Their father had deserted them. Yes, he'd been kind, but he'd also betrayed the ones he should have protected. She shook the hurtful thoughts from her mind.

Both Dinah and Clayton stood staring at her. "Oh, I'm sorry. I was woolgathering." She hurried to the door and pulled it open. The feeling of heat entering her face betrayed her.

As he passed, the scent of his shaving lotion drifted down and filled her nostrils.

Dinah followed close behind him. "Clayton, you smell good," she said.

"I tried a little of the shaving lotion that the store carries." His rich voice filled Maggie's ears. He flashed a full smile at Dinah. "You smell pretty good yourself."

Maggie heard her little sister giggle. "I smell like Sissy."

His voice deepened. "Yes, you do."

She felt her face burst into even hotter flames and continued walking toward the wagon. How was it that he could do that? Make her feel as if he really did notice things about her? Maggie knew he was only playing with Dinah, but for a brief moment she enjoyed the fact that he'd noticed her perfume.

Baby James began to kick his little legs and cry.

Clayton looked at her. His gaze moved to the baby and worry etched his brow.

Maggie said, "If you are going to be a doctor, you need to learn the different cries of a baby." Even though she'd been a mother for only a few weeks, Maggie knew that this was a hunger cry.

"He's either hungry or wet," Clayton answered, placing the boxes into the bed of the wagon. He reached down and took the smaller box from Dinah and placed it with the other two.

"He's hungry," Maggie answered.

"I'm hungry, too," Dinah said.

Clayton bent over and picked up the little girl. "Then let's go find something to eat." He strolled away from the horse and wagon.

Maggie had no choice but to follow them. Clayton walked at a fast clip toward the hotel. She listened as he and Dinah chattered about lunch. Was it wise to let Dinah get so close to Clayton? Would he leave them as soon as the Pony Express closed its doors? Or had the recent thoughts of her father's behavior simply made her even more wary of being hurt again?

Her sister had been only a year old when Papa had left. In the short time she'd been married to James's father, Dinah and Jack had never bonded in the way that she and Clayton seemed to be doing. Why, Dinah's smile could light up a room each time she saw Clayton. But could they trust him not to betray them as their father had? Maggie hated the thought that Dinah could be hurt by Clayton's leaving.

Confusion filled her. She hesitated, torn by conflicting emotions. Perhaps she and Dinah shouldn't get as close to Clayton as they were doing. She didn't intend to fall in love with her new husband but knew in her heart her little sister already had. Dinah seemed to confirm her thoughts right then by laying her head on his shoulder. She stopped suddenly and slowly turned in a circle. What had she gotten them into?

Clayton looked into the back of the wagon where Dinah was curled up in a tight ball under a blanket that Maggie had brought. The little girl was clutching her doll and sucking on her thumb. His gaze moved to a now-content James, in his mother's arms and also sleeping. Maggie looked deep in thought, but a soft smile twitched at her lips. This was his family.

He cleared his throat and then said, "Maggie, I'd like to talk to you about something."

Her pretty hazel eyes moved to his face. "I'd like to talk to you, too. I've missed adult conversations."

"I'm sorry. I should have known." Clayton felt bad that he'd not thought about the fact that Maggie had no women to talk to. His mother, Rebecca, had two friends living with her, but before they came she was a lone woman in a house full of boys. After her friends moved in, she'd become more carefree and happy.

"What do you want to talk about?" she asked, ducking her head and fidgeting with the baby's blanket.

He focused on the road ahead. "Well, I went to Doc's today to tell him I was giving up my dream of being a doctor. But, after talking to him and going with him to treat a patient, I've decided not to give it up. Doctoring is what I've always wanted to do." Would she understand? Would it matter if she didn't? Clayton knew it mattered to him more than he wanted to admit.

Maggie touched his arm. "I'm glad you decided not

to give up." Her voice sounded low and husky. "Everyone should strive to meet their dreams." She sighed.

Clayton stared into her pretty eyes and asked, "What's your dream, Maggie?"

She rocked James gently in her arms. "I don't have one." Maggie fiddled with a string on the baby's blanket. "But I'm glad you do, and I think you should pursue it." She wiggled about on the seat.

Clayton turned his head from Maggie. He felt sure she had a dream, but it was more than obvious Maggie didn't want to talk about it with him. Instead of pressing her, he said, "Me, too, but I have to give up something." He chanced a look in her direction.

At his words, her head snapped up and her features hardened. He studied her for several moments before pressing on. "I'd like for us to hire a foreman to take over the running of the ranch. That way I can focus on the Pony Express, my new family and my medical studies." He looked at her to see what she thought of his confession.

Relief and confusion filled her pretty face. "You aren't going to leave?" She tilted her head and stared him in the eyes.

So, that was what had been troubling her. Did she really think he was about to tell her he was leaving? Clayton pulled the wagon to the side of the dirt road. He set the brake and turned to face her fully. Taking her gloved hand into his, Clayton vowed, "Maggie, even when the Pony Express has run its course, I will not leave you and the kids. I thought you understood, unless you ask me to leave, I am not going anywhere."

She looked back down at baby James. Maggie pulled her hand from his. "Look, Clayton. I have every reason to believe that you will leave us whenever the going gets tough. My pa left his family for another life, one that didn't involve us or our mother. So please try to understand that men have a habit of leaving me. In a way, Jack left by way of the grave. I realize he couldn't help it but it still felt like abandonment to me. Why should I think you will be any different?" Tear-filled eyes dared him to argue that he wouldn't.

Clayton sighed. "All I can do is give you my word that I am not going nowhere." He looked out over the field. The grass was showing signs of new growth. Perhaps over time, his and Maggie's relationship would show similar signs. But would she ever trust him?

She sighed. "If you want to hire a new foreman, I see no reason why we shouldn't. You could still act as the ranch manager and let the foreman do the actual running of the ranch."

His gaze returned to hers. "I agree. I'll be happy to speak to him every evening about the day's work and plans for the next day. Then you and I can sit down after the children are in bed and discuss what he has reported. Does that sound fair?"

"More than fair," she agreed.

Clayton nodded. "I'm hoping to meet with the doctor a couple of times a week also and follow him around as he visits patients or they visit him. I've done a little doctoring on my brothers, but what Doc Anderson is doing is revolutionary." He turned to face forward once more, aware of the excitement in his voice. "He has his patients wash their wounds with soap and water to kill infections. As far as I know there are only a few docs who do that."

He released the brake and clicked his tongue to get the horse moving once more. His mind raced with all the things that Doc Anderson had told him in just a few minutes. The older gentleman had so much wisdom to share. For a brief moment, Clayton wished he lived in town where he could spend every day learning how to care for others.

"That sounds very interesting and something every mother should know." Maggie cuddled James close. She nuzzled her face in the crook of his little neck.

Clayton grinned. She really was a wonderful mother. Maggie hadn't asked for his help with the children. She'd taken care of them and the house. Now that he realized how lonesome that must have been for her, he wished he'd spent more time with the family in the evenings.

She looked up and caught him staring at her.

He nodded. "You know, I think you're right. I'll tell all mothers to make sure and wash their children's cuts and scrapes with soap and water." He returned his attention back to the road.

They traveled along in silence for a few more minutes. Finally, Maggie asked, "If you aren't working on the ranch, does that mean you will be spending more time with the children and me?"

"Yes, I'll be in and out of the house during the day. Plus, we'll discuss the ranch business in the evenings. I'm really sorry I left you alone so much before."

She smiled. "It's all right. I understand you had a lot to do."

Clayton thought that was no excuse but was grateful that she was allowing him to use it. To take her thoughts away from him being too busy to be with her and the kids, he said, "Yes. And I've been thinking that instead of hiring a foreman from outside the ranch, perhaps we should offer the job to one of the men who is already working for us. I'd prefer one of the men who already knows the ranch. I believe the other men would be more open to working for one of their own. Is that all right with you?"

Maggie nodded. "I think that's a good idea. Then when you do hire the extra men, they will have a fore-man in place to show them what needs to be done."

"I plan on working around the ranch, too, but it will be nice to give most of the responsibility over to Abraham, if he'll take the position." Clayton heard her intake of breath. He glanced in her direction and saw that she was frowning. "Something wrong with Abraham being the new foreman?"

"Well, I just thought George would be the best choice. Jack always said that George was his best and oldest man. What made you decide on Abraham?" She glanced in the back where Dinah was sleeping. With her free arm, Maggie reached back and rearranged the blanket over her little sister.

"George is getting older and likes what he's doing." He paused to let that sink in, then continued. "Hal is a nice young man, but he'd rather stay close to the house and take care of the barnyard animals." Clay-ton didn't see the need to explain that Hal was also a little slow in the thinking department. "And Abra-ham was the first one to say he'd stay on and make sure the ranch was taken care of when I told them Gus would no longer be working there. He's young and I believe he'll do a good job. But if you want to ask George first, I understand."

She shook her head. "No, I trust that you know the men better than I. All I know is what Jack and later Bill shared with me. Which really wasn't much." Maggie rearranged her skirts around her legs.

Clayton wondered if she was always this fidgety or if she was just trying to get comfortable. "Do you want to stop and stretch your legs a little?" he asked.

"No. But if you need to stop, we can." She shifted in the seat once more.

He frowned and pulled the mare to a stop. "Is something bothering you?" Clayton turned to face her.

A flush filled her face. "The wood is just a little splintered and it—" she paused "—keeps sticking to my skirt."

Clayton set the brake. "Stand up and I'll see if I can't smooth the wood out."

Maggie did as he asked. Sure enough, the boards had weathered and several thick splinters filled the spot she'd been sitting on. Clayton jumped from the wagon and went to the tailgate. He pulled a bag of flour from one of the boxes and returned to where she still stood. Putting the bag on the bench, he grinned up at her. "There you go." Then he returned to his side of the wagon and pulled himself back up.

She sat down and grinned. "That's much better, thank you."

Clayton released the brake once more and then clicked his tongue. The little mare moved forward. Maggie's pleased smile caused his heart to skip a couple of beats. Clayton frowned. Maybe he was more tired than he realized. Why else would his heart do those crazy flutters? He refused to admit that it had anything to do with Maggie and her pretty smiles.

Chapter Ten

The next morning, Maggie placed James in his wash-tub. "Dinah, watch James for me for a couple of minutes. He's sleeping so I'm going to go check for eggs."

"All right, Sissy." Dinah sat on the kitchen rug off to the side of the stove. She played with her doll and a cup and saucer. "Would you like a cup of coffee?" the little girl asked the doll.

Maggie slipped out of the kitchen without waiting to hear if the doll drank coffee or not. She pulled on her coat and stepped out into the brisk morning air. Swinging the egg basket, she walked toward the chicken coop.

Hal came around the house from the pigpen. "Good morning, Mrs. Young."

"Good morning, Hal. How are you this morning?" Maggie liked Hal. He was a talkative young man with a big heart for animals.

He sniffled. "I'm doing good. My nose is a little runny, but I think I've developed a touch of hay fever."

"Have you told Clayton you aren't feeling well?"

"Oh, no, ma'am. I'm not too sickly to not work."

He carried the slop bucket to the back door and put it down.

Maggie smiled. She continued to the henhouse. The hens clucked their morning greetings. Setting her basket down, Maggie opened the barrel that held corn. She pulled out a tin scoop and filled it with the corn, then tossed it into the chicken yard. While the hens chased after the food, Maggie picked up her basket and slipped inside the henhouse. She checked each nest and discovered she had six eggs.

When she came out of the henhouse, Maggie inhaled the fresh air. Hal stood beside the gate, his grin lopsided. "I'll clean out those nests today, Mrs. Young. I meant to do it yesterday but then had a run-in with the pigs." He opened the gate and she slipped past him.

"What kind of run-in?" She waited for him to fall into step with her and then walked back to the house.

"Aw, nothing too serious. Someone left the gate open and they got out. I spent all afternoon chasing the pigs down and putting them back inside." He slapped his hat against his thigh. "I can't imagine who would do such a thing to me."

Maggie knew Hal's mind was a little slower than some and figured he'd just forgotten to latch the gate. "It's all right, Hal. You got all the pigs back in." Maggie paused as a thought occurred to her. "You did get them all back in, right?"

That big grin came back. "Oh, yes, ma'am. And had fun doing it, too."

"Good. Thanks for walking me to the house, Hal. I'm going to make two cakes today. If you come back after supper, I'll send one out to the men, too."

She pulled the screen door open and looked into the kitchen.

"Thank you, Mrs. Young. I'll get to work on the henhouse right now." Hal spun on his heel and hurried back across the yard.

Dinah still played by the stove with her doll. The little girl glanced her way when she set the eggs on the sideboard. "Sissy, can I have two cookies? One for me and one for my dolly?"

"Yes, but you have to save them until after breakfast." She washed her hands and then started slicing bacon. Maggie laid it in a cast-iron skillet.

The little girl scrambled up on a stool and reached into the cookie jar to pull out two sugar cookies. "Can we make more cookies this afternoon?" she asked.

"No, we're making two spice cakes today. One for the family and one for the men." Maggie checked on the baby, who still slept soundly. His little face relaxed in sleep was the most precious sight she'd ever seen.

"Can I lick the spoon?" Dinah's eyes were bright with anticipation.

Maggie laughed. "Only if you are a good girl."

Dinah climbed down from the stool and placed the two cookies on the dessert plate. "Oh, that's easy. I'm always a good girl."

It was true most of the time, so Maggie agreed. "Yes, and since you've been so good, I'll even let you lick the bowl." It wasn't like the child would be licking the actual dish. Maggie wondered where such a saying had come from. She'd make sure Dinah used the spoon to get the extra batter out of the bowl.

"Is Clayton going to have lunch with us today?"

Dinah asked, moving her doll, cup and saucer with the cookies on it to the table.

Maggie shrugged. "I'm not sure. He might be too busy working to come in. George will make sure he eats, if he doesn't come to the house." She sat down at the table and yawned. The baby had been fussier last night than normal and now that it was midmorning, Maggie was beginning to feel the effects of her sleepless night.

"I hope he has lunch with us." Dinah pretended her doll was eating the sugar cookie.

She didn't want to admit it but Maggie hoped Clayton would have lunch with them, too. The night before she had been aware of his lantern light shining under the door. Was he reading his medical books? Or had he been unable to sleep because of James's fussing?

Maggie's body had refused to relax long after James had quit fussing. It wasn't until Clayton had turned the light out and the soft sounds of his snoring had traveled through the walls did she relax and gently drift off to sleep. What was it about knowing Clayton was close that gave her a sense of security?

Clayton frowned. He'd hoped to get back to the house and have lunch with Maggie and Dinah, but it looked as if that wasn't going to happen today. The sky was darkening at an alarming rate. If they didn't hurry they would all be drenched. "Do you think we can get her to the barn?" He stared at the brown-and-white cow. She had to weigh over half a ton. If she didn't want to walk to the barn, he didn't know how they could persuade her to.

Abraham tilted his head to the side and sighed

heavily. "We can try, but that calf is ready to come at any moment."

Bud joined them. "We could move her to the spring house barn. It's not that far away and would give her some shelter from the rain."

Abraham nodded. "I wish Gus had kept a better eye on that bull. We wouldn't be having this problem in early February."

Clayton ignored the Gus reference. What was done, was done. He remembered seeing a structure that looked more like a lean-to than a barn when he'd scouted out the ranch. It was as good a place as any to birth a calf. "Are you talking about the lean-to, over in that direction?" He pointed to the east. At their nods, he said, "All right, we need to get her up and moving."

The cow let out a miserable bawl as if to say she wasn't in the mood to stand up and walk to a safe place to have her baby. Clayton couldn't help but think of Maggie having baby James alone. Had she been as scared as this first-time-calving mom looked? He was sure she had been.

Bud walked down to the stream and filled his hat with water. He returned and poured it on the cow's head. She got to her feet. Abraham gently pulled her along behind his horse. Bud and Clayton each got on his horse. Bud took the left side of the cow and Clayton took the right. Together they kept her upright by keeping the horses close enough she couldn't lie down.

The men took it slow, and within half an hour they'd arrived at the lean-to. Abraham climbed down from his horse and walked the cow inside. The sky chose that moment to open, and rain began to shower down. Clayton pulled Bones inside the lean-to with the cow and said, "Why don't you two go on to lunch?"

Abraham took the rope from around the cow's neck and then looked at Clayton for several long minutes. "You sure, boss? I can stay with her."

"I'm sure. I've never helped a cow give birth before, but I've read how to do it. I'm just hoping that with a little rest, she'll be able to deliver without assistance." Clayton watched the cow settle down inside the shelter with a deep sigh.

"That's more than I've ever done. Gus was always the one who assisted with the birthing, if it needed to be done," Abraham said. He pulled himself up on his horse and looked down at Clayton. "I'll eat and get back here real fast."

Bud had already turned his horse toward the ranch house. He applied his heels to the side of the horse and shot off into the rain.

Abraham shook his head. "Didn't have to tell him twice, did you?"

Clayton chuckled. "Nope. But since he's gone I'd like to ask you something."

Wariness filled the young man's brown eyes. "Sure, boss." He pushed his hat back, revealing the tan line on his forehead.

"Maggie and I have been talking and we decided we'd like to offer you the job of ranch foreman. Do you think that you'd be interested in taking the job?" Clayton watched Abraham's shoulders relax, and he smiled.

"Yes, I would. When do I start?"

"How about tomorrow?" Clayton's gaze moved

to the cow as she stood up again. Then he turned his attention back to Abraham. He quickly outlined the new foreman's duties and made sure that he wouldn't change Hal's or George's responsibilities.

After Abraham nodded his understanding, Clayton said, "Tonight I'll tell the other men you are the new foreman."

Abraham nodded. "Then I'll keep the information to myself until then."

"Good. Go on now and grab some grub."

The young man couldn't keep his smile from reappearing. He climbed back on his horse. "I'll be back as quick as possible."

"Take your time. If it's still raining when you finish eating, just stay out of the weather. I'll be up to the house as soon as she has the calf."

Abraham nodded, then left.

Clayton settled down to wait. The rain pattered on the tin roof, creating a singsong rhythm. An hour ago he was sure the calf was going to be born any minute. Now the cow simply lay on her side and breathed heavily.

His thoughts went to Maggie once more. He could only imagine that her labor had been long and difficult, but she had endured and produced a beautiful baby boy. What would she think being compared to a cow? Clayton grinned at the thought. He was pretty sure no one would appreciate being likened to a cow. Least of all his pretty, young wife.

The cow began to move about as if ready to give birth. Clayton planted his feet firmly on the ground and waited for the calf to be born.

A little over an hour later both Clayton and the

mother cow were exhausted but happy. She stood nursing a small bull with the same markings as the one in the left pasture. He was sturdy with big brown eyes.

Clayton led Bones out into the rain and then locked the door on the lean-to. Mother and calf would be fine until the rain let up, and then one of the men could come out and take care of them. He climbed into the wet saddle and pulled his hat down low on his head. A smile touched his lips as he said, "Let's go, ole boy."

Bones shot off like a too-tightly strung arrow toward the ranch house. Clayton whooped and laughed. His doctoring skills had come in handy today while delivering the calf. He couldn't wait to get back to his books tonight and learn more about how to help others.

Within minutes, Clayton was sliding off his horse in front of the barn. He and Bones walked side by side inside the warm, dry interior. Clayton shook the rain from his hat and wiped the water from his horse's face.

George came in the side door. "I figured you'd stay out of the rain, at least until it lets up a mite," he said, taking Bones's reins and leading him to the nearest stall.

"Naw, that ole cow had us a nice little bull and then wanted her privacy so my buddy and I headed for home." He walked to the bag of oats and filled a feeding bucket with the sweet-smelling grain.

George poured water into the trough from a bucket that he kept handy in the barn. "The boys are all holed up in the bunkhouse waiting out the storm."

"Good. I'll mosey over there in a few. I'd like for

you to come with me." Clayton pulled the saddle and blanket off Bones and then began to rub him down.

The horse grunted his thanks and continued eating.

"Can we wait for the rain to let up?" George asked as he walked to the big doors and looked out into the falling sheets of water.

"I don't see why not." He really wanted to go inside and see how the kids were reacting to the storm. James was probably sleeping through it, but Dinah might be afraid of the thunder and occasional lightning.

"Good. I kept a bowl of soup hot for you, if you're hungry." George turned from the doorway and led him to the small room that, for a few brief days, Clayton had called home.

As they entered the door, Clayton asked, "How are you liking this quieter space?"

George grunted. "It's nice not to hear all that wheezing and snoring every night."

Clayton laughed. "I know just what you mean. When my brothers all get to snoring at the same time, it's like listening to a bunch of hogs at the feeding trough."

The older gentleman handed Clayton a big bowl of steaming soup. "Speaking of hogs, did Hal tell you that all the pigs got out of the pen yesterday?"

"No, can't say that he did. Anything I should be worried about?"

George shrugged. "I don't reckon so. But it isn't like Hal to leave a gate open. I'm a little worried about him."

Clayton sampled the soup. It wasn't Maggie's cooking, but it wasn't all bad either. He glanced up to see the older man studying him. "Soup's good," he murmured.

The other man laughed. "I'm not concerned about my cooking. I'm concerned about Hal."

"Oh. Well, we all make mistakes. I'm sure that it was just an accident."

"You're probably right," George agreed. He sat down in the rocker Maggie had sent out to him the day before. "I'll have to let the missus know how much I like this chair." He grinned up at Clayton. "You're welcome to sit on my bunk, if you want to rest a spell."

Clayton sat and ate the rest of the soup. His mind returned to Maggie and the kids. What were they doing to pass the time while it rained outside? He imagined James would still be sleeping, tucked either into his dresser drawer or in the washtub in the kitchen. Poor kid needed a real bed. His gaze moved to George, who had stopped rocking. His head was thrown back and his eyes closed. Gentle snores rose and fell.

Careful not to wake the old man, Clayton eased off the cot. He set his bowl down on the floor and slipped out of the room, closing the door behind him. His gaze darted about the barn. What would Maggie think if he built James a crib? Thanks to his brother Philip, who loved to make furniture, Clayton was pretty sure he could build a fine crib for the baby.

He walked to the door and looked out into the now-light drizzle. His gaze moved back to the room where George was napping. Should Clayton go and wake him? Or leave him be and tell him later that Abraham was the new foreman? Clayton knew that the old man's feelings would be hurt if he was left out of this important announcement. He returned to George's room to find the old man waking. "Rain's about stopped. Ready to go have a word with the rest of the men?" Clayton asked.

George pushed up from the rocker. "As long as it's not to announce I'm being fired, sure." He yawned and stretched. "Rain has always made me sleepy. Resting my eyes seems to help keep me from sleeping in the middle of the day."

Clayton hid his smile by turning away. "I'll have to try that sometime."

"My pappy swore by the resting-of-the-eyes method."

This time he couldn't contain his laugh. "I'm sure he did."

George grunted and followed him out into the light rain.

Clayton hurried to the bunkhouse and knocked quickly before entering without an answer. Hal and Bud sat in front of the checkerboard. Abraham sat beside the stove whittling on a piece of kindling.

"Sorry to barge in on you boys like this, but we had no desire to get any wetter than we already are." Clayton stepped aside to let George in behind him.

Hal grinned. "You can come in anytime you want to, boss."

Clayton smiled at the young man. "Thank you, Hal."

George walked over and sat down beside Abraham. He glanced at the game board. "Looks like Hal is beating you today, Bud."

"Yeah, guess my mind's not on the game today." Bud jumped at the sudden clap of thunder.

"You sure are jumpy today," Hal said with a frown.

Bud shrugged. "Never cared much for thunder or lightning."

"Aw, that's all right. We're all scared of something," Hal said, looking down at the game again.

"Didn't say I was scared. Said I didn't like them," Bud growled, as if ready to fight over the simple words.

Clayton cleared his throat. "I didn't come in here to listen to you bicker." That seemed to catch everyone's attention. He looked to Abraham, who continued to whittle on the stick. Clayton couldn't tell what the young man was thinking so pressed on. "I came in to tell you that I am no longer going to be the foreman of this ranch."

Bud and Hal turned at his words. Abraham continued flicking curls of wood with his knife. Hal was the one who asked, "Have you hired someone to take your place?"

"I have." He looked at each of the men in turn. His gaze connected with Abraham's, and he gave the young man what he hoped was a subtle nod.

George frowned. "Care to tell us who you hired?" He sounded wary.

Abraham stood up and looked at each of them. "He hired me."

Bud's mouth opened and closed. Hal grinned as if he were at a church picnic and had just been served a plate of fried chicken. George simply looked relieved.

Clayton nodded. "Yes, I hired Abraham. Maggie and I agreed that he would be best for the job, since he's been here almost as long as George."

George stood and thumped Abraham on the back. "Congratulations, son. I'm glad it's you and not me."

Hal laughed. "Me, too." He walked over and shook Abraham's hand.

Bud slowly pushed his chair back and walked across the room. "Couldn't ask to work with a better man." He also shook hands with Abraham.

Clayton watched Abraham's whiskered cheeks turn a light pink. He looked about the room. "You fellas need to straighten up in here. Abraham and I will be hiring a few new hands and they will need a cleaner place to live. Be sure you are in the bunk you want because whatever is left over will belong to the new men."

"We'll do it," Hal answered.

George walked over to the door. "Well, if this meeting is done, I'm heading back to the barn." He waited for Clayton's nod and then left.

Abraham moved to his bunk and began carrying his few things over to Gus's old bunk. He looked to Clayton. "Is there something more you wanted to talk to me about?" he asked.

"No, I was just thinking about the space in here. At home we built partitions so that each of us could have some privacy. What do you think of building walls and creating each man his own area to live in? You'd still all be under the same roof, but you'd have space to feel like you were alone."

Bud, who had returned to his and Hal's board game, answered, "I wouldn't mind having some alone time from time to time." He grinned at Hal. "Don't get me wrong, but there are times when I'd like to read and not feel like everyone is watching me."

Hal chuckled. "I like watching your lips move."

"See what I mean? I'd be willing to help build some walls."

Abraham nodded. "Sounds like a project we can do now, since winter keeps us inside much of the time anyway."

"Good. I'm glad you are all in agreement." Thunder boomed, causing Clayton to jump. "Let's all take the rest of the day off." He looked at Abraham. "I left the cow and new bull in the lean-to. Someone will need to go out in the morning and move her."

Abraham nodded as he stripped the cot of its sheets and then proceeded to take them to the other side of the room. He answered, "I'll see to it."

Clayton opened the door and looked out into the falling rain. His gaze moved to the house, where he knew Maggie had a warm fire going and his medical books awaited him. He longed to see the baby and Dinah. Clayton admitted to himself that he missed them.

His thoughts turned warmly to Maggie, and he had to admit that he had missed her today. Admitting it didn't make him feel very good. Was he falling in love with his bride? No, it was a simple longing to be with a friend. Nothing more. He made a wild dash for the house and the warmth it offered all the while ignoring the swift beating of his heart at the thought of being with his new family once more.

Chapter Eleven

Maggie saw Clayton splashing across the yard and opened the door. She laughed as he slid across the porch. "Wipe your feet good before traipsing into the house."

"How about I just pull my boots off out here on the porch?"

"Even better." She walked back into the sitting room.

Dinah sat on the couch holding her doll tightly. She offered a weak smile to Clayton as he entered the house in his stocking feet. "Hi, Clayton. Will you sit by me? I'm scared."

Maggie watched as he walked to the little girl. Clayton sat down beside her and gathered Dinah close to his side. "You don't feel scared," he teased.

"I am. The rain is loud." She pressed against his side.

Maggie felt his gaze upon her but had no advice for him. As long as she could remember, Dinah had feared storms. And nothing she'd ever said seemed to take the fears away.

"You know what we need, Dinah?" Clayton asked.

She pressed her face deeper into his side and shook her head.

"We need to read a story from the Bible. Maybe Sissy could get us the Bible."

Maggie hurried to get the Bible. Clayton's soothing voice and calm behavior had her wondering what he was going to read that could possibly help her little sister overcome her fear of storms. She'd taken the Bible up to her room earlier in the day, so she hurried up the stairs to retrieve it. A large clap of thunder had her racing back to the sitting room, where Clayton and Dinah waited.

Clayton pulled Dinah up into his lap and then took the Bible from Maggie. "Maggie, why don't you get baby James so he can hear our story, too?"

She didn't know why but Maggie found herself doing as Clayton requested. James had been lying in the washtub. His eyes were big as he listened to the thunder and falling rain on the tin roof of the house. Maggie picked him up and cuddled him close.

"Our story is from the book of Mark, chapter four, verses thirty-five through forty-one." Dinah sucked her thumb as she watched him find the story and then begin to read: *"And the same day, when the even was come, he saith unto them, Let us pass over unto the other side. And when they had sent away the multitude, they took him even as he was in the ship. And there were also with him other little ships. And there arose a great storm of wind, and the waves beat into the ship, so that it was now full. And he was in the hinder part of the ship, asleep on a pillow: and they awake him, and say unto him, Master, carest thou not that we perish? And he arose, and rebuked the wind, and said unto the sea, Peace, be still. And the wind ceased, and there was a great calm. And he said unto them, Why are ye so fearful? how is it that ye have no faith?*

"And they feared exceedingly, and said one to another, What manner of man is this, that even the wind and the sea obey him?" Clayton stopped reading and looked down at Dinah. "Do you understand the story?"

She pulled her thumb from between her lips and answered, "A little."

Clayton set her up straighter and pointed to each verse as he told the story in a way she could understand. "Well, it was like this. It was about this time of day when Jesus told his disciples to take him over to the other side of the sea in their boats. And they all got in the boats and Jesus went to sleep." He pulled his finger away and asked Dinah, "Do you know what happened next?"

Dinah nodded. "It rained and made loud noise."

"That's right." He put his finger back on the page and ran it along the words, and continued telling the story in his own words. "And like you the disciples were afraid so they woke up Jesus. Well, Jesus stood up and told that wind and rain to stop. And it did."

Dinah continued to stare at his finger and the words on the page. Maggie knew that her sister couldn't read, but she seemed to have calmed down as Clayton read to her. She tilted her head back and looked at Clayton. "He made it stop?"

"He sure did."

She looked back at the page and touched the Scriptures. "And were the disciples still scared?" Dinah asked in a small voice.

Clayton hugged her close. "They weren't afraid of the wind and water anymore. Jesus was watching out for them."

A smile tugged at Dinah's lips. "Jesus watches out for us, too, huh, Clayton?"

"He sure does, half-pint."

"And if Jesus tells it to stop, it will stop?"

"It sure will."

Dinah scrambled off his lap. She walked over to Maggie and baby James. Touching his small hand, Dinah said, "Did you hear that, baby? We don't have to be scared of the rain and noise. Jesus is taking care of us and when he says stop, it stops."

Maggie marveled that at that moment, the storm stopped. It quit raining, and for the rest of the evening there was no more thunder or lightning. Clayton knew exactly what Dinah needed to hear and believe. How could a man who had no children of his own comfort someone else's child so easily? Had God brought him into their lives to do more than save James's life? The thought both comforted her and worried her.

Maggie stood in the doorway and watched as a Pony Express rider raced from the yard. She sighed heavily. Over the last couple of weeks, Maggie and Clayton had created a routine. She got up early and made sure that Clayton had a hot breakfast before heading out to the barn to do his morning chores. Then once he was out of the house, she took care of the children's basic needs, cleaned, cooked and did laundry. Each evening he came in and, true to his 'word, played with Dinah and even baby James. After the children were in bed, Clayton told her what was happening on the ranch and praised Abraham on a fine job. They now had three additional hired men who were helping with the repairs on the place as well as taking care of the newborn calves and their mothers. After about an hour, Clayton would excuse himself to go read his medical books.

She told herself her life was full. But if it were so full, why did she feel so empty? Maggie walked back into the kitchen and began washing the noon-day dishes. As she scrubbed, her thoughts went to the ranch. Yes, Clayton told her what was going on, but she wanted to see for herself. Hadn't Gus told her things were going well and then almost succeeded in taking the ranch from her?

Not that she could compare Clayton to Gus. Clayton had a way with both the children that left her in awe of him. Dinah had fallen deeply in love with the Pony Express manager. She waited each evening by the front door for his return. On the days that he went into town the little girl moped around the house as if she'd lost her best friend.

Not that she blamed Dinah. She felt his absences from the ranch also. Maggie hated to admit it, but she missed him as soon as he left the house. She told herself it was because he was the only adult companionship that she had. Was she starting to care for Clayton more than she should? Or were they simply becoming good friends?

Maggie heard the kitchen door open behind her and looked to see who was coming in. Clayton grinned and whispered, "Maggie, are the children lying down for a nap?"

"Yes, why?"

Clayton ignored her question and asked one of his own. "How long will they be down for?"

She frowned. "Probably another hour. If James doesn't wake up hungry before then." The little boy was growing and eating much more than he had in the past. "Why?"

He stepped back and allowed Hal to come into the door. "I want to show you something. Hal has agreed to call if either one of the children wake up, if you will come with me."

Maggie looked from Clayton to Hal. "How long would we be gone from the house?"

Hal said, "I promise to be real quiet, Mrs. Young."

"And I promise to have you back in an hour."

She wanted to go and see what Clayton had to show her but she also worried that Hal might not know what to do if the children were to wake up.

"Come on, Maggie. You haven't been away from this house in two weeks."

It was true. She pulled her apron off and hung it by the back door. Just as she started to follow Clayton out the door, she stopped. "Wait." Maggie turned to Hal. "How will you let me know if the children wake up?"

He grinned. "I'll ring the old dinner bell. Remember? We used to use it all the time."

Maggie did remember. But it wasn't really a bell. More like a large chunk of metal that she would hit with another piece of metal Jack had found. It made the loudest noise. She hated that thing, and after several weeks of using it, Maggie had told Jack she would never use it again.

She smiled at Hal. "That's a great plan." Still, as she left the house, Maggie felt uncomfortable.

As soon as they were at the barn, Clayton took her to two saddled horses, Bones and another one that she'd named Snowball. After she'd climbed up on the horse, George handed her the reins. Maggie looked toward the house, where Hal stood in the back door watching them.

The older gentleman said, "Don't worry, Mrs. Young. I'll keep an eye on Hal and the young'uns." He patted her leg reassuringly.

"Come on, Maggie. The children will be fine for a few minutes." Clayton turned Bones away from the house and toward the west pasture. "I'm not sure you've ever been where I'm taking you, but I think you'll like it."

"Thank you, George. I feel better knowing you are watching out for the children and Hal." Maggie turned Snowball so that she followed Bones.

The sun shone and after some dreary days inside, being outside in the sunshine was a true blessing she welcomed. The cold wind whipped at her cheeks and nose. Maggie felt like throwing her head back and racing across the pasture. Being able to ride again after so many long months was exhilarating.

Clayton slowed Bones down until she was riding beside him, instead of behind him. "We should do this every day while the kids are napping."

Maggie laughed. Was he saying he'd like to spend alone time with her every day? She decided to make light of the suggestion. "Don't you think Hal and George would get tired of playing nursemaids?"

"Doubt it. This is probably the easiest hour's work they've done in years." He grinned across at her.

"Where is this mystery place you are taking me?" she asked.

He made a tsking sound. "Patience, Maggie. Just enjoy the ride."

"We have less than an hour now. Shouldn't we be riding a little faster?"

A mischievous glint entered his eyes. "Sure, catch me, if you can." Clayton patted Bones on the neck. "Let's go, ole boy."

Maggie watched in surprise as the horse sped away. "Hey! No fair! That's a Pony Express horse!" she yelled after him even as she urged Snowball to follow.

His laughter flowed back to her. For the first time in weeks, Maggie felt carefree. Joy traveled through her veins as the sunshine shone on her face and the wind blew through her hair. Maggie found herself laughing also. What would it be like to feel this light-hearted always? If only she didn't have a lingering fear of abandonment, Maggie could almost see herself falling in love with her handsome husband.

Chapter Twelve

Clayton led her to the small cove that was tucked away on the back side of the ranch. Over the last few weeks, he'd packed one or both of the medical books in his saddlebags and come to the cove to study. Its peacefulness welcomed him like an old friend.

Clayton had entertained the idea of bringing Maggie and the kids to the cove and having a family picnic, but first he wanted to show it to Maggie. George had said that he never recalled Maggie going out to the cove. That was all Clayton needed to hear. He'd decided then and there to share his special place with Maggie first.

He slid off Bones's back and stood waiting for Maggie and her mount to catch up to him. Her hair had come down from the braid she'd been wearing earlier. Strands of blond silk framed her laughing face. She was probably the most beautiful woman he'd ever met.

"Oh, Clayton. This is a beautiful spot." She allowed him to pull her from the horse.

His hands lingered on her tiny waist for a moment

too long. Maggie looked up at him with startled hazel eyes. Had she felt the connection that he'd just felt? That need to be closer to her? Clayton released her and took a step away. She was his wife. Why shouldn't he get closer to her? He turned his back and looked out onto the water. Where had such a thought come from?

He didn't want to fall in love. He didn't think it was fair to get close to a woman unless he was willing to give her his heart. Clayton knew he wasn't there yet.

"It's beautiful here, Clayton." Her voice sounded soft and unsure.

He turned with a smile. "It is, isn't it?"

She nodded. "It will be even more beautiful in another month." Maggie bent down and picked up a rock. She turned sideways and sent it across the water in two little hops. Then the rock sank.

Clayton laughed and joined her. "That was sad. I can skip a rock four times before it sinks," he bragged.

Maggie bent for another rock. "Let's see you do it." She handed him the stone, stood back and gave him space.

Clayton took his time and aimed the rock across the water. It did three skips and sank to the bottom. He groaned loudly. "I will pick out my own rocks next time."

Her laughter drifted over him like sugar on a cookie. He playfully growled, "If you can do better, step on up." Clayton moved away and let her into his spot.

She scooped up another small stone, moved to where he stood, wiggled her body and twisted the little rock in her fingers. Then she let it fly. "One, two, three and four!" Maggie jumped up and laughed. "Four. Beat that."

Clayton couldn't believe that he was playing a game of skipping rocks with a girl. Not just any girl, but his wife. He laughed and stepped up for his turn.

Half an hour later, Maggie called their game to an end. She smiled broadly at him. "You win this time. I'll do better next time, but we have to head back to the house now."

He laughed. "Thanks for letting me win." Clayton stood behind her as Maggie pulled herself up into the saddle. Once she was seated, he grinned up at her. "I look forward to a rematch."

Maggie's voice softened. "Me, too. This has been fun."

Clayton felt sure Maggie hadn't had fun in a long time. He felt as if he'd do anything to see her relaxed and smiling again.

They rode back to the ranch in comfortable silence. Clayton dismounted beside her at the front of the porch. He took her reins. "I'll be in after I put the horses away."

"Really?"

The shock on her face gave him pause. Had he neglected her? Since they'd come from town, he'd spent his evenings with her and the children.

"Boss!"

Clayton turned at the sound of George's voice. He called back to him. "George, call me Clayton. I'm not the boss."

George ran across the yard from the barn. "Clayton, Abraham said to tell you that the fence in the back west pasture has been knocked down. He said someone took an ax to part of it. He wants you to come out and help him round up the cattle."

"Where's Bud?"

"He's fixing the fence."

Clayton looked at Maggie.

"Go. We'll be here when you get home."

He wanted to stay with his family but knew his duty was to help on the ranch. He nodded and swung up on his horse. "George, please put Snowball back in her stall." Clayton turned to Maggie. "Please ask Hal to meet us in the west pasture."

George started back to the barn with the white mare. He stopped. "B— Clayton, do you want me to let Hal have this horse so that he can get out there faster?"

Clayton nodded. "That's a good plan." He turned to find Maggie already gone.

Hal came rushing from the house. "You need me, boss?"

Clayton groaned. He'd have to tell every man on the place that he was not their boss. "Yes, we have fences to fix and cows to chase. And stop calling me boss."

Hal looked to George, who shrugged.

"You can take Snowball." George held out the mare's reins.

Clayton turned Bones toward the west pasture.

Hal rode up beside him and asked, "You want me to chase cows or fix fences?"

He shook his head. "Which one are you better at?"

The other man rubbed his chin. "I'm pretty good at chasing cows."

"Then you'll go with me to find Abraham. We'll

see Bud first and find out which way Abraham went."
He glanced over at Hal.

The young man had a frown on his face.

"What's wrong?" Clayton asked.

Hal looked over at him. "Why are we chasing
cows?"

Clayton realized that Hal had been in the house
when George had told him about the fence. "Someone tore down the fence in the west pasture, so we
have to go catch the cows that got out."

"They tore it down?"

"That's what Abraham said." Clayton watched the
young man's forehead furrow deeper. He waited while
Hal worked through his thoughts.

Hal looked across at him. "Who would tear up the
fence?" He worried his bottom lip between his teeth.

"I'm not sure. Could be cattle rustlers." His first re-
sponse was to think it was Gus, but they hadn't heard
from Jack's cousin since they'd told him to leave the
ranch.

"Do cattle rustlers also let pigs out of their pens?"

"What?" Had he been daydreaming or had Hal
really just asked if cattle rustlers let pigs out of their
pens? He remembered George mentioning the pig incident.

Clayton allowed Bones to walk once more. "It's
probably not the same person." His gaze moved to
Hal. Like him, she probably thought the young man
had forgotten to close the gate well and didn't feel the
incident was worth mentioning.

"Maybe not." Hal didn't look convinced.

They'd wasted enough time. Clayton grinned at
him. "We'd best get to the west pasture. Those cattle

aren't going to round up themselves." He touched his boot heels to Bones's sides.

Within a few minutes, they saw Bud working on the fence. He was putting the logs back into place. Those that had been chopped in half lay off to one side. Clayton stopped and leaned on the saddle horn. "Any idea what happened here?" he asked.

"Abraham and I were riding the fence lines and came across this. Looks like someone took an ax to the logs." Bud leaned against the undamaged wood.

Clayton nodded. His gaze moved to the cow tracks. He didn't need Bud to tell him which direction Abraham had gone to follow the cows. "Come on, Hal. Let's go find the cattle." He led the way over the lower part of the still-down fence.

As he followed the trail, Clayton worried. Was Gus the cattle rustler? Or had it simply been a mischievous passerby? What would Maggie think when he told her about the damage? And, even though he thought Hal probably forgot to close the gate to the pigpen, what if he was wrong? Had someone let the pigs out to distract Hal? Worry etched into his being. Was his family in danger?

Maggie sat up waiting for Clayton. She'd put the children to bed and walked to the barn to see if George had heard anything from the men. After plying him with fresh cookies, Maggie was no closer to knowing what was going on than when she'd walked over. He'd assured her it would take them a while to get all the cows rounded up.

She settled into her chair. Would Clayton spend all night rounding up livestock? Maggie hated the thought of going upstairs without him in the house. She'd gotten used to him being there.

A bump sounded at the back of the house. Was Clayton back? She pushed out of her chair and walked to the kitchen. Maggie knew he'd be starving. He'd missed dinner, which had consisted of ham and potatoes. A plate sat at the back of the stove warming for him.

Maggie stopped at the stove. She tilted her head and listened. If he were coming through the back door, Clayton should have already come inside. Another bumping sound met her ears. Her heartbeat picked up.

Was someone outside? And if so, why didn't he knock at the door? Or simply come inside? She called out, "Clayton is that you?" Then realized her mistake. If someone was out there, he now knew she was alone in the house.

She tiptoed to the back door and dropped the large bar across it. Then Maggie walked as quietly as she could to the front door. Just as she got to the door it opened.

Maggie screamed.

Clayton pulled his gun from the holster on his hip. He took in the empty room and stared at her as if she'd grown two heads. "Why are you screaming?"

Maggie had already covered her mouth. Her hands shook as she pulled them away to answer. How foolish she was going to look to him. "You scared me."

"I scared you? Woman, you took ten years off my life screaming like that." He holstered his gun.

"Since when do you wear a gun on your hip?" Maggie demanded.

"Sissy? Are you all right?" Dinah stood at the top of the stairs. Her eyes were wide and full of fear.

Maggie nodded. "Yes, go back to bed. Clayton just came home."

The little girl turned back toward the bedrooms.

Clayton shut the door with a tired sigh. "We're all going to be wearing them for a while," he answered once Dinah was no longer standing at the head of the stairs.

"Why?" Maggie walked to the kitchen. He'd scared the living liver out of her. She hoped by asking him questions he wouldn't ask her why she was so jumpy.

"Someone deliberately damaged a fence and ran our cattle off." He followed her into the kitchen and sat down at the table.

Maggie took his plate from the stove and carried it to him. Clayton lowered his head and said a quick silent blessing over his food, then she said, "Did you round them all up?"

"Yes, and I spoke with our neighbors. Seems all of them have had their fences meddled with. They aren't any happier about it than we are." His shoulders slumped as he ate.

"I would say not," Maggie agreed. She poured him a hot cup of coffee.

Clayton ate several bites. "I also spoke to Mr. Morris about taking our cows to market with his. He said he'd welcome the help on the trip."

Maggie sliced a generous portion of cake for Clayton. She set the dessert beside him and then poured herself a cup of coffee. "Good. I was hoping that would be the case."

He continued eating.

She sat quietly sipping on the hot coffee. Who would benefit from tearing down fences? If it had been just their ranch, Maggie would have thought it was Gus. But since it was others, too, she was at a loss as to who would do such a thing.

Clayton finished the ham and potatoes and then pulled the cake toward him. He stuffed a generous portion into his mouth. "So, what was the screaming really about earlier?"

His tired eyes seemed to tease her. Maggie frowned. She'd hoped to have distracted him.

Now she would just have to be honest. "I heard something by the back door and thought it might be you, but you didn't come inside. Then, I heard it again, got scared and locked the back door. I was about to lock the front door when you came barging in and scared the living daylights out of me."

He shook his head. "What does that even mean?"

Maggie knew he was tired, but he wasn't making any sense. "What does what mean?"

"Living daylights?" He drank deeply of the black coffee.

She frowned. "It means you scared me half to death."

"Half to death? Really? That has to be the stupidest saying I ever heard. How can anyone be scared half to death?" He continued eating, without looking up.

Maggie couldn't read his face since she couldn't see it. Was he teasing her? Or being serious? She picked up his dirty plate and set it in the pan of water. "Are you trying to pick a fight with me, Clayton Young?"

He looked up, startled. "No, why would you think that?"

She couldn't believe he was so thick. "Oh, never mind. We are both tired and need to get some rest." Maggie glanced at the dirty dish in her pan. It would be fine soaking in the water. She was tired and her nerves were shot. She pulled her apron off and hung it on a hook beside the stove. "Good night, Clayton."

Maggie had almost made it out the door when he called, "Maggie?"

Tired, cranky and a little out of sorts, she snapped, "What?"

"Tomorrow morning, let me or Hal collect the chicken eggs. I'd like for you to stay inside." He sounded tired and unsure.

She turned to face him. Collecting the morning eggs always gave her a little time outdoors, and she enjoyed the fresh air. Maggie didn't want to be cooped up inside all day like a brooding hen. "Why?"

"Because I want to make sure you stay safe." He stood up and took his dirty dishes to the washtub and eased them into the water.

Was he trying to protect her? It was a sweet gesture, but Maggie had no intention of hiding in her house. "Safe from what, or should I say whom?"

Clayton walked over to her. He titled her chin up with his hand. His blue eyes melded with hers. In a soft voice, he answered, "I don't know, but it's important that you do as I say."

She felt as if she might drown in the blue of his gaze. He was close enough she could smell the earthy scent that was purely Clayton Young. His hand felt warm on her chin, and she leaned into it.

He ran his tongue over his lips. Mesmerized by the sight, Maggie watched as his face leaned close to hers. His breath felt warm against her face. She closed her eyes and waited.

Nothing happened. She cracked her left eye open and found him watching her closely. Heat filled her cheeks. Maggie moved to pull her chin from his hand, but he refused to release her.

His thumb swept back and forth on the underside of her chin. What was he doing? "Clayton, we're both tired and need to go to bed." She attempted to pull away once more.

Clayton leaned forward and kissed her lips softly. Then drew away. "All right. Good night, Maggie." He turned and walked away.

Maggie stood in the kitchen doorway feeling stunned. How could he do that? Make her feel silly for wanting his kiss and then kiss her and leave? It hadn't been an earth-shattering kiss, but her lips still tingled where his had touched them.

She reached up and touched her chin where he'd held her in place. No man had ever made her feel the way Clayton did. He drew her in like a partner at a taffy pull but then released her just as quickly.

His lips had left hers tasting sweet like the icing on the cake. Would she be able to avoid having feelings for him, if he continued to kiss her in such a sweet way?

Chapter Thirteen

Clayton watched as the Pony Express rider switched horses. The boy handed him a letter from his breast pocket. "A note from your family." He put his heels into the Pony Express horse and then sped away before Clayton could react.

He called after the boy, "Thanks, Peter. Godspeed!"

Peter waved above his head but didn't turn around. His job was to get the mail through.

Clayton looked down at the envelope in his hand. It was addressed in his adoptive mother's beautiful handwriting. He glanced at the house.

Maggie, Dinah and baby James were on the front porch. Tucking the letter into his front shirt pocket, he walked into the barn and called for George.

The older gentleman looked over a stall door. "I'm here."

Clayton walked to Bones and quickly pulled him from his stall. "Keep an eye on the family for me?"

George nodded. "I always do."

Clayton cinched up the belt under the horse's

belly. "Thank you." He double-checked to make sure the gear was on the horse properly.

"If the missus asks where you are off to, what do I tell her?" George asked.

He answered, "I'm going to check fence lines." Clayton led Bones out into the yard. He didn't look to the house. After last night, he wasn't sure he trusted himself in Maggie's presence.

Clayton traveled the fence. The soft sounds of cows lowing in the pasture gave him a sense of peace. He pulled the letter from his pocket. What had his mother written? Was she angry she hadn't heard from him? The little boy in him wanted to avoid opening the envelope.

He turned the letter over and over in his gloved hand. Clayton wanted to open it but also feared its contents. What if something had happened to one of his adoptive brothers? They were Pony Express riders. What if one of them had gotten hurt or killed on the trail? Or what if something was wrong with Joy or Ben, his younger adoptive sister and brother?

Clayton found himself riding to the hidden cove. He dismounted and walked to a nearby rock. The peacefulness of the place warred with the inner turmoil of what could be in the letter. His brother Andrew would scold him for worrying and tell him to just open the letter.

He took his pocketknife out and ran the blade under the flap of the envelope. Once it was open, he put the knife away and pulled the letter out. Clayton swallowed hard and then began to read.

Dear Clayton,
I hope this note finds you doing well. We miss

you here at the farm. Your brothers are all doing well and are happy. Ben is doing well in school. He's smart like you and has discovered he loves reading. Joy is baking up a storm. She told me the other day that she wants to open a bakery in town when she grows up.

Clayton stopped reading. Joy's baking reminded him of Maggie's cake, which led his thoughts back to kissing her. That kiss had kept him tossing and turning all night. She hadn't pushed him away, and that bothered him almost as much as knowing he enjoyed kissing her. He brushed the thoughts away and continued with his letter.

All the new mamas are doing well. Seth is treating me like one of those porcelain dolls that were in the general store at Christmas. Now that I've caught you up on the family, I would love it if you would drop us a line and let us know how you are doing.

Love from home, Ma.

Clayton folded the paper back up and put it into the envelope. He swallowed. Relief that his family was safe washed over him. What would Ma say when she found out she'd missed his wedding? And that he was responsible for not only a wife but two children? He pushed off the rock and looked to Bones. "I miss my simple life of just riding you for hours on end."

The horse bobbed his head as if in agreement.

He climbed back in the saddle and went in search of Abraham. While Clayton had been tossing and turning, he'd forced himself to think of other things besides kissing Maggie.

Abraham was down in the west pasture. Clayton sat on the top of a small rise and watched as the younger man rode in the midst of a group of cattle. He took his time looking at each cow in turn. Bones eased down the rise.

Clayton pulled Bones to a stop at the foot of the hill. He waited for Abraham to work his way back to him. The other man waved, indicating that he saw him.

When Abraham came even with Clayton, he said, "Looks like we might have a couple more calves born later this month."

He sighed. "I figured as much. Seems ole Gus let that bull in with more than one cow. What do you suggest we do?"

"Let's move these to the pasture closest to the house. That way we'll be able to keep a good eye on them and assist the mamas if we need to."

Clayton's thoughts went back to when he'd first met Maggie. The memory of her large tear-filled eyes at the thought that her son was dead made a protectiveness swell within him. He'd protect her and the children with his life, if need be.

"Are you all right?" Abraham leaned on his saddle horn, studying him.

He nodded. "Yeah, was just thinking. That sounds like a good plan to me, too. I'll help you cut the cows out of the herd."

Together they rounded up the cows. It was an easy ride back to the front pasture. Clayton watched as the round-bellied cows moved slowly into the new pasture. They didn't seem to mind being moved from one place to another.

Clayton found his thoughts taking him once more to when he'd first arrived here. He'd looked forward to new beginnings. Only in his wildest dreams could he have imagined the twists and turns his life had taken. He'd gone from being a single man with one responsibility, to being married with two small children in his care, with a ranch to oversee and his medical studies to complete. His plate had filled up in a hurry.

"I'm going to check the other pastures and see if we have any more early births coming our way," Abraham told him.

"Do you want me to come with you?"

Abraham looked him over. "You are the owner of this ranch. You are welcome to come any time you want and you don't need my permission." He tilted his hat back on his head.

Clayton laughed. "Let's get a couple of things straight here. I am not the owner of this ranch—James Fillmore and his mother are the owners. I am only an overseer."

"Do you seriously expect me to believe that?"

Clayton felt his eyes narrow. "What's that supposed to mean?" Did Abraham and the men think he'd married Maggie to take over the ranch? Was Abraham insinuating that he was no better than Gus? His hands tightened on the reins. Bones twitched under him.

Abraham held his hands up. "I only meant that James is a baby and Mrs. Young is a woman. You are the man and the head of the house and this ranch. No disrespect to Mrs. Young, but she doesn't know the first thing about running a farm, let alone a ranch."

He forced his body to relax. Everything Abraham had said was true. "Well, you are the foreman and I expect you to make ranch decisions. If I need to be doing something to help out, you are free to tell me you'd like my help. As for James and Maggie, you're right. James is a baby, but we will teach him how to run the ranch when he's old enough to start learning." Clayton rubbed his chin. "I suppose we should start educating Maggie now, but with the baby and Dinah, I'm not sure how we can do that. So for now, you are the foreman, I am the overseer..." Abraham's laugh stopped him in midsentence. "What's so funny?"

"Boss, 'overseer' is a fancy word for 'boss.'"

Clayton knew Abraham was right. It was another responsibility that he hadn't wanted to acknowledge. He sighed heavily and nodded. "Okay, for now I'm the boss, but don't call me boss. Clayton is my name, and that's what I expect all the men to call me. Be sure to mention that to the others."

"Deal." Abraham's horse stomped his foot. "Now, are you coming with me?"

"Yep, I want to talk to you about hiring some more men. I'm thinking maybe three or four. I know we've already hired some, so you may have other ideas. What do you think?"

Abraham turned his horse with a nod. "I was thinking about that, too. The more men we have on the land, the better our chances are of keeping highwaymen and the like off the ranch. I can send Bud to town tomorrow morning to get the word out that we are still hiring."

"That sounds good. I'll ask Maggie to make a few fliers to hang about town."

Clayton spent the rest of the afternoon checking the cows and taking the ones that they suspected of having early births to the front pasture. As he worked, Clayton wondered what Maggie and the children were doing. He spent an awful lot of time thinking about them, and he didn't know if that was a good thing or not. Would things change between him and Maggie since he'd kissed her?

Maggie loved her weekly trips into town. A week had passed since Clayton's kiss. She hated to admit it but there wasn't a day gone by that she didn't think of that sweet moment. Of course, neither of them mentioned the kiss, but the tension between them was as thick as molasses on a cold winter's day.

Clayton had ridden Bones into town, leaving her to drive the wagon. His excuse was that he wanted to take the horse to the blacksmith to get new shoes. Maggie suspected it was so that they wouldn't need to ride side by side on the wagon bench.

Pulling up in front of the general store, Maggie glanced over her shoulder at baby James and Dinah. The baby had been tucked into a basket and had been content to play with his feet while Dinah strung wooden beads on a piece of yarn.

Clayton jumped from Bones's back and hurried to help her down from the wagon. He placed a hand on her back as she climbed down. "Do you want me to take the baby with me while I go to the blacksmith's and then over to visit with Doc?"

Ignoring the warmth where his hand had rested, Maggie turned to face him. "Thank you, but no, I'll take him with me." She waited for Clayton to hand her the baby.

His gaze met hers. "I don't mind taking him, Maggie." He turned to help Dinah from the wagon bed.

It would be easier to shop if the baby wasn't in her arms.

"Or, Dinah here can go with me if she wants to." He placed Dinah on the boardwalk beside Maggie.

"I don't want to go to the doctor's," Dinah said, clutching her skirt.

Maggie patted the little girl's head with her free hand. "You don't have to go." She handed James to Clayton.

With ease, he placed the baby in the crook of his arm, tilting him just so that James could look about. Clayton tucked the blankets tighter around the baby and then turned with a grin. "You ladies have fun shopping while us men go take care of manly things."

"We'll try," Maggie said, walking to the door.

She turned in surprise when he reached over her head and pushed the door open for her and Dinah to enter. Maggie had thought he'd leave immediately, but instead he had followed them. "Did you need me to pick up something for you?" she asked.

"No, I thought I'd see if they had any store-bought shirts in my size." He walked toward the back where men's clothing, boots and other necessaries were.

Maggie followed. "I can make you new shirts, Clayton. I am a pretty good seamstress, if I do say so myself."

He turned to look at her. "Are you sure? I don't want to be any bother."

"Sewing for one's husband is hardly a bother." She giggled. "Most husbands insist."

Clayton looked at her as if he were about to say, "Well, I'm not most husbands." But instead he clamped his lips closed.

Ignoring his sour look, Maggie said, "Follow me to the fabric. You can pick out the colors you like." She turned around and walked away. Maggie held her breath as she walked, then exhaled once she heard his boots following her.

Dinah skipped ahead of them both. She went straight to the candy counter when Maggie thought she'd stop at the fabric.

Maggie ran her hand over the cotton fabric. "Which colors do you like?"

Clayton's gaze searched the table. "Nothing with flowers," he grunted.

She giggled. "No flowers for you. Got it."

"I like these two." He pointed to a solid white and a light brown.

If it had been her choice, she would have gotten the light blue and the green. "All right." Maggie carried the two bolts to the counter.

"Sissy? Can I have some lemon drops?"

Maggie laid the bolts down. "Not right now. Maybe after I'm all done with my shopping."

"Oh, then I'll keep looking." Dinah pressed her nose to the glass that separated her from the jars of colorful candy.

Clayton had followed her once more. He knelt beside Dinah. "I like those." He pointed to a jar with big red balls in it.

"Me, too." Dinah looked at him with big eyes.

"If you are a good girl, maybe we'll get you a few of both."

Mrs. Fisher came from behind a curtain and stood behind the counter. "I'd be especially good, if I were you, Dinah. Those red balls are solid and take a week or more to eat. You'll have candy for a long time." She winked at Clayton as he stood.

Maggie felt anger begin to boil in the pit of her stomach. What was Mrs. Fisher doing winking at Clayton? The woman was married!

"Oh, hello, Maggie. I didn't see you standing there. Do you have a list I can help you with?" She came around the counter and walked over to Clayton. Mrs. Fisher touched the baby's little face and grinned. "This little man is getting bigger every time I see him." She smiled up into Clayton's eyes.

"Clayton, don't you and James have a doctor to visit?" Maggie snapped the words, causing four pairs of eyes to shift in her direction.

He grinned. "Yes, I suppose we'll be on our way." Clayton closed the distance between them. His blue eyes danced as he bent down and planted a soft kiss on her cheek and then whispered, "Easy, honey. She's harmless."

Maggie gasped at his words. She heard him chuckle softly as he left the store.

Mrs. Fisher looked to Dinah. "Dinah, we got a new doll in. Would you like to see her?"

"Oh, yes." Dinah stood up. "Sissy, can I look at the new doll?"

She touched her burning cheek where Clayton had kissed her. Absentmindedly, Maggie answered, "Uh, yeah." What was wrong with her? Had she really been jealous of Mrs. Fisher and Clayton?

Yes, she had.

Her cheeks felt as if they were on fire. Maggie walked back to the fabric table. She chose the blue and the green and added them to the other two bolts. Dinah and Mrs. Fisher were talking about the doll, so Maggie moved to the spools of thread.

Mrs. Fisher joined her. In a soft voice, she said, "I suppose I owe you an apology."

"No, you don't. I should be the one apologizing. I don't know what came over me." Maggie's cheeks grew even warmer.

Mrs. Fisher picked up a black spool of thread and rubbed it between her hands. "No, I spend so much time talking to men that I tend to get carried away. I meant no harm."

Maggie took a deep breath and faced her. "Mrs. Fisher, I overreacted. Please, let's forget the whole thing."

The other woman smiled at her. "Thank you."

Impulsively, Maggie hugged her. She didn't know the other woman very well but knew that once someone asked for forgiveness it was her duty to do just that. Maggie released her and said, "Please tell me that the doll you showed Dinah isn't a glass one."

A grin spread across Mrs. Fisher's face. "No, it's not. But it is something to consider for her birthday."

"Oh, that's a thought and a good excuse to get her to leave the doll here today."

Mrs. Fisher nodded. "I let all the kids play with it. If you decide you want one later, I'll special order it so that it's new and pretty."

"Thank you."

"Well, if I can't help you find anything, I'll go put out more candy for Dinah to drool over." She giggled and left Maggie standing with four spools of thread in her hands.

Half an hour later, Maggie and Dinah left the store. Maggie still couldn't believe she'd been jealous of Mrs. Fisher. It was the woman's job to be nice to everyone. Her cheeks warmed at Clayton's kiss and teasing words.

"Sissy? Can we go to the bakery?" Dinah skipped ahead of her and turned around with a twirl.

"Maybe after we pick up the baby from Clayton." Maggie pointed in the direction of Doc Anderson's office.

Dinah skipped back to her. "Do we have to go to the doctor's?"

"Yes. He's not going to examine you, Dinah. You aren't sick." She took the little girl's hand in hers. The last time Dinah had been in the doctor's office she'd had a bad cold and the doctor had made her take a medicine that must have tasted awful because Dinah hated going there now.

Maggie saw Clayton walking toward the doctor's office from the opposite direction. He had his head down and was talking to baby James. She stopped and waited for him beside the gate.

"Clayton!" Dinah called, getting his attention.

When he looked up, his eyes sparkled with merriment. "You missed me already?" His question was directed toward Dinah, but Maggie knew he was teasing her.

"No, we came to get the baby. Sissy is taking us to the bakery."

"She is, is she?"

Dinah bent over and picked up a shiny rock. "Uh-huh. I was a good girl at the store so she got me one of those big red balls and some lemon drops." She turned the stone over in her hands. "But I had to leave the new baby doll. I might get it for my birthday."

Clayton grinned down at James. "Sounds like the girls had a good time."

Again it was Dinah who answered. "We did."

Maggie felt as if the cat had gotten her tongue. She reached for James and forced the words, "We'll be at the bakery for a while. Maybe you can join us when you get done visiting the doctor."

James gurgled as his mother took him. He worked a chubby hand out of the blanket. Before Maggie could tuck it back in, Clayton bent over and took the baby's hand in his larger one. "Keep that in there," he told the baby.

His warm breath caressed Maggie's face. She felt as if her own breath was trapped in her chest. Clayton smiled at her. "Did you have a good time at the store?"

"Yes. I got everything I needed to make your shirts and a few other supplies." Her gaze clashed with his blue one.

Clayton reached up and tucked a strand of her hair behind her ear. "I think I might have found another man to hire at the blacksmith's."

She swallowed hard. "That's good."

"I'll see you at the bakery." He dropped his hand.

Dinah tugged on Clayton's pant leg. "Look at my pretty rock." She held it up for him to gaze upon.

He bent over at the waist and looked into her hands. "It's very pretty."

Maggie admired the way he gave the children his total attention when he was with them. He'd make a great father. Only they'd agreed that their marriage would be in name only. Would he regret being married to her someday? Probably. And when that day came, Clayton Young would leave her just as her father had. Maggie turned away from the sight of her sister and husband. She didn't want them to see the tears in her eyes.

Chapter Fourteen

"Maggie Fillmore? Is that really you?"

Maggie turned to see Mrs. Morris come across the room toward her. "Hello, Mrs. Morris. How are you?" She cuddled James close as she waited for her nearest neighbor to walk to their table.

Dinah looked up from her sweet roll and smiled. "Hello, Mrs. Morris."

The older woman patted Dinah on the head. "Hello, Dinah. How are you?"

"I'm fine." She picked up her glass of milk and drank deeply.

"Hello, Maggie."

Maggie smiled at Sally, Mrs. Morris's sixteen-year-old daughter. "Hi, Sally."

Sally shyly looked down on James. "He is beautiful, Maggie."

Maggie turned her motherly gaze on her son. "Thank you." She hugged him close.

"Can I sit by you for a moment, Dinah?" Sally asked.

Dinah nodded. "Clayton's not here yet."

Mrs. Morris smiled. "We really shouldn't intrude, Sally," she said as Sally sat.

Maggie motioned for the older woman to sit also. "It's not intruding. How have you been?"

"I was going to ask you the same. Mr. Morris tells me that you married not too long ago." Mrs. Morris eased into the chair.

Maggie nodded. Sally and Dinah chatted in quiet tones. "I did."

Sally looked across at her. "Can I hold the baby?" she asked.

"I don't see why not." Maggie passed the baby across the table to Sally.

The young girl oohed and aahed over James. She touched his fingers and felt the silkiness of his hair. "He really is beautiful." Sally finally looked up. She smiled at Dinah. "Your hair is so pretty today, Dinah. Did you fix it yourself?"

Dinah, who had been looking as if she were feeling left out, smiled broadly. "I brushed it but Sissy braided it for me today."

Sally tugged on the braid. "She did a very good job. Braids look pretty on you."

The little girl took a big bite of her bread. "You look pretty, too."

"Thank you, but remember, you shouldn't talk with your mouth full of food. You might choke." She tweaked Dinah's nose playfully.

Mrs. Morris turned to Maggie once more. "Is your new husband running the ranch now?"

Maggie wasn't sure if her neighbor was being nosy or just trying to keep the conversation going. "He is. We have hired a new foreman and several other men to help out. With the fences being destroyed, we thought it wise to hire more men to keep an eye on the ranch."

Mrs. Morris touched the napkin with the tip of her finger. "Yes, we did the same. I mean, we hired more men. Mr. Morris still oversees the running of the ranch."

Maggie watched Sally give a quick kiss to the top of James's head. The young woman seemed to really enjoy holding the baby and keeping Dinah entertained while her mother and Maggie visited. "I'm concerned about the fences being torn down," she admitted to the other woman.

"Did you lose any of your cattle?" Mrs. Morris asked. She looked about and caught the waitress's eye.

Once the middle-aged woman had taken Mrs. Morris and Sally's order, Maggie answered, "No, Clayton and Abraham were able to find all of ours. You?"

A quizzical look came over the older woman's face. "You know, I didn't think to ask. I suppose we did, since Mr. Morris didn't mention it."

Maggie took a sip of her coffee. "You're probably right."

"We have been missing you at the quilting bees."

"I've missed going, too, but with the baby it isn't as easy to get to town as it used to be." Maggie smiled at the sleeping baby.

Sally raised her head. "I'll be happy to watch him for you, Maggie, if you ever need me to."

Maggie smiled. "Sally, I'd love to take you up on that."

Shrewdness entered Mrs. Morris's eyes. "We came into town today to see if Sally might find a job."

"What kind of work are you looking for?" Maggie asked.

Sally shrugged. "I thought I would enjoy working at the general store, but Mrs. Fisher said she didn't need extra help right now." She looked about. "Ma thought this might be a nice place to work."

Maggie's gaze moved about the small bakery. There were four small tables in the dining area. They were each covered with a blue-and-white-checked tablecloth. A large window at the front let light shine in, giving the place a warm feeling even in the coldest of weather.

The waitress chose that moment to return to their table. Mrs. Morris leaned forward. "Do you know if the owner is hiring any new help?" she asked.

Maggie watched Sally's face. The young girl looked down at James. Pink filled her cheeks.

"I don't think she is, but I will be happy to ask. Do you want a fresh coffee?"

"No, I believe we're all good here."

Maggie looked into her near-empty cup. She would have liked more but decided to wait until the girl came back, since she'd already turned from their table and headed for the kitchen.

"Ma, I'm not sure I want to work here," Sally whispered across the table.

Mrs. Morris frowned at her. "Girl, you need a job. Someplace where you can meet a nice young man." She paused and then pressed on. "You aren't getting any younger, you know."

"I'm not that old," Sally protested.

Maggie leaned forward. "If there aren't any openings here, how would you like to come out in the afternoons and work at my place, Sally?"

Dinah yawned. "I'd like that." The little girl's eyelids drooped lower. Dinah had gotten up early due to her excitement of coming to town again.

Mrs. Morris stuttered. "What is there at your ranch for a sixteen-year-old girl to do?" Her green eyes shined with curiosity.

"She can help with the children, household chores and laundry," Maggie answered.

Sally opened her mouth to answer, but Mrs. Morris cut her off. "She's looking for a husband. How will she find one working in your house with children?"

Maggie smiled. "We have several single young men working for us. I can arrange for Sally to meet them. Send her out to fetch eggs or go to the barn and ask questions I might need answers to, that sort of thing."

The server returned. "I'm sorry, Sally. Mrs. Cole says she has all the help she can afford."

Sally grinned at Maggie. "I think I'd like working out at your place." She turned to her mother. "Ma, I wouldn't need to ride into town every day either. I could take Stardust and ride over to the Fillmore place without having to hitch up the wagon."

"I don't know, Sally…"

Maggie interrupted. "I'll pay her well."

"Money isn't the reason she's seeking work," Mrs. Morris answered.

Sally gently rocked James. "No, you want me to get married. Wouldn't taking care of young children prepare me for married life, Ma?"

Maggie tried again. "I could use her help, Mrs. Morris."

The older woman sighed. "I'll give you until the fall. If you haven't found a young man by your birthday, I'll expect you to look for a job in town."

Sally smiled. "Thanks, Ma."

Maggie nodded. "Yes, thank you." She didn't know if they could find a husband for Sally in six short months, but Maggie knew it was six months that Sally could enjoy being with the children and she could explore the ranch.

Clayton entered the bakery. He swooped his hat off his head and, using his fingers, combed down the mass of light brown hair. His blue eyes searched the room. Upon seeing his family, he headed toward them.

She waited until he stood beside their table and said, "Clayton, have you met our neighbors, Mrs. Morris and her daughter, Sally?"

"Can't say that I have. It's nice to meet you ladies."

Mrs. Morris stood. "It's nice to meet you as well, but we really must be going." She fussed with the buttons of her coat while Sally handed James back to Maggie.

"When do you want me to start?" Sally asked. She turned and gave Dinah a quick hug.

Half-asleep, Dinah returned her hug. "Can she come tomorrow, Sissy?"

"Yes, she can, Dinah." Maggie turned to Mrs. Morris. "If it's all right with her mother."

Mrs. Morris nodded. "She'll be there, right after lunch."

The two ladies left the bakery, one all smiles, the other looking concerned.

Clayton slipped into the chair across from Maggie. "What was that about?"

She turned to the waitress, who stood beside the window looking outside. "Would you be so kind as to refill my coffee?"

"I'll be happy to." The young woman walked to the kitchen to grab the coffeepot. "Would you like a cup also, Mr. Young?"

"Yes, and maybe one of those sweet rolls I saw on the counter."

She smiled. "I'll be back with both."

Maggie turned to answer Clayton. "I hired Sally to come out to the ranch and help me with the kids and around the house."

Clayton frowned. "Oh. I didn't realize you needed help."

She giggled. "I didn't either until I heard Sally was looking for work. With Sally watching the children, I can be available to help out around the ranch." Maggie watched his face. Clayton didn't seem to care one way or the other.

Dinah leaned her head against Clayton's shoulder. "Sissy? If you go ride Snowball again, can I come, too?" She yawned and closed her eyes.

"We'll see," Maggie answered in a soft whisper.

Clayton moved his shoulder and pulled Dinah to his side. He wrapped an arm around her small body. His gaze met Maggie's. "Seems only fair that if I'm going to be a bed that we both should be comfortable."

Maggie chuckled. "Sounds reasonable to me." Now that Clayton was with them, Maggie felt as if a weight had been lifted from her shoulders. She felt carefree and happy. What was it about this man that made her forget that she was a mother and older sister? That she didn't want to fall in love and live a life of solitude?

Clayton enjoyed the sweet roll and coffee. He grinned at the little girl pressed against his side, sucking her thumb in her sleep. Maggie had grown quiet but seemed content just to sip her coffee and watch the people pass by.

He cleared his throat. "I hired the man I told you about earlier, the one I met at the blacksmith's shop. He's on his way now out to the ranch to claim a bunk."

"Is he young and single?"

"Um, that wasn't one of the requirements of working on a ranch so I didn't ask. Why?" Was she already looking to replace him? Clayton frowned at her.

She shifted James in her arms. "I told Mrs. Morris that I'd make sure Sally met our single men."

He choked on his coffee. Clayton tried to cough without jostling Dinah. He was finally able to squeak out, "What?"

"Sally's mother wants her to meet a nice young man and get married. She's worried the sixteen-year-old is going to become an old maid." Maggie held his gaze across the table.

Well, at least Maggie wasn't looking for a new man for herself. "You're serious?" Clayton hissed. What was Maggie thinking, trying to play matchmaker with his ranch hands and their neighbor's daughter?

"As a Pony Express rider in a snowstorm." She grinned, then smiled broadly.

Clayton enjoyed the teasing glint that entered her

eyes. He thought about taking another drink of his coffee, but since they were still talking about the Morris women, decided against it in fear he might not be able to control his shock and Maggie would wear the lukewarm beverage home. "What are your plans? It's not like the men work around the house."

"True. But I thought maybe we could invite the preacher out one Sunday for afternoon services. The men could come up to the house, hear the Word of God and then have supper." Maggie's eyes changed color as she spoke her thoughts. "And I'm sure there are a few things they could do for me around the house, such as chop wood or repair the chicken coop."

"Is something wrong with the chicken coop?" he asked, feeling confused and dismayed at the way Maggie could come up with things for the men to do.

She shook her head. "Not yet." Maggie's eyes flashed as she thought of something new. "How about we have a barn raising?"

Would she go so far as to damage the chicken coop? Surely not. "Maggie, we don't need a new barn." He picked up his cup and quickly took a drink before she came up with something else that might have him spewing coffee in her direction.

"Are you sure?"

Clayton smirked. "Pretty sure. Think of the expense and add to the mix that it's winter."

Her brow furrowed. "I'll think on it. I'm sure we'll find ways to get the men closer to the house where Sally can meet them."

"And what if the men aren't interested in courting? Then what?" Clayton shifted to his other hip. Dinah snuggled closer.

Maggie waved her hand as if dismissing his concerns. "Oh, I'm sure one of them will find her attractive enough to start courting. We just have to get them to the house."

Clayton shook his head and eased Dinah into a sitting position. Holding her upright with one hand, he slid off his chair. Once standing, he scooped up the little girl. "We need to be getting back to the ranch. Are you finished with your shopping?"

She stood also. "Yes, but I would like to buy a loaf of cinnamon nut bread before we go."

He carried Dinah to the display case. She rested her little head on his shoulder and wrapped her arm around his neck while still sucking the thumb on her other hand. Clayton paid for the bread and then walked to the wagon.

Maggie tucked the bread into her bag and followed him. When he slowed his steps, she caught up. Her gaze moved to her sister. "Do you have any suggestions on how to get her to stop sucking her thumb?"

If he grew to be one hundred years old, Clayton didn't think he'd be able to keep up with the way Maggie switched from one subject to another. "Let her grow up at her own pace. She'll stop when she's ready."

She nodded. "You never did answer my question."

Clayton frowned. What question? All the woman had been doing for the past hour was trying to figure out ways to entrap a man for Sally Morris.

"Is the man you hired today young and single?"

Hadn't he told her he didn't know? Well, he did know the man was probably a few years older than Sally, but he didn't know if he was single. Although, he probably was. Clayton shook his head to clear it. He was starting to think like Maggie talked.

"That's too bad."

"What's too bad?" He repositioned Dinah in his arms, aware that several middle-aged women were watching them.

She sighed heavily. "That he's not young and single."

"I didn't say that."

Now she frowned at him. "Yes, you did."

"When?"

"Just now. You shook your head." Maggie walked up to the wagon and gently laid James in his box filled with blankets.

Clayton shook his head. "Woman, I shook my head trying to make sense of what you are talking about." He heard a woman's giggle behind him and turned to see an older couple walking past them. The man smiled at Clayton with understanding. Clayton smiled back, even though he didn't feel much like smiling. Maggie was driving him crazy.

The gentleman approached Clayton. "You two are bickering like a couple of old married folks. Son, can I give you some advice?"

Clayton felt the tops of his ears grow hot from embarrassment. "Yes, sir."

He slapped Clayton on the back. "First off, never try to understand them, and second, just agree. It will save you time in the long run." After dispensing his advice, the man walked back to his wife and offered her his arm.

Clayton watched the couple walk away arm in arm. Would he and Maggie ever walk together like that?

At the moment, she was busy building a pallet of blankets to lay Dinah on. Her pretty blond hair shone in the sun, and when she looked up at him, Clayton was sure he'd drown in the pools of her eyes. The air was turning colder, giving her cheeks a pretty tint of pink. Clayton waited for her to motion for him to lay Dinah down, then turned away from the sight of his pretty wife.

His job wasn't to admire Maggie but to work the ranch, manage the Pony Express and to study. *Do not add falling in love with your wife to the mix*, he commanded himself as he climbed up on the wagon seat.

Chapter Fifteen

The next morning, Maggie felt as giddy as a school-girl. It was fun to think of ways to help Sally meet the single men at the ranch. After they'd stopped at the blacksmith's and picked up Bones, Clayton had become even quieter than normal, giving her time to think of ways to bring the young people together.

Maggie cleaned the kitchen of the breakfast dishes and then turned to Dinah. "How would you like to help me bake sugar cookies?"

Dinah pushed away from the table where she'd been sorting beans. "I love making cookies. I'll help."

"Go wash your hands well." Maggie smiled as the little girl skipped to the washbasin. "Can I make them have faces?"

"Um, you can make some like that, but I want the rest to be real pretty."

"How come?" Dinah dried her hands.

Maggie smiled. "Well, I thought we might share them with the men."

Dinah pushed her stool up to the counter. "How come?"

"To be nice." Maggie slid a bowl toward Dinah. "Start stirring this together," she instructed.

Dinah stirred the flour mixture. She smiled. "Can I go when you take them to the men?"

Maggie grinned. "Well, I was going to ask Sally to take them, but I'm sure she won't mind if you go with her." She watched Dinah stirring. Her heart ached as she recalled helping their mother make cookies. Dinah would never have the pleasure of those memories.

"Sally is nice, isn't she, Sissy?"

"I think so," Maggie agreed. She brought a cookie sheet over to where Dinah stood.

Clayton came through the kitchen door. Cold air announced his arrival shortly after his boots entered the room. "Good morning, ladies. What are you doing?" His smile said he knew it was baking and couldn't wait to hear what kind.

Dinah looked over her small shoulder at him. "We're making sugar cookies."

He hung his coat beside the back door. "I love sugar cookies."

Maggie admired the way the muscles in Clayton's shoulders rippled under his shirt as he lifted the coffeepot from the back of the stove. She quickly looked away.

"Me, too," Dinah agreed. She looked to Maggie. "Is this stirred enough?"

Thankful for something to do, Maggie considered the bowl of dough. "I think it's about right." She pulled the bowl to her and added the remaining ingredients, aware that Dinah watched her every move.

"Where's the little man?" Clayton asked.

"He's napping upstairs," Maggie answered. She

worked the dough until it was the perfect consistency for sugar cookies.

Clayton leaned a hip against the counter. "I'm heading upstairs to read. I'll keep an ear open for him." He pushed away from the counter.

"Thank you." Maggie handed Dinah a small spoon.

He nodded. "Half-pint, you can bring me a couple of those cookies when they are done." Clayton winked at the little girl.

"All right. But Sissy says we have to save most of them for the men that live outside."

Clayton's gaze flew to Maggie. "And why is that?"

Dinah giggled. "We're being nice."

Maggie averted her eyes but felt him looking at her.

"That is nice. Just put them on a plate and I'll take them out for you."

Sadness filled Dinah's voice. "But I thought me and Sally were going to take them out."

Clayton's voice held a hint of amusement. "Oh, I didn't know that."

"That's what Sissy said." Disappointment sounded in her little voice.

Maggie heard the thud of his boots as he walked back to where she and Dinah stood. She glanced in his direction.

His face beamed with amusement. "Maggie, why aren't you taking the cookies out to the men? After all, Sally has never met them."

"I thought this would be a sweet way to meet them," she answered.

He chuckled. "I hope you know what you're doing." He turned and left the kitchen.

Maggie hoped so, too. Here she was meddling in

Sally's life, and why? So that she could help the girl get away from her mother for a while? Or was she hoping Sally could find a man who wouldn't run at the first sign of hardship or another woman?

Dinah chattered as she shaped the dough into soft balls. The little girl flattened a few of them and then used her fingers to give them eyes, noses and mouths, all the while telling Maggie who they were for. She even made one for her dolly.

She was thankful her little sister could entertain herself. Maggie placed a tray of cookies into the oven. "Thanks for helping me, Dinah. If you want to, you can go play in the sitting room now."

"Can I go upstairs and play in my room, Sissy?" Dinah climbed down from her stool. She untied the small apron from around her waist. "I want to play with my dolly."

"Play quietly. Baby James is still sleeping and Clayton is trying to study. Do not disturb him." Maggie wiped off the counter. Her thoughts were on Sally and her own matchmaking skills.

"I will, Sissy." Dinah skipped out of the kitchen.

Maggie turned. Did that mean Dinah was going to disturb Clayton? Or play quietly? She sighed and leaned against the kitchen counter. What was wrong with her? Was she so determined to help Sally find a husband that she was no longer paying attention to her sister?

She poured herself a cup of coffee and sat down at the table. Maggie asked herself why she was so excited about helping Sally look for a husband. She took a sip of her coffee. Sally hadn't seemed as interested in finding a husband as her mother had. Was it possible there was a reason Sally hadn't found a beau?

The sweet scent of baking cookies filled the warm kitchen. Maggie pulled them from the oven. She walked to the kitchen window and stared out at the cloudy day. Cold air whipped about the house, but she was comfortable in her cozy kitchen.

"You seem deep in thought." Clayton stood in the doorway. He cradled the baby in his arms. "Someone woke from his nap."

Maggie stared. Clayton had slipped his boots off and stood in stocking feet. His shirttails were out and the sleeves of his shirt rolled up, revealing muscular arms. Baby James stared up at him with serious eyes, comfortable with Clayton. She took a step toward Clayton, but he stopped her.

"Stay, I'll bring him to you." Clayton crossed the floor and handed the baby to Maggie.

"Thank you." It seemed she was always thanking him for something. Maggie cuddled James close and breathed his baby scent in deeply.

Clayton sat down. "Are you all right?"

"I believe so. I was just asking myself why I want to find Sally a husband." Using two fingers, she caressed the side of James's small face. His skin felt silky soft.

"I've been wondering that myself," Clayton admitted. "She's young and if I understood correctly, will be working at least six months out here. So why the rush?"

James began to fuss.

Maggie cradled the baby in her arms and started to pace. "I don't know." She stopped in front of the window again and looked out into the yard. "I guess I thought of Sally as a project. You know, something that would keep me busy. Finding new ways to bring her and the men together." Maggie frowned. "That didn't come out the way I meant for it to."

Clayton laughed. "I know. I'm just glad Mrs. Morris wasn't here to hear it."

She started giggling. "Yes, that would have been horrible. She would never let Sally come to the ranch."

Moisture seeped through James's blanket around his bottom. "Excuse me, I need to change the baby." Maggie carried her son up the stairs. She went into her room where his diapers were and quickly got rid of the soiled one.

James was now dry but he released a cry that screamed, "I'm hungry."

Maggie sat down to nurse him. She rocked the baby and thought about Clayton. He'd been sweet to bring the baby to her. With the new hired men handling ranch duties, Clayton had taken the morning to read a chapter from one of the doctor's books. She had just finished feeding the baby when Clayton knocked on the bedroom door.

"I hate to disturb you, but I wanted to let you know I'm heading out. I've a Pony Express rider coming in here in a bit." He kept his gaze locked on the floor.

She loved that he cared about her feelings. "Come in. James and I are ready to go back downstairs and work on the sugar cookies. We made enough dough to feed a church picnic crowd."

Clayton looked up. "Are you still going to share them with the men?"

Maggie grinned. "Yes, but I think Dinah and I will

deliver them while Sally gets used to the house. She can watch James for me for a few minutes."

He leaned against the doorjamb. "What about playing matchmaker?"

She stood and cuddled the baby close. "I still want to help her but will try to let things happen naturally instead of forcing them."

He walked over to them and touched the baby's soft hair on his head. James reached out with a chubby hand and grasped Clayton's finger. Clayton looked deeply into Maggie's eyes. "I think that is wise. Things should happen naturally between a man and a woman. It's my opinion that God never meant for men and women to be forced into a relationship."

Maggie swallowed hard. She felt the same way but had never put it into words. When she'd met Jack, she'd felt like she had no choice. She nodded. "I agree."

Clayton gently pulled his hand from the baby and brushed the hair off Maggie's forehead. "I'm glad." Then he turned to go into his room.

Her forehead tingled where his fingers had touched. Maggie left the room feeling as if he'd been trying to tell her something. But what?

Clayton watched the gentle sway of Maggie's skirts as she walked away. His fingers had felt as if he'd touched a warm fire when he'd brushed her forehead. Her pretty eyes had flickered with some emotion that he couldn't read. He worked the laces of his boots with trembling hands.

Clayton knew he cared for Maggie and that she affected him like no one else ever had in his life. Even his fiancée had never made him feel hot and cold at the same time. What was it about his wife that he found so appealing? Was she the woman God had always intended to be his?

He stood and walked out of his bedroom and into hers and James's. She'd added a pretty quilt made of brown and blue squares to the bed. In the center of each square was a smaller red square. Clayton walked to the side table. A light blue cloth runner covered the dark wood, giving the room a cheerful look. His gaze moved to the window. New brown-and-blue curtains covered it. As he looked about, Clayton realized that her favorite colors were blues and browns.

As he walked down the stairs, Clayton looked about her home. When he'd first moved in, he hadn't noticed all the little touches that screamed Maggie's doing. He stopped at the foot of the stairs and glanced into the warm, inviting kitchen.

Maggie had changed things in there, as well. The kitchen table now sat closer to the stove, away from the window and back door. She'd placed a cabinet that he knew held plates and cups under the window. On top of the table was another quilted table runner, only it held yellows and reds in the fabric. Dinah sat off to the side of the stove, not too close but close enough she could play and be warm and still be out of the way of Maggie's cooking. With her box of toys, she had her own space in the kitchen.

James still rested in his washtub, but now it too had its own special place on the counter, within reach of both Maggie and Dinah. The baby's hands and feet could be seen waving above the rim of the tub.

Everything and everyone had a place in Maggie's

home. Even him. She never entered his bedroom, but in the sitting room she'd given him the rocker by the fireplace with a table beside the rocker. Maggie had placed a Bible there and even given him a fancy doily to put his coffee cup on.

She looked up from the oven and smiled at him. Clayton wanted to go gather her up in his arms and thank her for the home that she was creating for them, but instead he waved and continued out the door. He couldn't let her see that she was thawing out his heart.

Cold air snagged his open coat. Clayton looked up into the darkening sky. His gaze moved to the bunkhouse, where smoke rose from the chimney. He hurried to the barn to prepare the Pony Express horse for its future rider.

George met him at the door. "It's getting colder out there by the minute."

"I'll say." Clayton walked to the horse's stall and gave her another cup of oats. It wouldn't do to send a Pony Express horse out on an empty stomach. She'd be ridden hard. The least he could do was prevent her from feeling hunger on the trip.

"Do you think we'll get snow?" George asked as he pulled the barn doors closed.

Clayton hoped not. So far, the winter had been mild. Cold, but not extremely wet like many of the previous winters. "We might. We've had an easy winter of it so far this year."

The older man nodded. "Yep. My left elbow is aching something fierce. I'm afraid we might be in for a big one."

The horse stomped her foot as if saying she'd do her job and fight through the wind and snow to get the mail delivered. Clayton pulled her out of the stall and began to saddle her. He said soothing words to the little mustang as he worked. Once the horse was ready, he led her to the doors. He looked to George. "Does your elbow always hurt when it snows?"

"Nine times out of ten it does." George rubbed the elbow in question.

The sound of a bugle announced the arrival of the express rider. Clayton didn't need to encourage the little mustang. She had heard the sound, too, and practically pushed him out the barn doors. He walked her to the right spot and held her head, waiting for the exchange. Not all Pony Express riders still used the bugle but some did. Most thought the added weight wasn't needed and they would just whoop or yell as they got closer to the station. But if a young man had a cold and no voice, the bugle was his way of announcing his arrival.

Clayton watched the rider as he came in. His pale face told of his weariness. Clayton looked to the house, his thoughts on relieving the rider, but he knew he couldn't. For one thing, he wasn't dressed appropriately, and for another, he'd not warned Maggie that he'd be leaving.

As soon as the rider came to a stop, Clayton asked, "Are you well enough to continue?"

"I'll make it to the next stop." He jumped on the mustang.

Clayton wasn't so sure. "Pete?"

"Don't coddle me, Clayton. I have a job to do." He spurred the little horse and away they flew down the Pony Express trail.

George chuckled behind him. "You can't help but doctor folks, can you?"

Clayton took the reins of the mare. Her head drooped and her sides heaved. He walked back to the barn. "I suppose not. It's in my nature to try to keep them from killing themselves."

George slapped him on the back. "Well, I, for one, am glad you know a little something about doctorin'."

Clayton spent the rest of the afternoon taking care of the horses and mucking out stalls. George talked his ear off about the new men and what fine young fellas they were. According to George, each man could eat more than a family of six.

Clayton had chuckled at that reference. He'd remembered himself and his brothers eating as if it were their last supper at every meal. His mother, Rebecca, would beam with delight at their compliments on her cooking.

The sound of a horse arriving drew Clayton and George back to the barn doors. They opened them enough to look out. Snow drifted softly from the sky, and cold air swirled it about on the frozen ground.

Sally Morris rode her horse up to the barn with a grin. "Howdy, Mr. Young. Would it be all right with you if I left Stardust in the barn? I don't want her out in this weather."

Clayton pulled the door open farther and helped Sally off the horse once she was inside. "I'm surprised your ma let you come over with the weather the way it is."

George hurried to shut the barn doors.

Sally pulled her coat tighter around her slender waist. She cast her eyes to the ground.

"Well, she wasn't home when I left." The young girl looked up quickly and said in a reassuring voice, "But I told our cook where I was going and asked her to let Ma know when she returned from her quilting bee."

Clayton felt an uneasy feeling growing in his stomach. What if Sally got stuck here at the ranch because of the storm? "Um, Sally, I think we'd best get you back home. This storm looks like it might be blowing for a spell."

Clayton turned to retrieve Bones from his stall. He stopped at the high pitch in Sally's voice.

Sally protested, "But I just got here and Maggie is expecting me." Disappointment filled her eyes.

"Yes, but your ma will be worried sick."

Sally shook her head. "No, she knows I'm here."

Clayton opened his mouth to argue but quickly shut it as the barn door opened, letting snow and cold air inside. He looked to see who had just entered. Maggie walked inside. She wrapped her cloak tighter around her body. "Sally, what are you doing here? You shouldn't have come in this weather."

"That's what I was trying to tell her," Clayton said, folding his arms over his chest and trying to look stern to the girl.

Sally frowned. "I came because you offered me a job yesterday. Did you change your mind about me working here?"

"No, of course not. But that storm looks like it is here to stay. Why in the world would your ma send you out in a storm like this?" Maggie searched the girl's face, and as the answer dawned on her she frowned. "She doesn't know, does she? Or worse, she told you that you couldn't come and you snuck out."

Sally tossed her hair over her shoulder. "I did not sneak over here. Ma knew I was supposed to come to work today."

Clayton watched Maggie as she studied the younger woman. It was as if she knew what the girl was thinking and what she wasn't saying. "Look, Sally. I'm pretty sure your ma does not know you are here." She imitated Clayton's stance.

"Yes, she does. I'm sure Cook has told her by now."

Maggie gasped. "You get back on that horse. I'm taking you home."

Sally stared in disbelief. "You're firing me?"

"No, I'm taking you home before this storm gets worse and you get stuck here. Your ma is probably worried silly." Maggie turned to Clayton. "Would you saddle Snowball for me and keep an eye on the children while I'm gone?"

"No, I will not." Clayton sighed. "I'll take her back."

"But she's my responsibility."

"And you are mine."

Maggie straightened her shoulders. "I most certainly am not your responsibility."

George chuckled, reminding them all that the old man was still there. They all turned to look at him with a frown. "Sorry. This is the best entertainment I've had in weeks."

Clayton decided to ignore George and focus on Maggie. Her eyes narrowed and she placed her fists on her waist. Before she could say more, he reminded her, "You are my wife. That makes you my responsibility. I can't have you catching your death of a cold in this weather, or worse, getting lost in the storm."

The wind howled about the barn. Clayton saw Maggie shiver. Her eyes remained narrowed on him as she said, "Sally, get on that horse. You are going home now." She continued staring at him. "George, saddle Snowball."

Clayton felt George's gaze swing to him. He answered the man's unspoken question. "No. Maggie, you are staying here. I'm going."

"How about we all just stay here?" Sally asked. She looked uncomfortable and a little nervous.

"Clayton, you can't stop me from taking her home." Maggie ground the words out through clenched teeth.

Clayton sighed. "No, I can't stop you, but I'd like to think you'd give some thought to the children." He waited for her to stop grinding her teeth. "What if something happened to you in that storm? What would become of James and Dinah? Have you thought about that?"

Maggie stood her ground.

He could see she was warring with herself. To help her not look weak in front of Sally and George, Clayton walked to her. He pulled her stiff body into his embrace. Softening his voice as he'd heard his adoptive father, Seth, do with his ma, Clayton said, "Honey, I couldn't bear it if something happened to you in that storm. I'll take her home and be back before you have time to miss me." He kissed the top of her head as if it were the most natural action between them.

Maggie stiffened even more in his arms. "But what

about you? Maybe we should just all stay home." She sounded confused.

"I want nothing more than to stay home, but Sally's ma is going to be worried sick. It's best I take her home now before the storm gets worse." Clayton tilted Maggie's head back and looked deeply into her eyes.

Maggie relaxed in his arms. "All right, but promise you will come straight to the house as soon as you get back." Her eyes told him that this was an act and she was angrier than a bull that had just sat on a burr.

Clayton released her. Was she angry because he had won their argument? Or was she angry that he'd dared to display affection for her in front of George and Sally?

Chapter Sixteen

Maggie paced the kitchen, certain she was going to wear right through the planked pine floor if Clayton didn't return soon. He had been gone much longer than he needed to be. Dinner sat on the back of the stove waiting for his return. Snow continued to fall. It covered the ground and turned the world a brilliant white. Its beauty was lost on Maggie as she worried and paced.

His words, "Honey, I couldn't bear it if something happened to you in that storm. I'll take her home and be back before you have time to miss me," echoed through her tired mind. Had he meant them? Or was it simply a show for George and Sally?

At first, she'd been angry with Clayton for insisting she stay home with the kids, but now that his lingering absence continued and her mind thought up all sorts of reasons he might be running late, she understood what he was saying. If anything had happened to her, James wouldn't have a mother and Dinah wouldn't have a sister.

Where was he?

The question ripped through her overactive mind. She silently prayed. *Lord, please keep and protect him.*

Maggie had to admit that she loved Clayton. She'd hold his words close to her heart even if she'd never know how he'd meant them. She would never let him know how she felt. What good would it do? She'd entered this marriage thinking she'd never trust a man enough to fall in love with him. And Clayton had made it clear he had no intentions of falling in love either. But whether or not he could love her, she did love him, and that love magnified her worry about his safe return in the storm.

As the little clock ticked on the side table, her heart raced with worry all the faster. She tried to sidetrack her thoughts of him lost or frozen in the snow by returning to her sewing. The blue material in her hands was turning into a beautiful shirt for Clayton, and she had enough material left over to make a matching one for baby James. Her heart warmed at the picture in her mind of the two of them together in their matching shirts. At least, it would be a touching picture if Clayton returned. Maggie continued to sew, each stitch a prayer, a plea, for her husband's safe return.

Her gaze moved to the children. Both were napping. She should wake Dinah up or the little girl might not sleep tonight. Maggie's gaze moved to the window once more. Dinah would want to know where Clayton was, and Maggie wasn't sure she wanted to answer the little girl's many questions. Questions she didn't have answers to.

Maggie set the shirt to the side and quietly left the room. She pulled the door closed behind her and walked down the stairs. The aroma of beef stew and corn bread filled her senses. She continued into the kitchen. Maggie needed to keep busy.

The coffeepot was almost empty. Clayton would be cold and would need a hot beverage to help warm him up. Maggie made fresh coffee and then turned to the platter of cookies that sat on the counter. She looked to her coat that hung by the door. They'd made the cookies for the men, so they should have them. Maggie knew George provided hearty meals, but she feared the men didn't get many treats. The cookies would cheer them on this dreary winter day. Maggie put on her coat, scarf and gloves then picked up the cookies and walked to the front door.

Her gaze moved up the stairs. She wouldn't be gone long and felt the children would be safe for the few minutes she'd be out. Frigid air and snow blew into her face as she opened the door. Maggie sank deeper into her coat and closed the door behind her.

Ducking her head, Maggie walked to the steps. The boards felt slick under her boots. The thought that she probably should go back inside tried to sway her. She ignored the inner voice and stepped off the porch. Her leg sank up to her knee in the snow. Maggie shivered but pressed on.

Trudging through the snow seemed to take forever. Ten minutes later, Maggie raised her hand and knocked on the bunkhouse door. Weariness pulled at her, and it seemed the cold had seeped into her bones. She shivered. She should have listened to her inner voice and stayed in the house, where it was warm and cozy.

The door opened. Hal gasped when he saw her.

"Mrs. Young, ma'am, what are you doing out in this weather?"

Maggie held the plate out to him. Her teeth chattered as she said, "I made these for you men earlier and I wanted you to have them tonight."

He took the plate. "Do you want to come in and warm up?" Hal stepped back to give her room to enter.

"No, thanks. I need to get back to the children." Maggie turned, dreading the return trip to the house.

Hal turned and handed the plate to one of the other men. He grabbed his coat and hat and stepped out onto the stoop with her. "I'll walk you back to the house."

The wind picked up, whipping snow about them. Maggie shook her head. "That's not necessary. I'll follow my footprints back to the house. There is no reason for you to be out in this weather, too."

Hal pulled his hat down farther and squinted at her. "Clayton would have my hide if I didn't escort you back." He tucked his hands into his coat pockets and then stepped into her earlier footprints. "Just follow me. My boots are bigger than your tiny feet. It will be easier on you."

Maggie nodded. Easier would be good. George came out of the barn. He shook his head when he saw the two of them out in the storm. His action made Maggie feel worse than she had before. She'd been foolish coming out in the storm. Not only was she out in the weather but now Hal was, too.

Maggie had no choice but to follow Hal. His head was down and his shoulders hunched as he pressed through the wind and falling snow. Her ears burned from the cold.

The sound of a horse snorting off to her right drew

Maggie's attention from her miserable thoughts. She'd know the form of Clayton anywhere. Even hunched over the horse and with his head down, Maggie knew it was him.

Hal called over the wind, "Looks like Clayton has made it back."

He must have heard his name because Clayton sat up straighter atop Bones. The horse covered the ground between them at a remarkably fast pace, considering the depth of the snow. He stopped beside them. "Maggie, what are you doing out in this weather?"

"I'll explain later." Her legs felt as if she couldn't lift them another step, and she could hardly feel her feet. Snow and ice clung to her skirts, making the effort even harder than it had been before.

Clayton kicked his foot out of the stirrup and ordered, "Climb up here. Bones and I will take you the rest of the way to the house."

Maggie tried to lift her heavy, snow-laden skirts and put her foot in the stirrup. After two failed attempts, Maggie looked at Hal, who was watching her from where he stood. He stepped forward and said, "Mrs. Young, I'd be honored if you would allow me to give you a hand up."

Shame filled her but Maggie nodded. "Thank you." Within moments, she was in the saddle behind Clayton.

Clayton looked to Hal. "Head on back to the bunkhouse. I appreciate your helping Maggie."

The young man nodded. He dropped his head to avoid the flying snow and then proceeded back the way he and Maggie had come. He stopped and turned. "Thank you, Mrs. Young, for bringing us that plate."

Maggie grinned. Hal had no idea what she'd brought and yet he still expressed his thanks, when she should be the one thanking him. "You're welcome, Hal. Tell the men I said you get extra for helping me get home."

Hal turned and began the short walk back to the bunkhouse. Clayton slipped his booted foot back into the stirrup and prompted Bones to take them to the house.

She buried her face against his back and wrapped her arms around his waist. Maggie knew Clayton was angry with her and he had every right to be, but she didn't care. Her relief that he was home outweighed his irritation at her.

Clayton patted her hands. "Missed me, did you?" he called over his shoulder above the howling wind.

Maggie answered, "You have no idea how worried I was when you didn't return earlier." She snuggled closer, seeking his warmth.

When they were beside the porch, Clayton removed his boot from the stirrup once more and helped her off the horse. "I'll be in shortly." He lowered her to the ground and then waited for her to get back on the porch before turning Bones toward the barn.

Maggie walked as quickly as she dared on the slippery porch. Warm air welcomed her into the house, and she sagged against the door. Taking off her coat, scarf and gloves, she looked down at her skirt. The hem was caked with snow. It took her a few minutes, but she managed to get her boots and skirt off.

Water pooled at her feet where the snow was

quickly melting. Maggie set the boots beside the door on the small rug and then scooped up her skirt. She hurried up the stairs, hoping she'd make it to the top before Clayton entered the house.

At the top, she giggled. Clayton was home. Relief washed over her with such force she felt tears enter her eyes. Tears of happiness? Not sorrow, for sure. She went into her room and put on a fresh skirt.

Maggie had already admitted to herself that she loved Clayton. She hadn't wanted to feel this way toward him. How was she going to hide it from him? He wasn't looking for love. If he suspected how she felt, would he leave? Abandon her like her father had? Maggie determined in her heart that Clayton would never know how she felt.

Over the next couple of days, Clayton and the men did the basic chores but spent most of their time indoors. Clayton had read, played tea party with Dinah, enjoyed desserts that Maggie baked and simply enjoyed life as he now knew it.

He sat at the kitchen table with pencil and paper in hand. Clayton tapped the pencil against his chin. How did you tell your ma that you were married? And that you also had two children in your care? He sighed. Clayton knew his ma would be worried. He should have written this letter days ago, but each time he'd tried, he just didn't have the words.

"You've been sitting there for an hour sighing. What are you trying to write?" Maggie wiped the counter, then picked up her coffee mug and walked over and sat down.

Clayton studied her. She'd been quiet, even reserved, over the last few days. "I'm writing a letter to my ma."

She stood. "Oh, I'm sorry. I'll go to my room and give you some peace."

He motioned for her to sit back down. "Nonsense. You aren't disturbing me. I just don't know how to tell her we are married."

Maggie sank back into the chair. "Oh, I see."

Clayton glanced back at the paper. He'd written about the Pony Express and about ranch life. He placed the tip of the pencil to the paper then lifted it again. Why couldn't he just say it?

Her soft voice drew his gaze from the page to her face. "Clayton, simply tell her. Explain it's a marriage of convenience and tell her you're sorry she wasn't at the ceremony. She'll understand."

He chuckled. "You make it sound so simple." Clayton noted the dark circles under her eyes.

"The truth is simple." She took a sip of coffee then asked, "Will you end the marriage if she doesn't approve?"

Clayton studied her. Was that what she'd been dwelling on for the past two days? He didn't know how he could convince her that he wasn't going to end their marriage or leave her and the children. "No." He leaned forward and continued. "The only way this marriage is going to end is if one of us dies or you ask for it to end."

"Then just tell her." Maggie got up and took her cup to the washtub. She placed it inside and then left the kitchen.

She was right. The truth was the best way. Still,

Clayton paused in his writing. He pushed the paper away and followed Maggie to the stairs.

"Maggie, it has quit snowing. Would you like to go outside and play?" Clayton tried not to grin at the expression on her face.

"What?"

"We've been cooped up in this house for two days. I thought it might be fun for Dinah if we went outside and played in the snow." He leaned against the post at the bottom of the stairs.

Dinah came running to the stairs' top landing. "Please, Sissy. I want to go play in the snow."

Clayton chuckled. There was nothing wrong with the girl's hearing.

Maggie looked from him to Dinah. She smiled at her little sister. "You need to change into your heavy skirt and boots." She watched Dinah run back to her bedroom, then turned to Clayton. "I'll need to change, too."

He chuckled. "We have all day and I don't think we'll be out there long, so take your time." Clayton smiled as a grin spread across her lips.

"I haven't played in the snow in years." Her eyes were sparkling with anticipation. Clayton was glad he could make her happy with something as simple as playing in the snow.

"Then this will be a treat," he answered.

Half an hour later, they all met down in the sitting room. Dinah bounced around with excitement. "Clayton, can I make a snow angel?"

Maggie buttoned Dinah's coat, helped her with her gloves and lastly pulled a stocking hat over the little girl's hair and ears. She then proceeded to dress herself the same way.

Clayton pulled on his gloves. "Sure, I'll make one, too. What about you, Maggie? Want to make a snow angel?" He held the door open while first Dinah ran out and then Maggie followed at a slower pace.

Maggie grinned over her shoulder at him. "Oh, yes, there is nothing like lying down in the snow and waving my arms back and forth."

He pulled the door shut and waited for it to click into place. Baby James rested in his washtub by the fireplace. Clayton didn't want to wake the baby and ruin Maggie's fun before it even started.

Dinah squealed as she jumped off the porch and into a pile of snow. She sank like a rock in a stream on a summer's day. Clayton's heart jumped into his throat. Had the child already hurt herself?

Maggie gasped and hurried to look into the hole the child had made. "Dinah, are you all right?"

The little girl popped up out of the snow. "This is great! I didn't know the snow was this soft." She plowed about, giggling.

Clayton laughed. Dinah had chosen the end of the porch where no one had walked. There was a beaten-down path to the barn and bunkhouse, but everywhere else the snow was fresh, untouched. Not only had she chosen a fresh pile of snow but also one of the tallest.

Maggie turned to Clayton, who now stood beside her looking down at Dinah. "How are we going to make snow angels? That snow is deep and soft." Her eyes sparkled at him with humor.

"Hmm." He rubbed his chin as if in deep thought. Clayton pretended to focus on Dinah, who burrowed through the snow like a puppy. He watched Maggie out of the corner of his eye. When she looked to Dinah, he pushed her over the side of the porch.

Her screech sounded over the silent yard.

Men poured from the bunkhouse door. Most were barefoot and half-dressed. Their heads turned toward the house. Abraham was the only one fully clothed, and he was carrying a shotgun.

Clayton placed his hands on his knees and laughed. Maggie came up out of the snow with fury in her eyes. He called to the men, "It's all right, boys. Maggie's just playing in the snow."

Her head turned in the direction of the men. She also called out. "Bring me that gun, Abraham. I'm going to shoot my husband."

Abraham called back with a grin, "I'd love to, ma'am, but I don't want to get out in that snow. Today's my day off."

Dinah had stopped burrowing and now stood by her sister. "Are you really angry with Clayton, Sissy?"

Maggie turned her back on him. She bent over and scooped up a handful of snow. Twisting her torso, she let the snow fly. "No, Dinah, I'm not angry." She laughed.

Clayton was thankful the snow wasn't packed. Its powder showered over him instead of pelting him as she'd planned. "Oh, trying to hit me with snow, are you?" He jumped in beside them.

They laughed and played for a good hour. Clayton loved Maggie's sense of humor. He loved that Dinah's imagination had them pretending to be prairie dogs and making tunnels in the snow. Clayton didn't want to admit it, but he loved his small family. Maybe that was the reason he was having trouble telling his mother that his marriage was a marriage of convenience.

He helped Dinah up the steps to the house.

"I don't want to go in," she whined. Dinah looked up at Maggie.

Maggie answered, "I know, but James will be waking up soon and he's sure to be hungry." She immediately went to her son. James gurgled up at her.

Clayton wondered at the boy's sweet disposition. From his experience with his brothers' babies, most of them were cranky when they woke up soiled and hungry. He put his hand on Dinah's shoulder. "I'm hungry, too. Maybe after we all change into dry clothes, we can make sandwiches with the ham from last night's dinner while Maggie takes care of the baby."

"All right." Dinah pulled her coat, gloves and hat off and handed them to Clayton to hang up. She walked to the stairs, dragging her feet as she went.

After hanging up everyone's coats, Clayton followed Maggie and Dinah upstairs. He went to his room and changed out of his cold, wet clothes. Maggie cooed to the baby in the next room, her voice soothing and sweet. Clayton pulled on his boots.

His thoughts went to the letter he knew he needed to finish. He wished his mother lived closer. Clayton didn't know how to make Maggie feel secure in knowing he wasn't going to abandon her and the children. Perhaps Ma would know what to say or do that would make Maggie feel more secure.

Chapter Seventeen

Maggie waited in the sitting room for Sally.

Dinah played outside in the melting snow while James lay on a blanket in front of the fireplace. He was growing more and more every day. His gurgles filled the quiet room, and Maggie's heart filled with love for her precious little boy.

She finished sewing the last button onto Clayton's shirt. Maggie had finished his other two shirts earlier but because she worked on this one in secret, it had taken a little longer. Now that it was finished, Maggie looked forward to surprising him.

Dinah and Sally came into the house. "Sorry I'm running late today, Maggie." Sally hung up her coat and swirled about. She made her way to James. "How are you today, little man?" she asked.

"Sissy, can I have a piece of cake?" Dinah asked.

Maggie shook her head. "No, you should have eaten your lunch."

"But I don't like fish." Dinah hung up her coat. Clayton had installed a hook at just the right height for Dinah to reach, and the little girl loved hanging up her own hat, scarf and coat.

"You can have a slice of buttered bread. And, if you eat all your dinner tonight, then you can have a piece of cake."

"But—"

Sally interrupted. "Dinah, I wouldn't argue. My ma would have made you wait until dinnertime and you still wouldn't have gotten a piece of cake." She folded her arms over her chest and frowned.

Dinah nodded. "Thanks, Sissy." Then she skipped off to the kitchen.

Maggie smiled. Sally had been coming every day for a week. The young girl loved James and Dinah and took very good care of them. She'd learned Maggie's afternoon routines and had insisted that she would be fine if Maggie wanted to take a ride on Snowball. "Thanks for helping with Dinah."

Sally relaxed. "My pleasure." She focused on the baby grabbing at her skirt hem.

"I finished Clayton's shirt today. What do you think?" Maggie held it up for Sally to see.

The girl picked up James and, cuddling him close, looked at the shirt. "It's very pretty. Is he going to wear it to the winter dance?"

"The winter dance?"

Sally nodded. "Uh-huh. I heard Ma and Mrs. Parker talking about it the other day when Mrs. Parker came by. I'll be happy to watch the children if you and Mr. Young want to go."

Maggie wished she lived a little closer to town. Sometimes she felt isolated out on the ranch. "That's very sweet of you, Sally. But don't you want to go?"

"I'm not going. I hate standing around waiting for someone to ask me to dance."

Maggie wondered what Mrs. Morris thought of her daughter not attending. She could just imagine that Sally's mother had plans of parading Sally before all the available young men. "Well, we haven't been invited."

"Everyone is invited. The whole town turns out for it." Sally buried her face in James's neck. "Babies smell so good."

Maggie laughed. "That baby needs a bath." She folded Clayton's shirt and placed it on top of her sewing basket.

"Would you like for me to give him one?" Sally made a funny face at the baby.

"That's nice of you to offer, but I think I'll give him one tonight so he'll sleep well." Maggie smiled. "If you don't mind, just play with the children today. I have a roast in the oven for tonight's dinner." She lowered her voice. "I'm not a fan of fish either, but don't tell Dinah."

Sally giggled. "It's our secret. I'll keep an eye on the children and the roast. You enjoy your afternoon out in the fresh air."

Maggie pulled her cloak from the hook and smiled. "Thank you, I will." She hurried out the door and across the yard to the barn.

George sat on a bench, oiling a saddle. He looked up. "Hello, Mrs. Young. What are you doing out here today?"

She made her way to Snowball's stall. "I came to take Snowball out for a little run today."

He put the oil and rag away, then came to her. "I

wouldn't run her if I were you. That ground is still pretty icy."

Maggie smiled. She hadn't planned on running the horse. It was a bad choice of words on her part. "I'll try to keep her from running then."

George saddled Snowball and then led her to the front of the barn. "You two have fun. Clayton is in the east pasture."

She turned Snowball in that direction. "Thank you." Maggie wondered what Clayton was doing and if her arrival would interfere with his work. The air felt good on her cheeks as she rode. Snow still covered much of the land, but the sun had decided to come out and help melt what remained.

As she crossed the ranch she noted the cows and pools of water. Thankfully with the snow melting, the men wouldn't have to be out breaking the ice on the ponds and stream to supply the animals with water. She'd listened to Abraham's reports each evening and knew that eight of the nine men working the ranch went out every day and broke through the ice so that the cattle would have fresh water to drink.

Ranching wasn't for the faint of heart. Jack had loved it. Clayton hadn't seemed impressed one way or the other. His love lay with medicine. Abraham seemed to love working the ranch. His reports were always positive. Maggie had heard Abraham complain only once and that was because Bud, the youngest in the group, couldn't seem to stay on task and was often found in a pasture he wasn't assigned to.

Maggie waved a greeting to Clayton when she came upon him. He was pouring bags of corn into troughs as Bud drove the horse and wagon up the fence line. She watched for several minutes. It was a slow process.

Maggie watched as Clayton lifted the bags of feed from the wagon. She knew they were heavy, but he hauled them as if they were filled with feathers.

She hopped off Snowball and asked, "Is there anything I can do to help?"

"You can tie Snowball to the back of the wagon and drive it so that Bud and I can get these gals fed." He grinned at her. "Many hands make the job go faster."

Maggie did as he asked and then hurried to the wagon. Bud set the brake and hopped down from the wagon. He waited until she was seated before jumping into the back. She drove slowly, giving Bud time to hand the bags to Clayton and then continuing to the next set of troughs.

"This is going much faster," Bud remarked, grinning at her. "I'll be sure and tell Abraham that three men on the job beats two any day."

Clayton frowned. "I'm sure if he could have spared another man, he would have."

Maggie wondered if Clayton was overly tired. She'd never heard him snap at anyone before.

They continued working. After about thirty minutes, Bud announced, "That's it." He handed Clayton the last bag.

She set the brake and waited for Clayton to tell them what to do. He finished emptying the bag and turned to face her and Bud. His jaw was set. "Bud, take Snowball to the south pasture and see if you can help Abraham. We got finished here faster than we expected." He smiled at Maggie. "Thanks to you."

"I'm glad I could help," she answered.

Bud jumped from the wagon and untied Snowball. He was in the saddle within a few minutes and started to leave.

Clayton called after him, "Bud, be sure to go straight to Abraham. I'm sure he'll be happy for your help."

Bud didn't answer. He just rode away.

Clayton sighed heavily. "That boy is in danger of losing his job, and I don't think my talk with him today is going to change that." He motioned for Maggie to scoot over on the wagon seat.

Maggie moved over. "He's still young. Maybe he needs more time to mature."

"How old do you reckon he is?" he asked, releasing the brake and turning the wagon back toward the house.

"Sixteen, maybe?"

Clayton grinned. "No, he's twenty."

"He doesn't look twenty." Maggie frowned. "Honestly, he looks like a young kid."

"And he kind of acts like a young kid, too. But twenty isn't all that old."

Maggie wondered how old Clayton was. It had never dawned on her to ask. She'd always just known that he was older than her. Or was he?

He laughed. "I'm twenty years old, Maggie."

Had he read her mind? "How did you know what I was thinking?"

Clayton shrugged. "I don't know. I guess I just read the question on your face." He maneuvered the horse and wagon around a shrub covered in icicles.

Maggie felt a moment of panic. Could he read on

her face that she loved him? She pushed the thought away. "Oh, well, you're right. Twenty isn't old at all."

He laughed. "No, it isn't."

"Do you mind if I change the subject?" Maggie picked at a piece of lint on her cloak.

Clayton turned his head and looked at her. "Is something wrong?"

She sighed with relief. He couldn't read her mind. "No, I wanted to ask if you've heard of the winter dance."

He nodded. "Yes, Abraham asked me this morning if I thought it would be all right to let the men go."

"What did you tell him?" Since the dance was at night, she really didn't see the harm in letting the men attend, but then again, there were a lot of things she needed to learn about ranching. Maybe there was something going on at night that would keep them from going.

Clayton turned the mare away from the house and more toward the hidden cove. "I told him I didn't see any harm in their going." His glance moved to her face. "Unless you want them to stay."

Maggie shook her head. "No, I think that will be fine. Although, I was hoping you and I might go."

"Us?"

She grinned. "Yes, us. But with all the men gone, I wouldn't feel comfortable leaving Sally with the children alone on the ranch. So, forget I mentioned it."

Clayton nodded. "All right."

Sadness entered Maggie's heart. Until this moment, she hadn't realized how badly she'd hoped to go. The backs of her eyes began to burn. Averting her eyes from Clayton, Maggie focused on the upcoming cove. Winter coated it much like the disappointment coated her heart. *Stop being silly*, Maggie told herself. It wasn't like she and Clayton were a young married couple looking for an evening where they could court each other or express their undying love. Still, she wanted to attend the dance.

Clayton didn't want to build up her hopes so didn't tell Maggie that he would ask George if he intended to go to the dance. If George wasn't attending, then he and Maggie could go. Her eyes had shone when she'd asked about the dance, but now they looked glassy with tears. He pulled the wagon up beside the cove and set the brake.

"What are we doing here?" she asked, looking about.

He reached up to help her down from the wagon. "I just thought we could both use a little break from everyone."

Maggie placed her gloved hand into his. "I do love this spot."

When she was firmly on the ground, he tucked her hand into the crook of his arm. "I was thinking that tomorrow I'd run into town and see the doctor. Would you like to come along?"

"It would be nice but no, I don't want to take the children out in this cold weather. Besides, if you leave early enough, Doc Anderson might take you out on his home visits." She leaned her head on his shoulder. Clayton had been studying the medical books every night.

He patted her hand. "It would be nice to have you along, but I agree. Breathing this cold air all day wouldn't be good for the children." Clayton enjoyed the feel of Maggie pressed against his arm and side. She smelled of cinnamon and sugar.

They continued to walk in comfortable silence. Clayton stepped around the patches of snow and ice. He didn't mind the cold air on his cheeks or the mud on his boots. All he cared about at the moment was spending quiet time with Maggie.

The sound of a horse coming in fast drew his attention. He turned to find Bud racing Snowball across the frozen ground. That boy was going to kill himself and the horse if he didn't slow down. Bud was not an experienced Pony Express rider.

When Bud and Snowball slid to a stop in front of him, Clayton demanded, "What are you doing? You could kill yourself and that horse racing about like that."

He ignored Clayton's outburst. "Abraham is hurt. You need to get to him as soon as possible. I'll go get the doctor."

Clayton grabbed Snowball's bridle. "Get down." He waited for Bud to do as he'd been told and then jumped into the saddle. "Take Maggie home and then ride into town for the doctor." He turned the horse and headed toward the south pasture.

What could have happened to Abraham? He should have asked Bud what was wrong with his foreman but instead had acted impulsively. As the little mare raced back to Abraham, Clayton realized he should have told Bud to send Hal or George back with the wagon to get Abraham home.

He saw Abraham propped up against the fence. Clayton jumped off Snowball and ran to the fallen man. He pulled off his gloves and ran his hands over Abraham's arms, legs and back. There were no injuries that he could feel. His breathing was steady, but he seemed to be out cold. Clayton leaned back on his heels. Had his heart gone out? Or had he fallen off his horse and hit his head?

Where was Abraham's horse? He looked about the area but didn't see the stallion anywhere. It probably headed back to the barn. Clayton focused on Abraham. His needs were more important than worrying about a horse.

Clayton leaned forward once more and ran his fingers over the back of Abraham's head. When he pulled them away, they were covered in blood. He set the other man up and searched for the wound. It was a large gash and felt deep.

The sound of a wagon traveling across the pasture drew his attention. He watched as Bud whipped the horse toward him. Clayton gently lowered Abraham back to the cold ground and stood.

"Mrs. Young said you might need the wagon to get Abraham back to the house." Bud set the brake and jumped down.

Clayton nodded. "Where is she?"

"She's walking back to the house."

Clayton growled deep in his throat. The last thing he needed Maggie to do was get sick and die, like his parents had. He pushed the thought away. "We'll pick her up on our way back."

"What happened to him, Clayton?" Bud asked. He stood over Abraham, frowning.

Clayton pulled the tailgate off the wagon and set it to the side. He joined Bud. "Help me get him to the wagon. He has a nasty cut on the back of his head, so be careful laying him down."

He lifted Abraham by the shoulders and Bud took his feet. Together they carried the foreman to the wagon.

As soon as they got him inside and the tailgate back in place, Clayton climbed into the wagon and turned it back toward the house. Aware that going too fast would shake Abraham about, Clayton kept the little mare at a slow clip. He pulled his gloves back on.

"Bud, go find Maggie and take her to the house. But don't ride so carelessly this time. Then switch horses and go to town and find Doc. Take one of the Pony Express horses. They know how to run on this ice and snow."

"All right, boss."

He watched the young man ride away. Why did this ranch have to be so big? Why had Maggie decided she would be better off walking home than riding with Bud? And what had happened to Abraham? Clayton hadn't seen any rocks that Abraham could have hit his head on.

The thought came to him that Abraham might have been attacked. Clayton should have checked the ground for other footprints. Then a bone-chilling thought came to him. If Abraham had been attacked because he was alone, what did that mean for Maggie? She was alone now, too.

Chapter Eighteen

Maggie trudged toward home. Now that Clayton was gone, the cold sank into her bones. She wrapped her cloak tighter about her body and prayed for Abraham to be all right. Clayton would make a great doctor someday. Abraham was blessed that her husband was on the ranch.

It hadn't seemed like she was that far from the house when she'd been riding a horse. Even though she was now cold and tired, Maggie wouldn't have given up the last hour spent with her husband. She'd enjoyed listening to his voice and feeling his gloved hand on top of hers.

Her boots slipped on a clear slab of ice. Maggie used her arms like windmills and tried to keep her feet beneath her. It was no use. Maggie went down hard, landing on her back. She lay on the cold ground for several moments. Other than the fall knocking the air out of her, she didn't think she was hurt.

Thankfully, there had been no one around to witness her fall. She imagined she'd looked far from graceful as she'd flailed her arms and slipped on the ice. She pushed herself up into a sitting position and looked about, just to make sure she was truly alone. After several long moments, Maggie stood and began walking once more, taking greater care now about where she put her feet.

Her thoughts went to the dance that she would be missing. It would have been fun to attend. Before her mother had died, they had gone to a barn-raising dance every year. She closed her eyes and imagined the new barn, smelling of freshly cut wood, decorated with hay and benches. Images of the large dance floor and the musicians filled her tired mind.

Her favorite part was being swirled about the dirt floor to the sound of fiddles and violins. Maggie had been sixteen, the same age as Sally now, when she'd attended the last dance. The young men had kept her dancing all night. Perhaps she should talk Sally into going. It had been fun.

She heard a rider coming and opened her eyes. How long had she been standing in this same spot daydreaming? Maggie looked to her right and saw Snowball and Bud coming toward her. She waved.

Bud stopped the horse and kicked his foot out of the stirrup. "Come on, the boss says I'm to take you home." He extended his hand down to her.

Maggie started to put her gloved hand in his but then realized it was covered in mud. She looked down at her dress. It too was covered in the sticky clay of the land. "I fell," she said needlessly.

The young man laughed. "I can see that. Wipe your hand off on Snowball's hip."

"I'm sorry, ole girl." Maggie did as Bud instructed,

then placed her hand in his and swung onto the horse's rump.

"Ready?" Bud asked, glancing over his shoulder and placing his boot in the stirrup.

Maggie couldn't bring herself to wrap her arms around his waist as she'd done with Clayton. Instead she gripped the seat of the saddle and held on. "Ready," she answered.

Bud nodded and then took off.

Maggie bounced along on the horse's hindquarters, wishing for the life of her that she'd just walked home. Bud seemed unaware of her discomfort and pressed the horse harder to race back to the barn. Snowball's hooves thundered across snow and ice.

The little mare pitched forward when her front feet hit a spot of ice. Maggie feared the horse was going to lose her footing and the three of them would all go down. "Don't you think we should slow down?" she called to Bud.

"No, ma'am. Abraham is hurt bad and Clayton told me to get the doctor out here quick. I have to leave this nag at the barn and get one of the Pony Express horses saddled and be on my way before he gets back to the house with Abraham." Bud pressed the horse harder.

Maggie hung on tighter and wondered what Clayton had been thinking to give Bud such orders. Didn't he realize how bad the ground was? Or had he been so concerned for the foreman that he hadn't thought of what could happen to her and Bud should Snowball lose her footing?

"We're here," Bud said needlessly when they arrived at the barn. He kicked his foot out of the stirrup. "You should get off first."

George came out of the barn. His gaze shot from Maggie to Bud. "What's going on here?"

Bud answered, "Abraham is hurt. I need to get to town for the doctor."

Maggie reached out to George. She wasn't sure how to get off Snowball without falling unless the older man helped. George hurried to the side of the horse and assisted Maggie. Her legs felt like jelly. She leaned heavily on George.

"Mrs. Young, are you all right?" George asked, wrapping an arm around her waist to better hold her up.

She nodded. "I think so. It's just been a hard day."

Bud had already jumped from Snowball's back and entered the barn, leaving the little mare standing out in the cold. He called from inside, "George, which one of these horses is the fastest?"

George frowned and looked to Maggie.

In a low voice, she answered his unasked question. "Bud says Clayton told him to take one of the Pony Express horses."

"What do you think?" George asked, his worried gaze on the barn.

Maggie sighed and tested her legs. "I don't know. Those horses are Clayton's babies. But if Abraham is hurt as bad as Bud says, I suppose it's possible Clayton told him to take one of the Pony Express horses."

"George!" Bud's voice sounded irritated.

George looked into Maggie's eyes. He called back, "Take the solid black." He turned back to Maggie, concern in his faded blue eyes. "Do you want me to help you to the house?"

Maggie shook her head. "No, I'm fine. My legs

were just shaky from trying to stay on the back of
Snowball without falling off." She took a careful step
away from George. The last thing she needed was to
fall again.

"If you don't mind my saying so, it looks like you
took a roll in the mud." George's eyes were still filled
with concern.

She giggled. "I did. Hurt my pride more than anything else."

Bud came thundering through the barn doors. He
sat atop the black mustang with a wide grin. "I'm
headed to town to get the doctor."

Snowball whinnied and stepped sideways to get
out of Bud's path.

Maggie frowned.

Bud's eyes shone. He looked anything but concerned for Abraham. The hired hand seemed more
excited to be riding a Pony Express horse than anx-
ious to get help for the injured man. He spurred the
mare into action.

She sighed as he sped down the road toward town.
Maggie looked to George. "I hope he makes it to town
without breaking his neck on that horse."

George shook his head. "That boy has been a handful since Gus left."

Maggie nodded. She was beginning to see that.
"Thank you for helping me down from Snowball."
She walked over to the little mare and rubbed her
nose while telling her what a good girl she was. Taking hold of the bridle, Maggie began leading the horse
into the barn.

"Here, Mrs. Young, let me take care of her for

you. You head on into the house and get cleaned up."
George placed his hand over her gloved one.

"George, please call me Maggie." She released the
bridle. "Thank you."

He smiled at her. "It's my pleasure, Maggie."

She smiled and turned to the house. Baby James
wasn't the only one who would be getting a bath tonight. Her smile dissolved as she thought of Abraham.
Had he lay in mud and ice? He'd probably need a bath,
too. Maggie turned back to the barn.

Her footsteps felt weighted. She entered the barn
just as George released Snowball into her stall.

"Is there something else I can do for you?" George
asked.

Maggie nodded. "Yes, please tell Clayton to bring
Abraham up to the house. I'll have a place fixed for
him."

"Yes, ma'am." George pulled a feed bag from a
hook.

She turned and walked to the house.

Sally and Dinah sat at the kitchen table. Baby
James lay on a blanket beside the stove. The two girls
looked up as Maggie entered the room.

"What happened to you? Did you fall off the
horse?" Sally asked. She pushed her chair back and
stood.

"I'm fine, Sally, and no, I did not fall off the horse.
I slipped and fell in the mud." Maggie pulled her
gloves off. Dinah hurried to her side. The little girl
was about to hug her, but Maggie stopped her by putting her hands out. She smiled at her sister. "No hugs
just yet. I'm a filthy mess, but I promise I'm fine."

Dinah looked up at her. "Good."

Sally tsked and walked over to Maggie and Dinah. "You should go on upstairs and get cleaned up. I'll make sure these two stay out of trouble." She pulled on one of Dinah's freshly woven braids.

Maggie nodded. "I will, if you will put a large pot of water on the stove and throw a sheet over the settee. One of the men was hurt out in the pasture. I'm not sure how badly, but I want to make him comfortable until the doctor arrives." She wanted to go pick up James and give him a quick hug but decided against it.

"We'll take care of it, won't we, Dinah?"

The little girl grinned. "Uh-huh."

"All right. Then I'll go clean up and be right back down."

Maggie started to climb the stairs. A muscle in the back of her right leg protested the movement. Would she be too sore to move tomorrow? Her body protested each step she took to her bedroom.

Her thoughts went to Clayton and Abraham. How far were they from the house? What had happened to Abraham?

Clayton's thoughts were on Maggie. Had Bud found her and taken her home? He looked over his shoulder. Abraham lay in the same position he and Bud had placed him. It bothered Clayton that Abraham hadn't woken and hadn't made a sound. Clayton knew Abraham was breathing, but the man was out cold.

The ranch yard and house came into view. It was all Clayton could do to keep from racing the horse toward home. He forced himself to drive slowly, avoid ruts and bumps and focus on getting Abraham to the bunkhouse in one piece.

George stepped out of the barn as soon as Clayton got to the bunkhouse. "Maggie said to take him up to the house. Says she'll have a place fixed for him." He walked beside the wagon.

Thank the good Lord that Maggie was all right. Clayton continued to the house.

George met him at the back of the wagon. "I'll help you get him inside."

Maggie stepped out of the house. Her hand fluttered to her heart and rested there.

Clayton called to Maggie, "Bring a blanket, please." She hurried into the house and returned with an old blanket. Clayton rolled Abraham onto his side and then placed the blanket where he'd been lying. Then he let Abraham back down onto the blanket. This way, they could use the blanket to carry the unconscious man into the house. Clayton grabbed one end of the blanket and George took the other.

Maggie held the door open. "I hope the settee is big enough for him." She followed the men into the sitting room.

Sally stood in the kitchen doorway. "Maggie, I know earlier you said Dinah couldn't have cake, but it might be enough distraction to keep her in the kitchen for a while."

Maggie nodded. "I believe you're right. Cut a piece for yourself, too."

Clayton and George carried Abraham to the settee. "Maggie, can you get a towel for his head? He has a nasty cut, and I don't want to get blood on the settee."

He watched as she hurried to the kitchen. Was she

limping? Clayton looked to George. "Let's get him on the settee."

George lowered Abraham's legs onto the piece of furniture.

Maggie came back with a large piece of cloth. She folded it and placed it on the arm of the settee.

Clayton lowered Abraham's upper body the rest of the way down. He worried that Abraham still hadn't shown any signs of waking up. "I wish I knew what happened to him." Saying the words out loud didn't make him feel any better.

Maggie moved to his feet. "Do you think we should take his boots off?"

Thinking she didn't want the mud on her sheet, he nodded. "We can take them off, if you want to."

"I just thought he might be a little more comfortable." Maggie looked up at him with wide eyes.

Sally came into the room. "Dinah is happily eating cake. Is there anything I can do to help in here?" She looked at Abraham. "He's a big one, isn't he?"

Clayton chuckled. "I don't think there is much any of us can do until he wakes up, and to answer your question, I suppose Abraham could be considered a big man."

"Oh, I don't mean big as in fat. I meant that he's tall." Her voice trailed off as she studied his face.

Clayton moved to Abraham's feet and pulled off one boot and then the next. He placed each stockinged foot back onto the sheet. "I wish he'd wake up. In all my studies, it says that the longer a man is knocked out, the worse the injury could be."

Silence filled the room as each person stared at the patient.

"Have you tried to get him to wake up?" Sally asked.

Maggie giggled. "Yeah, have you tried to wake him up?"

George shook his head. "You'd think that being jostled around in the bed of a wagon would wake him."

Clayton agreed with George.

Sally huffed. "Well, if none of you are going to try, then I will." She walked over and gently laid a hand on his shoulder. "Abraham. I need you to wake up. You're scaring Clayton." She gave him a cheeky grin.

Clayton couldn't deny her words. Maybe he wasn't scared, but he was definitely concerned. "Keep talking to him, Sally."

She shrugged. "Abraham? What color are your eyes? I bet they are blue. Most people have blue eyes. Are your eyes blue?"

Abraham groaned.

Clayton's pulse jumped. "Keep talking, Sally." His gaze flew to Maggie's hazel eyes.

They were filled with compassion and worry.

"Well, since you aren't answering me, I'm going to guess again. Maybe they are brown. Are they brown? Abraham, don't make me frown." She giggled at her own silliness. "Hey, that rhymes."

Abraham answered in a grumpy voice, "No, they are green."

"I don't believe you. I can't see them. I think they are brown. If your eyes are really green, open them and prove it." Sally leaned closer to Abraham.

"You smell good." He sighed and twisted his face toward Sally.

Clayton motioned for her to keep him talking. He wondered how much of this conversation his foreman would remember, and if the situation wasn't so serious, he'd probably laugh at the ridiculousness.

"Well, thank you." Sally lowered her voice and said in a firm tone, "Abraham, open your eyes."

His forehead furrowed above dark eyebrows. "I can't."

She placed her hand on his forehead. "Sure, you can, honey. Open your eyes so I can see if they are green."

Clayton watched as Abraham's face muscles worked. It was as if he were trying to open his eyes but couldn't. He asked, "What happened out there, Abraham?" ·

If Abraham heard Clayton, he ignored him. Clayton motioned for Sally to ask the same question.

"Abraham, what happened to you out in the pasture?" She spoke sweetly to him, as if trying to coax answers from him.

He sighed. "I don't know." Abraham slowly opened his eyes. He squinted as if the room were filled with brilliant light. "My head hurts."

Clayton felt all the pent-up air in his lungs release. "Thank you, Lord."

Abraham tried to sit up. He looked at Sally and grinned. "See? They are green."

She leaned forward and stared into his glassy green eyes. "Yep, they are a pretty grass green. Clayton, come look how pretty his eyes are."

Clayton looked at the vacant eyes. "What do you see, Abraham?"

"Nothing. It's dark in here. How about turning on a light?" He rubbed his eyes.

Sally put a hand over her mouth. Her gaze searched out Clayton's. He held a finger to his lips as if to silence everyone in the room. It wouldn't do for Abraham to realize he was blind.

"Hey, where is the lady with the pretty voice who smells so good?" Abraham asked, moving his head from side to side as if looking for her.

"I'm here." Sally placed her hand on his shoulder again. Tears filled her eyes. "Why don't you shut your eyes and try to get some sleep? You'll feel better in the morning."

Abraham did as she asked and shut his eyes. "Don't leave me. I want to see how pretty you are in the morning." He reached up and put a hand over Sally's.

She vowed as a tear slipped down her cheek, "I won't leave you. Go back to sleep."

Clayton wasn't sure they should be letting Abraham sleep, but he didn't know what more to do for the man. He felt helpless. What kind of doctor was he going to be if he didn't know what to do for the sick or injured?

Maggie placed her hand on his shoulder. "How about we all go to the kitchen until the doctor gets here? There's nothing more we can do."

"You two go on. I'll stay with him," Sally said. She sat down on the floor in front of the settee.

Clayton nodded. He and George followed Maggie into the warm kitchen. She was definitely limping.

Dinah sat at the table eating cake. She smiled broadly at Clayton.

"Would you like a cup of coffee and a slice of cake?" Maggie asked.

Both he and George nodded.

Maggie got the coffee and placed it in front of the men. Then she sliced large chunks of cake for each of them. Her hand shook. Did she feel as unnerved as he did by what had just happened in the sitting room?

Clayton looked back into the sitting room. He took the cake Maggie offered but didn't have the stomach to eat it.

Maggie limped back to the coffeepot and poured a cup for herself. Her face looked pinched and her lips tight.

"Maggie, honey, what's wrong with your leg?" he asked. Clayton stood and offered her his chair.

"Nothing."

George grunted. "Something's wrong with it. We can all see you are limping."

Maggie frowned at him. "I'm fine."

Clayton shook his head. "What happened?"

She sighed. "I fell, but I'm fine. Really." Her eyes pleaded with him to drop the subject.

"Well, when the doctor gets here, as soon as he's done looking at Abraham, I'm going to have him examine you." Clayton set his cup on the table and then returned to the sitting room.

"Sally?"

The girl looked up from where she sat.

"Would you help me clean the wound on the back of Abraham's head?"

Sally stood up. "What do I need to do?"

"Get me a bowl of hot water and a cloth, please."

She nodded and walked to the kitchen.

While she was gone, Clayton asked Abraham, "Abe, are you still awake?"

"Yep, but my head feels like it is going to explode." He sounded more like Abraham and less like a schoolboy with a crush.

Clayton nodded. "Good. I need you to sit up so we can clean this cut on the back of your head."

Sally returned with two bowls. She handed the one with hot water in it to Clayton. "Abraham, I brought you a bowl. Just in case you decide to get sick when we sit you up." She placed the bowl in his broad hands.

Together they sat Abraham up. He immediately lost his lunch in the bowl. Clayton watched as Sally wiped his face and mouth with another rag that she'd brought. She took the bowl and tossed the contents. When she returned, she gave him back the bowl.

Clayton cleaned the cut on the back of Abraham's head. He was pretty sure it would need to be sewn back up. Sally's soft voice soothed Abraham. She told him her name and began talking about her family. He sat still and listened to each word she spoke.

Once the wound was clean, Clayton asked, "Do you want to lie back down or sit up until the doctor gets here?"

"I'll sit up." Abraham sounded more like himself. "When is the doctor supposed to arrive?"

Clayton had been wondering the same thing. "He should be here any minute. I sent Bud out to get him."

A short nod of the head was all that told Clayton that Abraham had heard him. Clayton sat down in Maggie's rocker. This day hadn't turned out as he'd expected at all. Abraham was seriously injured, Maggie had been hurt in a fall and Clayton had realized just how much his wife meant to him.

Chapter Nineteen

The next morning, Maggie woke hurting all over. She eased out of bed and took tiny steps to James. Her arms ached as she picked him up and then walked to her rocker to feed him. The doctor had said nothing was broken. She was just bruised, but right now she felt as if someone had beaten her with a stick.

She heard Clayton moving about his room. His lamp had been on most of the night. Maggie knew he was concerned for Abraham. The doctor had said head injuries were odd and that everyone reacted to them differently.

Abraham was blind, but Doc had said that it might be temporary. Abraham also couldn't remember what had happened in the pasture. The doctor had claimed that was normal also. But no matter what the doctor said, they had a man in their sitting room who was blind and had no memory of what had happened to him.

She thought about Sally as James nursed. Sally hadn't wanted to leave Abraham's side. She'd kicked up a fuss when Clayton offered to take her home. She said she'd promised Abraham she'd stay by his side and refused to leave.

It was all one big mess. What were they going to do?

Clayton had sent Hal to the Morris place to tell them that Sally would be staying the night. Mr. Morris had come back with Hal and insisted Sally return home with him. She'd refused.

Maggie understood the girl's determination to keep her promise. Hadn't she been just as stubborn? Jack had made her promise to save the ranch for his son. And she had. Even though Gus had all but begged for the land and she didn't really want it, she'd stubbornly kept her promise.

Mr. Morris had gone home angry and without his daughter.

Sally had asked for blankets so she could sleep on the floor beside the couch where Abraham slept. The doctor had given him enough medicine to knock out two men, so Maggie had allowed the girl to stay unchaperoned with the foreman.

Maggie was sure that all these same thoughts had kept Clayton awake. That, and not knowing what had happened to Abraham. She heard Clayton's bedroom door open and close. She sighed, knowing as soon as James finished his breakfast she'd need to get dressed and start everyone else's breakfast.

Getting dressed took longer due to her sore muscles. Each step down the stairs was excruciating. At the bottom, she paused. Abraham's soft snores filled the room, but there was no sign of Sally.

The smell of bacon and eggs filled the house. Maggie inched her way to the kitchen to find Sally and

Clayton having a discussion over plates of food and coffee. She walked to the stove and lifted the coffeepot. Her muscles screamed in protest.

"Good morning, honey. I thought I'd let you sleep in. How are you feeling?" Clayton smiled at her over his cup.

Maggie frowned. What was this sugary sweetness that was pouring from his lips, and why did it happen only when other people were around? "I'm sore but I'll live," she answered.

Sally pushed her chair back. "I'll dish up some breakfast for you."

"What are your plans now, Sally?" Maggie asked, easing her bottom into the hardwood chair.

"Clayton and I were just discussing that. Pa is angry and told me if I stayed last night I'm not welcome home." Tears filled her eyes. "He just didn't understand."

"No, I reckon he didn't," Clayton agreed. "I'll ride over there this morning and see if I can talk some sense into him."

Sally set a plate of scrambled eggs, bacon and fresh biscuits in front of Maggie. "It won't do any good. Pa is a man of his word." She slipped into her chair.

The fork felt as if it weighed as much as a sack of sugar. "You are welcome to stay here," Maggie offered.

"I'm still going over there, even if he's as stubborn as you say he is. Is there anything I can get for you?"

Sally nodded. "See if Ma will pack a bag of clothes for me."

He nodded. Clayton looked at Maggie. "Maggie,

a hot bath might loosen your muscles some." She felt as if he had switched from husband to doctor.

"Maybe." She ate. A hot bath would probably do wonders, but with two grown men in the house, she didn't see it happening anytime soon.

Dinah came into the kitchen. She yawned and rubbed her eyes. "Sissy, I'm hungry."

Once more Sally pushed her chair back. "I'll get her a plate."

The little girl climbed up onto her chair. "Good morning, Clayton."

"Good morning, half-pint." He tugged at her braid. "Did you sleep well last night?"

"Uh-huh." Dinah looked at the plate Sally sat in front of her. "Thank you, Sally. Do you live here now?"

Sally caught her lower lip between her teeth. "I think so, Dinah. Is that all right?"

Dinah nodded. "You can stay in my room with me, if you want to."

Maggie smiled at her little sister. Dinah had a big heart. Wouldn't it be nice if everyone was as giving as her little sister?

"That is very sweet of you, Dinah. But Sally might like to have a room of her own. How about after breakfast you show her the room next to yours?" Maggie reached over and brushed the soft bangs out of Dinah's eyes.

"All right." Dinah nibbled on a piece of bacon.

Clayton pushed his chair back. "I'll head on over to your folks' place, Sally. I have an Express rider coming through this afternoon."

Maggie spoke up. "Clayton, what are we going to do about Abraham?"

He glanced into the sitting room. "He should sleep most of the day. Doc left medicine to give him for pain."

Maggie nodded. "Be careful."

Clayton walked around the table. "If the pain gets too bad today, you can take a little of Abraham's medicine and take a nap. I'm sure Sally wouldn't mind taking care of the children for a few hours." He leaned down and kissed her on the forehead. "I'll be back as quickly as I can."

Maggie's forehead tingled where he'd kissed her. She watched his shoulders sway as he walked out of the kitchen. Why had he kissed her? Was Clayton falling in love with her? Or had yesterday's events shaken him up more than she thought? Maggie hoped he was falling in love with her. She wanted him to love her so much that he'd never even consider leaving. Was that too much to ask?

The ride back from the Morrises' seemed to take forever. Sally had been right. Her father no longer welcomed her in his home. Personally, Clayton thought he was being a bit harsh. He didn't believe he would ever be able to do that to one of his children.

Dinah came to mind. She wasn't his daughter, but he cared for her as if she were. No, no matter what she did, she'd always have a home under his roof.

Clayton took Bones to the barn, where George waited. The older man seemed more shook up about Abraham than any of the other men. After Doc Anderson left the night before, Clayton had gone to the bunkhouse to tell the men about Abraham.

Each man had reacted differently. The four new men simply nodded their understanding of Abraham's condition, but since they really didn't know the man, their reactions were expected. Hal had nodded and asked Bud if he could read his Bible and say a prayer for Abraham. Bud had handed the book to Hal and then offered to run things until Abraham got back on his feet. It was all Clayton could do not to laugh at Bud. Of all the men, he was the least likely to be chosen to replace Abraham.

Maybe it was because George had seen Abraham at his worst that it affected him the most. The older man asked, "Clayton, what's to become of Abraham?"

Clayton shook his head. "You heard Doc. He might snap out of this and be as right as rain in a few days."

"Yep, I also heard him say that Abraham may never get his sight or memory back. Then what?" He leaned against the pitchfork he'd been using to muck out the stalls.

Clayton sighed. "I don't know. Let's give him time to heal and if worse comes to worst, we'll decide what to do then."

George nodded. "Fair enough." He went back to mucking out the stall.

After putting Bones back in his stall, Clayton walked up to the house. He carried the carpetbag full of Sally's personal belongings. Mrs. Morris had handed them to Clayton with tears streaming down her face. He could still hear her saying, "You tell my girl I love her and to be good."

Clayton opened the door to find Abraham sitting

up eating and smiling. Sally sat beside him working on a sampler. "It's good to see you sitting up."

"Wish I could say it's good to see you, too, but I can't. Seems I'm stuck in the dark at the moment." Abraham bit into the roll of bread in his hand.

Clayton hung his coat up and then walked to the settee. "Well, you'll be seeing again in no time."

Abraham nodded. "From your lips to God's ears." He tilted his head to the side. "That's a funny saying."

Clayton handed Sally the carpetbag. "Sally, your ma said to tell you she loves you and to be good." He offered her what he hoped was an encouraging smile.

"Thank you for trying. Pa can be stubborn. I didn't expect anything more from him." She laid the sampler on the end table and stood. "If you will excuse me, I'll just take this to my new room."

Clayton nodded. He looked into the kitchen. It was empty. "Abraham, do you know where Maggie and the children are?"

"No, I haven't been awake long. Is Sally gone now?" he asked with a frown.

Clayton nodded and then remembered that the other man couldn't see the movement. "She went upstairs to put away her things. Do you want me to call her?"

"No, my head is killing me." He held out the plate. "I think I'm going to be sick."

Clayton grabbed the bowl he'd used the other night and exchanged it for the plate. "Here, use this if you get sick."

Abraham's face went pale. "I hate this."

"I know. I would, too. But Doc says that being nauseated happens when you have a head injury." He pulled the brown bottle of liquid medicine off the end table. Clayton took the lid off and asked, "Do you still feel like you are going to be sick?"

"Not as badly as a few moments ago."

"Good. Let me have the bowl and you take this." Clayton took the bowl and put the brown bottle in Abraham's hand. "Take a swig of that."

Abraham did as he was instructed. He swallowed, then said, "Whatever that is, it's very sweet."

Clayton laughed and took the bottle back. He screwed the lid on and said, "Well, sweet medicine is better than bitter."

"I suppose." Abraham scooted back into the sofa. "I'll just be glad when my head quits hurting and the room stops spinning."

Clayton nodded and said, "This too shall pass."

"If you say so." He closed his eyes.

Clayton asked, "Abraham, do you have any family in these parts?"

Abraham tilted his head to the side. "Sadly, I have no idea." He yawned. "I think I'll lie down for a bit, if that's all right."

"Of course it's all right. Enjoy your rest." Clayton stood and took the plate into the kitchen. He emptied the remainder of Abraham's breakfast into the slop bucket.

Sally came into the kitchen. "He's lying down again. Is he all right?"

"I believe so. Doc Anderson said he might sleep a lot for a few days. I also gave him more medicine to help his headache." He put the plate into the washtub.

She nodded. "I'm sorry my actions of last night

caused you and Maggie grief." Sally walked to the window and looked outside.

"It's all right. We'll manage." He smiled at her. "Where is Maggie?"

Sally turned. "She's napping." Guilt pulled at her normally happy face.

Clayton crossed his arms over his chest and waited her out. He'd seen his ma do this to his youngest brother and sister many times. She had done something, but for the life of him Clayton couldn't figure out what.

"Um, I gave her a teaspoon of Abraham's medicine."

Clayton fought his facial muscles that wanted to break out in laughter. "How?" he asked, keeping his voice firm.

"I made her a very sweet cup of coffee, sugar and milk." Sally beseeched him with her eyes. "I know I shouldn't have, but she was in such pain that, well…"

Clayton did laugh. He couldn't stop himself. "You drugged her?"

Sally frowned. "Yes, but it was for her own good. And it wasn't enough to hurt her or the baby."

Impulsively, Clayton walked across the room and hugged her. "Thank you. That was probably just what she needed. But let's not do it again."

Sally pulled away. "You really think so? I mean, I thought she could use the rest, but I'm sure she wouldn't be happy if she finds out."

He held his hands up. "I'm not going to tell her."

Sally sank into one of the kitchen chairs. "Thank you."

"No, thank you. I'm glad you are here to take care

of my family." He glanced at the clock. "I'd better head out to the barn. I've got a rider coming through in half an hour." Clayton slipped into his coat and headed out to the barn.

He chuckled as he went. Maggie would want to wring Sally's neck if she knew what the girl had done. Clayton entered the warm barn with a sigh. Had life on the Fillmore Ranch always been this unpredictable? It seemed from the moment he set foot on the land, his life had changed several times. Or was it just his emotions and feelings?

Chapter Twenty

Maggie decided she needed fresh air. With Sally helping out around the house, she felt confident in leaving the girl in charge. Her muscles weren't as sore as they'd been three days ago, but they still protested as she climbed into the saddle. As she rode Snowball out to the cove, her thoughts rehashed the last few days.

Clayton helped out more on the ranch with Abraham slowly recovering and spent less time around the house. She noticed that he took one of the medical books with him everywhere he went. Maggie wished that things weren't so crazy at the ranch and that he could study more.

The foreman's headaches were less frequent, even though he hadn't regained his eyesight, and the wound on his head was healing nicely. The doctor was expected out again later in the day. Maggie would be back in time to hear what he thought of Abraham's progress.

Sally had settled in nicely and was a tremendous help with the children. Maggie worried about the closeness the young girl had developed with Abraham. Sally waited on him and stayed as close to him as she possibly could. The ranch foreman seemed to enjoy spending time with Sally also. They were building a sweet relationship based upon their newfound friendship. Still, Maggie worried it was developing a little faster than Sally's parents would like.

Maggie giggled at her last thought. Whom was she kidding? Mrs. Morris would probably be thrilled if Abraham and Sally were to marry. Wasn't that what the girl's mother had wanted?

The cove came into view. Since the snow had melted off, the ground was muddy and slick. She and Snowball took their time. The sun shone brightly, and the lack of wind almost made it feel like springtime. She pulled Snowball to a stop and slipped out of the saddle.

Quietness filled the midmorning air. Maggie closed her eyes and inhaled the freshness. Then she opened them and, taking the reins, walked with Snowball to the water's edge. The little mare drank deeply. Maggie rubbed the horse's shoulder. "We should do this more often," she told the animal.

Snowball snorted.

"I agree."

Maggie turned at the sound of Clayton's voice. She hadn't heard him approach.

Clayton walked Bones the rest of the way into the cove.

"Where did you come from?" Maggie asked. She admired the way he sat tall in the saddle. He smiled and the expression reached his eyes.

"This mud muffles the sound of the horse's hooves.

I'm sorry if I startled you." He stopped and dismounted from the horse.

Maggie smiled back. "We seem to keep meeting here."

Clayton moved in front of her. "You look very pretty today."

"Thank you." Maggie felt pretty. Her dress hadn't fit as snugly as it had since the baby had been born, and she'd gone out of her way to fix her hair in a loose style. Secretly she'd hoped to meet Clayton at the cove.

He reached out and touched a strand of hair. "I've always thought your hair was pretty."

She'd already thanked him so wasn't sure what to say. Maggie felt her cheeks begin to fill with heat. Clayton had a way of looking at her that made her feel giddy.

Clayton brushed his fingers down her cheek as he said, "I spoke with the men, and most of them are going to the winter dance." His hand dropped to his side. "All but George and now Abraham. I asked George if he'd keep an eye on Sally and the children, and he agreed. So…" He pushed his hat back and with teasing blue eyes said, "If you still want to go, I'd like to take you."

Maggie didn't even realize that she'd moved until she found herself wrapped in his strong arms. She hugged him close. In a breathless rush, she said, "Oh, thank you, Clayton. I'd love to go."

He hugged her close. The book pressed into her back as he buried his face in her hair. He nuzzled her neck. "I would have told you sooner, if I'd known I'd get this kind of reaction."

Maggie pulled away. She felt breathless and hot. Her eyes searched his as she said, "I should be getting back to the house. Doc Anderson is coming this afternoon." What was she saying? Maggie knew she had to get away from Clayton or she'd be declaring her love for him. It was one thing to hug him but another thing altogether to be alone and feeling emotions that she'd never felt before, not even with her late husband, Jack.

Clayton lowered his lips and kissed her lightly. He then released her. "Yeah, I should get back to the fence I was repairing when I saw you ride by." Clayton spun on his heels. He scooped up Bones's reins and then mounted. "I'll be back to the house by the time Doc gets there." Then he turned the horse back the way they had come.

Maggie felt as weak as a newborn calf. She pulled herself onto Snowball's back and turned her toward home. Why had he kissed her? She knew men didn't have to be in love to be romantic, but still, this was new territory for her and Clayton. Should she let it continue? Or put a stop to his affectionate ways now? How could she go on knowing that sooner or later, she'd let it slip that she loved him? Really loved him, like she'd never loved anyone else.

Clayton returned to the fence as he'd said he would, but now his mind couldn't focus on the job. What had gotten into him? He'd followed Maggie only so that he could invite her to the dance. Not so that he could kiss her.

He finished his work on the fence and then decided to go to the south pasture. Abraham still couldn't remember what had happened that day. Maybe if Clayton looked again, he'd figure out what happened. Abraham's horse had turned up in the north pasture the next day. It was a mystery that Clayton hoped to figure out.

A frown formed as he arrived at the place where Abraham had been hurt. Bud stood looking about. Clayton groaned. He'd told Bud to help Hal today. Why couldn't that boy just do as he was told? "Bud, did one of the pigs wander out here?"

Bud looked up and grinned sheepishly. "No. I just wanted to come out here and see if I could figure out what happened to Abraham. Besides, Hal knows what he's doing with those pigs. He didn't need me."

Clayton pushed his hat back on his head and leaned forward. "Look, Bud, I'm not sure what has happened to you since Gus left, but I've been told up until then you were a hard worker and followed orders. I expect you to continue to be a hard worker and follow orders or we will fire you." He hated confrontation, but Bud couldn't continue disobeying orders.

Bud nodded. "Sorry, boss." He climbed back on his horse. "Gus allowed us to work where we felt we were needed. I'll try to remember you are the boss." Bud shoved his hat onto his head and rode away.

The way he said "boss" made Clayton's skin crawl. He stepped down from Bones and looked about. Bud's horse's hooves and the mud had erased any signs of what had happened to Abraham. Clayton had meant to come back sooner, but the duties of the ranch had kept him busy.

He returned to Bones and sighed as he pulled himself into the saddle. Clayton didn't want to admit that he was avoiding the house and Maggie. His gaze moved to the sun. If he wanted to see the doctor, Clayton needed to go home. "Bones, I'm a coward." He turned the horse toward the ranch house. "Funny, as a Pony Express rider I had no fear. I could outrun, outshoot and outsmart any danger that came my way. But, give me one beautiful, smart lady, and I can't seem to hold my emotions in check. All I want to do is hold her, protect her and love her with all my heart."

Bones snorted and bobbed his head in agreement.

He patted the horse's neck. "What am I going to do? I know she's not Eunice. Maggie cares more about family than money. I don't believe she will ever leave me in pursuit of a richer husband, but she has said she isn't going to fall in love. I don't know if I can take her rejecting my love."

Clayton topped the hill and stopped Bones. So much had happened in such a small amount of time. He leaned on the saddle horn and watched the activity in the ranch house yard. Maggie had just left the henhouse. He assumed she carried eggs in her small basket. Dinah skipped along beside her. Maggie and the kids were his family, and although he'd tried to keep his heart at a distance, somehow he'd let himself grow to love them all. He wanted to be a true husband to Maggie and a father to Dinah and James. He waited for the doubts and worries to cloud his happiness. They didn't come.

He sat up straighter in the saddle. Next week, he'd confess his love to her at the winter dance. Clayton swallowed hard. His gaze shifted to movement coming down the main road. He recognized the doctor's buggy and urged Bones down the hill.

The doctor met him with a grin. "Good to see you, Clayton. How's our patient doing?" He pulled his buggy up in front of the barn and grabbed his black leather bag out of the seat.

"Good. But you are the real doctor. You'll have to tell me." Clayton slid off Bones. He handed the reins to George, who, as usual, was ready to take them. "Thanks, George."

George nodded. "Let me know how he's doing, won't ya?"

"Will do." Clayton walked with the doctor to the house. "I think the stitches are healing nicely, but I'm worried that he still can't remember what happened."

"It's not uncommon for a man to forget a few things when he's been conked over the head." Doc Anderson held on to the porch railing as he climbed the stairs. "Have you figured out what happened out there?"

Clayton stepped around him and opened the door. "No, and we may never know."

Doc followed him inside. "That's true enough."

Sally stood up when they entered. She'd been sitting close to Abraham reading out of the Bible. Baby James slept in his washtub. A glance in the kitchen revealed Maggie and Dinah at the counter mixing something.

The doctor hung his coat on a hook by the door, then turned to his patient. "Good afternoon, Sally, Abraham."

"Hello, Doc Anderson," Abraham said. He sat up a little taller.

Doc walked across the room. "How are you feeling today? Is the head still throbbing?"

"No, sir. The headache is gone." He turned his head in the direction of Doc's voice.

Clayton watched as the doctor picked up a lantern and lit it. "How are the eyes?" He held the lantern up and swung it from side to side in front of Abraham's face.

"I can see lights now."

The doctor nodded. "Yes, that's good. You'll have sight soon, I'm sure of it." He set the lamp back down and blew out the wick. "How about memories?"

Abraham sighed. "I can remember a lot of stuff about my past, just nothing about the past few days."

Clayton eased down into the chair by the fireplace. He reached down and picked up baby James. "What is the last thing you remember?" Clayton held the baby in his arms. James reached out and latched on to his finger.

"Same as before. I went to the south pasture to check on the cows up there. The next thing I knew, I was here." Abraham rubbed his eyes. "I can't stay here forever, Doc. Are you sure my eyesight will come back?"

Doc Anderson shook his head. "All I can say is that if you are seeing lights, you'll more than likely see better in a few days. But I can't guarantee your eyesight will come back fully. Only God can do that, son."

Abraham's jaw tightened.

Sally reached over and rested her hand over his. "I'll stay with you, Abraham. I can be your eyes."

He pulled his hand away. "I know you mean well, Sally. But I won't be a burden on anyone."

Doc Anderson interrupted. "Let's have a look at

my stitchery." He walked up behind Abraham and studied the wound on the back of his head. "This is looking good, too."

James tried to pull Clayton's finger into his mouth. Clayton gently turned the baby around and rested him on his shoulder. What was Abraham going to do if he didn't get his sight back?

Sally stood. "I think I'll go help Maggie in the kitchen."

Abraham's blank gaze followed the sound of her swishing skirts. He sighed. "Clayton, I'd like to move back into the bunkhouse, if that's all right with you."

"Of course it's all right with me, but you might want to check with Doc Anderson and make sure you are up to it." Clayton rubbed James's small back. The baby squirmed.

Doc Anderson asked Abraham several more questions but finally agreed that Abraham could leave the sitting room and go back to the bunkhouse. "Well, I'll be heading on down the road, since you are doing so well, Abraham." He picked up his bag and motioned for Clayton to follow him outside.

Clayton tucked James back into his washtub and stood up to follow the doctor. He thought the new crib was coming along nicely but wanted to finish it up with a little artwork. Unfortunately, Clayton couldn't decide what he wanted to put on it.

"Thanks for coming, Doc," Abraham said. "I'll pay you whatever I owe you next time I'm in town."

"There's no rush on payment, but I do want Clayton to bring you with him on his next visit." He pulled the door open and stepped outside.

Clayton turned to Abraham. "I'll walk the doctor

out and then come back to help you move back to the bunkhouse." At the other man's nod, Clayton closed the door behind him.

He'd seen the look in Sally's eyes when Abraham had pulled his hand from hers. There was despair and fear in their depths. It was clear that Sally loved the big man and pretty clear that he felt the same way about her. How were they going to make it work if Abraham never regained his sight?

Chapter Twenty-One

Two days later, Clayton came into the house carrying the cradle that he'd secretly been working on in the barn. He'd spent most of his time running the ranch and the Pony Express. Supplies had come in earlier, giving him the excuse he needed to stay in the barn and finish up the cradle.

Abraham's eyesight had remained the same. He spent most of his time indoors on his cot. Clayton could only imagine how miserable the foreman was feeling. He'd been thinking about the man most of the day and had decided Abraham needed a job. But, for the life of him, he couldn't think what.

Clayton set the cradle by the door and entered the house. He looked into the sitting room and kitchen, and not seeing Maggie or Sally around, he picked up the cradle and set it by the fireplace. Then he went to the foot of the stairs and called up, "Maggie, are you here?"

"I'll be right down," she called back.

He hurried to stand beside the fireplace and the cradle.

A few minutes later, Maggie came down the stairs wearing a pretty pink dress with ruffles around the hem. It swirled about her shoes as she descended. Her blond hair hung loosely down her back. Two shiny combs pulled back the sides. He smiled. "You look beautiful."

Maggie grinned shyly. "Thank you. It's been a long time since I've gone to a dance."

Clayton's smile faded. He swallowed hard. He'd forgotten about the dance. The two shirts Maggie had sewn for him were in the dirty clothes, and they were his finest. "Maggie, I forgot about the dance."

Joy drifted from her hazel eyes like fog in the morning sunlight. "You don't want to go anymore?" She rubbed her lips together.

Clayton walked forward and took her hands in his. "It's not that I don't want to go. It's just that my two nicest shirts aren't fit to wear to a social."

"That's the only reason?" she asked, staring into his eyes.

He nodded, wishing he'd remembered the dance was tonight.

Maggie pulled her hands from his and walked to her sewing basket. "I have a surprise for you." She bent over and pulled blue fabric from the basket.

Clayton grinned as she opened the material to reveal a brand-new blue shirt. "You made that for me? For the dance?"

She walked back to him. "I was going to give it to you the other night, but then Abraham had his accident and, well…"

He took the shirt in his hands and examined the buttons. They were fancier than those on his everyday shirts. "It will look great with my black jeans. Thank you."

Maggie blushed under his gaze. "You should probably go get dressed if we want to get there on time."

Clayton shook his head. "First, I have a gift for you, too. It's not as fancy as the shirt you made me, but I hope you like it." He took her by the hand and led her to the cradle.

Her smile filled her whole face. Maggie bent down and caressed the hemlock wood. Her finger traced the vines he'd carved into the headboard. "Oh, Clayton, it's beautiful!"

He chuckled. "I was hoping you would say that."

Maggie rose and kissed him on the cheek. "Thank you. It is the most beautiful piece of furniture I have ever seen."

Clayton felt his own cheeks flush. "Let's carry it upstairs and I'll get dressed so we can leave."

Maggie led the way.

He placed the cradle beside her bed and then hurried into his room. For several moments, he heard her puttering about. Then she left her room.

Clayton reached up and touched his cheek where she had kissed him. He loved that woman more than words could express. Tonight after the dance, he planned on finding a pretty moonlit spot and telling her. The question nagged at him. What would he do if she spurned that love?

Maggie had never told anyone how much she enjoyed going to barn dances. She smiled happily at Clayton as he swung her about the floor during the final dance. He looked so handsome in black jeans and boots. His eyes shone deeper than normal, picking up the blue from the shirt that she'd made for him.

Her cheeks felt warm from dancing. The music stopped and she laughed happily. "Thank you for bringing me. This evening has been fun."

Clayton placed an arm around her waist as they walked from the center of the barn. He leaned his head next to hers and said, "I had fun, too." Other couples were also leaving. The fiddle players were putting their instruments away. She enjoyed the feeling of Clayton being so close. He'd found reasons not to be around when the slow dances had played. Maggie told herself she didn't care, but the truth was she cared very much. Too much.

She stepped out of his embrace as soon as they were at the edge of the dance floor. "I'll go get my baking dish. Be right back." At Clayton's nod, Maggie hurried to the food table and located her plate.

"I'm glad you were able to come tonight," Mrs. Fisher said, handing her a cup filled with fruit punch. "Take one of these to Clayton. I have way too much left over."

"Thank you. The dance was lovely. Is there anything I can do to help you clean up?"

"No, thanks, Maggie." She looked about. "I think we have plenty who have already volunteered to stay and finish up." The other woman gave her a quick hug. "Besides, you have a long ride ahead of you and it's already getting late."

Maggie returned her hug and said, "Good night. And thanks again."

Mrs. Fisher turned away with a wave of her hand. Clayton stood where she'd left him. She exchanged his glass of punch and the plate for her coat. Maggie watched his Adam's apple bob as he drank deeply. She slipped her arms into the coat and buttoned it up.

"Ready?" he asked, placing his hand in the small of her back to guide her out to their wagon.

Maggie nodded. She smiled broadly. Today had been one of her happiest days in a long time. Clayton had proved his love for baby James by giving her the cradle. Then he'd taken her to the winter dance, where she'd had a wonderful evening. Nothing could make this day any more special.

Clayton helped her up onto the seat. His blue eyes searched out hers in the moonlight. A breeze threatened to take off his hat and reveal his light brown hair. He was by far the most handsome man she'd ever met. The only thing that would make this night more perfect would be if she told him she loved him and he returned that love.

Maggie sat up straight as Clayton fell in line with the other wagons driving away from the Fishers' home. She listened to others yelling between wagons and smiled. This was her home, she was with her handsome husband and nothing could spoil her evening.

Clayton remained silent as he directed the horse and buggy out of town. Maggie cut her eyes in his direction. Old fears raised their ugly head. She forced them away. There was no guarantee that Clayton would be with her for the rest of her life, but if Sally and Abraham's lost love had taught her anything, it was that she should express her love for Clayton while she had him in her life and stop living in fear.

Five of the Fillmore men rode up beside the wagon.

Maggie had seen them on the ranch but recognized only Hal. Four of them fell back while Hal stayed even with Clayton.

Hal tipped his hat at her and said, "Clayton, Mrs. Young, me and the fellas thought we might stay overnight in town this evening, if it's all right with you."

Clayton chuckled. "You are all grown men. Just be sure to show up tomorrow afternoon for evening chores."

Hal grinned like a little boy at Christmas. "Yes, sir. Thank you."

Clayton shook his head. "It's interesting how Hal has taken on the role of leader with that bunch," he said, clicking his tongue to get the little mare to travel faster.

The wind picked up. Maggie wrapped her coat tighter about her waist. She wanted to tell Clayton how she felt about him, but the words seemed stuck in her throat.

He looked to her and smiled. When she returned his gaze, he quickly ducked his head. If she didn't know better, Maggie would think he was shy.

They rode on in silence.

Clayton finally spoke. "This weather seems to be turning for the worse."

Maggie had to admit that the wind was blowing harder out here than in town. Her star-filled night was being covered by fast-moving clouds. "Do you think it's going to rain?" she asked, aware that they had reverted to talking about the weather. It was hardly the romantic conversation she'd hoped for.

He looked up. "Those look like snow clouds."

She nodded.

"We'd best get on home." He slapped the reins over the horse's back.

They weren't far from home when Maggie smelled smoke. She looked to Clayton, who was frowning. "Do you smell that?"

He nodded. "Maybe some highwayman has decided to set up camp close by."

Maggie didn't care much for highwaymen. They were usually robbers or murderers on the run from the law. She tucked her coat under her legs as a shiver ran down her spine. She was comforted in knowing Clayton would keep her safe.

The wind shifted and blew against them. The smoke in the air thickened. "Clayton, I don't think that's campfire smoke."

Worry etched his brow. He yelled, "Ya!" at the horse and sent it into a run.

Maggie held on to the seat for dear life. All the while her brain screamed that the children were in danger. Her house was directly in front of them. The Morris ranch was to the right. The wind wasn't blowing from the right.

They topped the hill. The same hill Clayton had sat upon two months earlier.

Maggie gasped. Her house was on fire!

Clayton's stomach turned. His only thought was for the children and Sally. He whipped the reins over the mare's back, mentally begging her to go faster. Just before they got to the house, he said, "Maggie, promise me you will stay away from the house."

She nodded as if in shock.

Sally stood by the barn holding baby James. Clayton searched the yard for Dinah. He pulled the wagon to the barn and barked, "Where's Dinah?"

With a shaky hand, Sally pointed to the house. Tears streamed down her face. "I think she's in her room."

Maggie ran for the house. Clayton chased her and caught her at the porch. The railing fell right in front of them. He pulled Maggie back kicking and screaming.

"Let me go. I have to save Dinah." She repeated herself and struggled against him.

Clayton looked to the men. He saw George with Bud running back and forth with buckets of water. They were throwing it at the fireplace where it looked like the blaze had begun. "George!"

The old man ran toward him. Clayton practically tossed Maggie at him. "Hold her."

George wrapped his muscular arms around Maggie and held her while she struggled.

Clayton shouted, "Maggie! Stop it!"

She stared at him wide-eyed, shocked at the force of his command.

"You have to stay here with James. He needs you. I'm going inside for Dinah." Clayton didn't give her time to respond. He ran around the house to the kitchen. Grabbing a chair, he placed it under the trapdoor in his bedroom and pushed up. The door popped open and he pulled himself through it.

Smoke threatened to strangle him as he shouted, "Dinah!"

He couldn't hear anything and raced from his room, through Maggie's, across the hall and into Dinah's room. She was nowhere to be seen. Had the little girl made it down the stairs? He turned to the stairs only to find them blocked by a wall of fire.

Clayton ran back to his room and jumped through the trapdoor once more. He rushed through the kitchen to the sitting room. The thick smoke and flames burned his eyes and throat. It was so thick that he could no longer see. Again, he called, "Dinah!"

A groan sounded close to the door. Clayton turned toward the sound, took two steps and tripped over something. He felt around with his hands. Confusion filled his mind as he felt a large arm under his hand.

He stood, grabbed the arm and began pulling a heavy body across the floor to the kitchen. Clayton got him to the kitchen door and yelled, "Bud! George!"

Bud appeared.

The man at Clayton's feet began to cough and moan.

Clayton pulled him closer to Bud, and between them they lifted the man. They carried him as far away from the house as they could. Once in the light of the fire, Clayton could see that they'd saved Abraham.

Sally came running to their side. She wrapped her arms around Abraham and wiped at his blackened face with her apron.

Clayton looked about for Maggie and the children. Maggie had her back to the house. Her shoulders shook, and he could tell that she was rocking James.

"Sally, did Dinah come out?"

She shook her head no.

Once more Clayton ran into the house. The fire had spread and would soon block him from entering or exiting the house through the kitchen door. He quietly pleaded, *Lord, help*. Clayton looked up at the still-open trapdoor. He pulled the chair under it again and climbed up.

Dropping to the floor to try to avoid some of the smoke, he crawled through Maggie's room and across the hall again. Clayton stopped in front of Dinah's room. He crawled to the closed door, stood, then pulled it open. "Dinah!"

"I'm here."

Clayton dropped to his hands and knees again where the air seemed cleaner. "Where?" The smoke billowed into the room.

"Here." Dinah reached out from under the bed and touched his arm.

He grabbed her and pulled her to him. Clayton hugged her close.

"I'm scared," Dinah whimpered against his shirt.

Clayton reached up and pulled the quilt from the bed. "I know you are but you have to trust me." He wrapped her up in the spread and said, "I'm going to cover your head up so that the smoke and fire can't get to you. Will you be all right?"

Dinah cried. "Uh-huh."

He hugged her again and then said, "Good girl." Clayton kissed her head and then finished wrapping her tightly in the quilt. He didn't know how he was going to get her down the trapdoor or if they were cut off from the back door.

Carrying the little girl, Clayton retraced his steps for the second time. When he got to the trapdoor he set Dinah down. The house popped and hissed with each lick of the fire's flames.

He looked down the hole and found Abraham standing on the chair.

"I was just coming up for you."

"Praise the Lord. Here, take Dinah." Clayton scooped the little girl up and lowered her wrapped body down to Abraham.

Once Abraham had her and was running for the door, Clayton lowered himself down to follow them. The beam over the door fell in front of him, blocking his path. He stood horrified as the flames traveled across the wall. Heat scorched his arms, and he backed up.

Clayton looked about. The ceiling would be coming down on him any minute now. He ducked his head, said a prayer and then burst through the back door, coughing. Two buckets of cold water slammed into his body. His eyes watered and tears ran freely down his face as he realized that God had saved both him and Dinah.

Maggie slammed into him so hard that what air he had left swiftly vacated his body. She'd wrapped a blanket around him. Together they tumbled onto the ground. "I was so afraid you were going to leave me," she cried.

Clayton laughed. "Honey, I am never leaving you."

A loud groan split the air as the burning house leaned. Clayton felt strong arms lift him up.

"You two lovebirds can chatter later. We've got to get farther away from the fire." Abraham half carried, half pulled Clayton and Maggie away from the falling house.

Clayton hated the weakness he felt. What he'd hoped would be a romantic evening of love and laughter had turned into a tragic night of sorrow and loss. How was Maggie going to feel once the smoke had cleared and she realized her home was gone? He wanted to make it all better. But how?

Chapter Twenty-Two

There was no saving the house. Clayton, Maggie, Sally, Abraham and George watched the building collapse into a burning heap. Dinah pressed against Clayton's leg. Sally rocked James in her arms while tears poured down her face.

What were they going to do now? Clayton looked about at the ragtag bunch. Soot-covered faces looked as lost as he felt. Only once before had he felt this lost, and that had been the day his little brother Benjamin had burned down the barn.

Everyone looked to him for guidance. He'd do the best he could, given the situation. "Let's go to the bunkhouse for now."

Clayton picked up Dinah and followed them into the men's quarters. Thankfully five of the men were in town. It wasn't a permanent solution, but for tonight they had a warm place to sleep.

His gaze moved to Abraham. "When did you get your sight back?"

Abraham grinned. "Tonight. I fell in the house and hit my head on something. When I got outside,

I could see again." He shrugged and hugged Sally to him. She snuggled against his side.

Clayton slapped him on the back. "God's timing."

"Yes, God's timing."

Maggie took over. "Let's get some sleep. Tomorrow, we'll rebuild."

Clayton waited until everyone was situated then went to the barn with George. "What happened tonight?"

The old man growled, "I didn't want to say anything in front of the women, but someone set that fire."

A shiver of fear traveled down Clayton's back. "Do you think it was Gus?"

"I don't know."

"Then how do you know it was set?"

George sat on the edge of his bed. "I was lured away from the house."

Clayton leaned against the door. "Tell me everything."

George rested his head in his hands and then looked up. "I was checking on Abraham when I heard the Pony Express horses. They sounded upset, so I hurried back to check on them. Someone shoved me into the tack room and locked me inside." He rubbed his hands down his face. "I don't know how I could have been so stupid."

"No, you weren't stupid. How did you get out?"

"Abraham. He heard the commotion and felt his way to the barn. It took him a few moments, but he got the door open. By then the fire was full blown. I went to get water."

George sighed.

Someone knocked on the door behind Clayton. He stepped to the side and answered it. "Can anyone come to your party?" Abraham asked.

Clayton nodded. "Come on in. We were just going over what happened tonight."

Abraham sat down beside George.

George turned guilt-filled eyes to him. "I'd just told him you'd gotten me out of the barn and I'd gone for water to put out the fire."

Abraham nodded. "I knew that Sally and the kids were upstairs, so I went looking for them, my thoughts being that since I'd managed to get George out of the tack room, I could get Sally to wake up by calling to her and get them out of the house."

It made sense to Clayton, but why hadn't Sally seen Abraham when she'd run out the front door? "Well, you must have gotten her awake."

"No, someone hit me from behind. I didn't even get her name out before everything went black." Abraham's hand went to the back of his head.

Clayton immediately went to the other man. "Let me look."

Abraham bowed his head. Clayton ran his fingers through the other man's hair. He felt an egg-sized knot behind Abraham's left ear. "I imagine when Sally did wake up and grabbed James, she didn't see me in the smoke-filled house."

George nodded. "Yep, and when I noticed him missing I didn't know where he was but assumed he'd sat down in the barn. Sally was frantic. She wanted to go back in after Dinah, but I told her she had to think about baby James. I didn't have time to hold him and get water."

Clayton frowned. "When did Bud get here?" Bud had said he was going to be at the dance, but Clayton couldn't remember seeing him there.

"Right before you. He seemed to appear out of nowhere. But I was sure glad to have his help."

Abraham stood. "So, which one of us is going to get the sheriff?"

Clayton pushed away from the door. "George, do you feel up to a ride to town?"

George stood. "Sure."

"Why don't I go?" Abraham stood also.

"Same reason I'm not going. George won't be missed because his room is in the barn. And the man who hit you, locked George in the tack room, and set the house on fire knowing that there were women and children inside is still out there. You and I are sleeping with one eye open tonight."

Abraham nodded. "I think Gus has been behind all of our troubles."

Clayton frowned. "Why's that?"

"We didn't have this kind of trouble before he left. Seems something has happened every week since. First the pigs being let out to waste a full afternoon of work for Hal. Then the fences being knocked down and the cattle run off the ranch. I can't prove it, but my gut says it was Gus who jumped me out on the range. And now this. It seems his actions just keep growing. If he isn't stopped soon, someone is going to be killed." Abraham rubbed his temples.

The doctor in Clayton asked, "Is your head hurting?"

"Yep, I got conked on the head again tonight. Remember?" He smiled for the first time that evening.

"But I have my sight back, so this little headache is worth that."

Clayton helped George saddle Bones. "He's fast and he's reliable. Of all the horses in this barn, this is the one that will get you home safely." He added a last warning. "Don't stop and talk to anyone until you see the sheriff. If someone does try to stop you, hang on tight and say, 'Let's go, ole boy.' He's fast and he'll get you where you're going safely."

They all agreed that George would walk Bones past the hill, then ride to town. Clayton and Abraham watched him go. Once he was out of earshot, Abraham said, "I think it's best we not say anything to Bud about George leaving also."

Clayton nodded. "Agreed. Go on to bed. I'll take first watch."

Abraham started to go into the bunkhouse but stopped short. He turned and looked at Clayton. "Thanks for..."

Clayton stopped him. "We're even. You saved my bacon, too."

Abraham nodded, then slipped inside the bunkhouse.

The night sounds were silent and the air hung thick with the smell of burning wood. Clayton felt the urge to go into the bunkhouse and gather his family close. If he and Maggie hadn't returned when they had, there was a good chance that Dinah and Abraham would be dead.

The next morning, Maggie's heart sank as she listened to the sheriff. "You have no proof that Gus did this."

She frowned. "Who else would want this ranch bad enough to burn me out of my home?"

The sheriff shook his head. "I've no idea, ma'am. All I can say is you need proof that it was Gus. I'm sorry for the loss of your home." He turned his horse and headed back to town.

"George, would you mind hitching up the wagon?" Maggie cuddled James close and held on to Dinah's hand. "We're going to town."

He nodded and went to get the little mare.

Maggie looked about at everyone. "Abraham, take Sally home."

Sally started to protest. "I don't…"

"Yes, you do," Abraham said. "I'm going to ask for your parents' permission to marry you. Whatever they say, we will be wed before the day's out."

Sally planted her hands on her hips. "Shouldn't you have asked me first?"

He smiled sweetly at her, bent down on one knee and said, "Sally Morris, will you marry me?"

Sally's cheeks filled with a pink tint. "Yes."

Abraham stood. "I don't know what all the fuss was about. I knew you'd say yes."

She playfully slapped him on the arm. "You heard the woman. Let's take me home." Sally pulled Abraham toward the barn to get his horse.

Clayton stood beside Maggie, grinning at the pair's retreat. Maggie's heart filled with love for him. Did he realize how handsome he was? He'd washed the soot and grime from his face, dunked his head in the watering trough and rolled the sleeves up on his blue shirt. Those sleeves and his coat were all that had stood between his skin and the blaze. Maggie thanked the Lord again for keeping him alive.

She tore her gaze from Clayton when George appeared with the wagon. Clayton picked Dinah up and put her in the bed of the wagon. He then turned to Maggie and took James from her arms. Maggie enjoyed the feel of his firm hand on her back as she climbed up on the wagon seat. She turned to take James from him.

Clayton handed the baby over and then pulled himself up. He looked to the men who stood around. "I'll be back tomorrow. George, you and a couple of men stay close to the barn and bunkhouse. The rest of you take care of the cows and make sure the fence lines are still intact."

Maggie loved the way he'd taken over the ranch. The men nodded and turned to do his bidding. She looked again at the rubble that once was her home. It could have been so much worse.

Clayton turned around and clicked his tongue to get the mare to pulling the wagon. He waited until they were out of earshot of the men and then asked, "What now?"

"Well, I was thinking we'd stay at the boardinghouse until we can find a home in town."

He frowned. "You are leaving the ranch?"

Maggie nodded. "Yes. We'll rebuild someday." She looked down at James's little face. "It's still James's ranch, and when he's older, he'll have the opportunity to run it if he wishes to, but right now I don't want to be out there." She looked over her shoulder at Dinah, who had remained quiet.

Clayton turned to look at the little girl also. "Dinah,

how would you like to go to the general store and get a new dolly and maybe a new dress?"

Dinah looked up at him. "All right."

They had lost everything. Would Dinah ever feel safe again? Would she? Maggie had to admit that her reason for wanting to move to town was because she feared what Gus might do next. Until he was caught and sent to jail, her baby and her sister were in danger.

The trip to town was made in silence.

Clayton drove the wagon to the boardinghouse. It was a tall building with whitewashed walls, but other than that the house was bare. She hadn't ever been inside and was disappointed at the coldness of the house. Maggie's heart ached for the warmth and comfort of the ranch house. Then she reminded herself that wherever she was with her family was home. Having her family with her was what mattered the most. Maggie put the children down for naps and then turned to Clayton. "Would you mind watching the children while I run to the general store and get a few things?"

He shook his head. "No, go ahead." His eyes had dark circles under them, and Maggie realized he'd had no rest himself the night before.

"Why don't you lie down with Dinah? It will give her comfort to have you beside her." Maggie hoped he'd lie down and rest.

He grinned. "I might just do that."

"Good. I'll be back as quick as I can." She took the key and locked her family inside before hurrying to the general store.

Maggie was about to push the door open to the

store when she heard her name being called. She turned to see the sheriff walking toward her.

"Mrs. Young, I'm glad I caught you."

She offered him a weak smile. "It's nice to see you again, Sheriff. What can I help you with?"

He stopped a few feet away. "I just thought you might like to know that Gus Fillmore and his cousin Bud are sitting in my jail."

"His cousin Bud?"

"Yes, ma'am. Didn't you know Bud and Gus are related?"

She shook her head.

"Seems Gus got a little drunk last night and told a few friends at the saloon that he'd be owner of the Fillmore Ranch by this afternoon. He bragged that he and his cousin Bud were going to burn you out."

Maggie smiled. This was the best news she'd had in weeks. "Thank you, Sheriff. I'll let Clayton know as soon as I get back to the boardinghouse."

He tipped his hat and continued down the boardwalk.

Maggie hurried into the general store and purchased a dress for herself and one for Dinah. She also bought Clayton a new shirt and James a baby outfit. Then she moved on to the toys. She bought Dinah a new dolly and a storybook.

Mrs. Fisher met her at the counter. "I heard you had some trouble out at your place last night."

"Yes, we did. I haven't had time to run to the bank. Would you mind putting these items on my account? Oh, and add a peppermint stick to the purchase, please." Maggie looked about the store. She'd have to start completely over and buy practically everything in the store. But not today.

Mrs. Fisher finished wrapping up her purchases and slid them across the counter to Maggie. "I'd like for you to have them, free of charge."

Maggie stuttered. "I can't ask you to do that."

The other woman smiled. "You didn't ask. Go ahead and take them."

"Thank you." Maggie left the store feeling dazed. Mrs. Fisher had always been nice but never that generous. She hurried back to the boardinghouse and found Clayton curled up on the bed.

Dinah sat by the window looking down at the street. "Sissy, is the man who burned down our house out there?"

"No, darling. The sheriff just told me that Gus is in jail." She hugged Dinah close. "He can never scare you again."

Dinah rested her head on Maggie's shoulder. "I'm glad. He is a bad man."

"Yes, he is. But even though he and Bud have done terrible things that have hurt people badly, one day, we will forgive them."

"That's what the Bible says, huh, Sissy?" Dinah asked.

"It does. We forgive because we are forgiven." Maggie's heart was grateful for the time Clayton had been spending reading and talking about the Bible with the children.

Clayton placed a hand on Maggie's shoulder. She jumped and looked over her shoulder at him. "I'm sorry. Did we wake you?"

He smiled at Dinah. "No. Did I hear you tell half-pint that Gus confessed to burning down the house?"

Maggie nodded. She smiled at Dinah. "Go look in the box I brought in. Your new dolly is sleepy and wants to lie down with you."

Dinah rushed to the box and pulled out the little rag doll. "Thanks, Sissy. She's beautiful." She climbed up on the bed and lay down with her new baby.

Clayton eased into the chair. "I'm glad Gus couldn't keep from bragging."

Maggie leaned forward. "He wasn't working alone."

"Bud?"

She sat back. "How did you know?"

"My gut told me so. Plus, when George said Bud just showed up out of nowhere, I figured he was the one who locked George up, started the fire and then knocked Abraham out. There really was no one else who could have done all that."

Maggie took a deep breath and blurted, "I love you, Clayton. I was so scared when you rushed in after Dinah. I thought you were going to die in that fire, and my heart broke." She held up her hand to keep him from saying anything. But her voice broke as she continued. "Thank you for saving Dinah and the ranch."

Clayton pulled her into his arms. Maggie listened to his heart beat rapidly. She was so afraid he would never love her like she loved him. Tears began to flow down her cheeks.

"I've been wanting to tell you I love you for a long time, Maggie. I was afraid you would reject me and, well, I'd planned on telling you after the dance but couldn't get my courage up." Clayton gently set her away from him. He used his thumbs and wiped the tears from her cheeks. "Maggie, I can't imagine life without you and the children."

Clayton cupped her face in his hands and began to pull her toward him. She stared deeply into his eyes and saw that he really did love her. When his lips touched hers, Maggie knew that this man would never leave her. He would love her until the day he died and he'd fight for her and the children. Maggie thanked the Lord above for sending her a Pony Express man when she needed him the most, and then she relaxed into Clayton's kiss.

Epilogue

Maggie smiled at Doc Anderson. She held one-year-old James in front of her while Dinah leaned against Clayton's leg.

"I don't know why you came to me. You already know you're with child."

Maggie giggled. "I did, but I wanted a professional opinion."

The doctor snorted. "Then why didn't you ask your husband? He's known for weeks."

Maggie looked up at Clayton. "You did?"

He nodded. "I didn't want to spoil your fun."

She made a face at him. "Morning sickness is not fun."

The doctor stood. "I'm glad you stopped by today. I was going to talk to Clayton tomorrow, but since you're both here, I'll talk to him today." He sighed and put a hand on Clayton's shoulder. "I've decided to move, and I want you to take over my practice."

Clayton looked from the doctor to Maggie. "I don't know, Doc. Maggie and I will need to discuss such a big change in our lives."

Maggie giggled. "I already knew the doctor was going to ask you to take over the practice."

"You did?"

She nodded. "You aren't the only one who can keep a secret." Maggie grinned and then her face became serious. "Even though Gus and Bud were caught, I don't want to move back out to the ranch. I love living in town and being around people. Dinah will start school soon, and it would be nice to be in town for that. I've already talked Abraham into staying on as the ranch manager. Sally is thrilled to live close to her ma, and I can continue to take care of the business end of the ranch. I know that you're meant to be a doctor, not a rancher. Doc Anderson is offering you the chance to be a doctor, Clayton."

He knelt beside her chair. "But what about the odd hours and the late nights?"

Maggie cupped his face in her hands like he had hers several months earlier. "Isn't that what doctors do? Keep strange hours and stay out late?" She leaned in and kissed him gently on the lips. "We are a strong family because you're a wonderful husband and father." She looked deeply into his eyes and then continued. "Have I told you how grateful I am to the Pony Express for sending you? Our lives have all changed because of it. And even though the Pony Express has ended, we are blessed to have you as a wonderful husband, father and doctor."

Clayton hugged her close. "I'm the one who is blessed. I love you, Maggie Young."

* * * * *

Dear Reader,

Clayton is one of those characters who leaped off the page and had me falling in love with him long before Maggie did. He understood the importance of getting the US mail through, but his true calling was to be a doctor. Maggie saw that dream and together they made it happen. But what I loved most about Clayton and Maggie was their love of God and family. I hope you enjoyed *Pony Express Special Delivery*.

Thank you so much for reading the Saddles and Spurs series. The Pony Express men have fascinated me for a long time, and it has been fun to fictionalize their stories.

For more information about my books, please visit my web page, www.rhondagibson.net. You can also join my newsletter or send me a note, by emailing me at rhondagibson65@hotmail.com.

Until next time,
Warmly,
Rhonda Gibson

Get 2 Free Books,
Plus 2 Free Gifts—
just for trying the Reader Service!

Love Inspired HISTORICAL

Love Inspired®

Inspirational Romance to Warm Your Heart and Soul

Join our social communities to connect with other readers who share your love!

Sign up for the Love Inspired newsletter at **www.LoveInspired.com** to be the first to find out about upcoming titles, special promotions and exclusive content.

CONNECT WITH US AT:

Harlequin.com/Community

 Facebook.com/LoveInspiredBooks

 Twitter.com/LoveInspiredBks

LISOCIAL2017